G000153889

Homo Derelictus

John Pether

Copyright © John Pether 2021
Published: 2021 by breind

ISBN: 9780645228809 - Paperback Edition
ISBN: 9780645228816 - eBook Edition

All rights reserved.

The right of John Pether to be identified as author of this Work has been
asserted by him in accordance with sections 77 and 78 of the
Copyright, Designs and Patents Act 1988.

**This book is a work of fiction and any resemblance to actual persons,
living or dead, is purely coincidental.**

No part of this publication may be reproduced, stored in a retrieval system,
copied in any form or by any means, electronic, mechanical, photocopying,
recording or otherwise transmitted without written permission from the
publisher. You must not circulate this book in any format.

To my wife, Sonia
For her encouragement

Also by John Pether

The Slow Apocalypse: ISBN 978-1780038094

A massive solar flare hits the Steppes of Mongolia, a mixing-bowl for devastating strains of the flu virus. Professor Jessica Patton struggles to control the outbreak but it is almost total. As one of the few survivors, Jessica leads a small band or people out of the catastrophe.

Deadly Botanicals: ISBN 978-1787197701

The horticultural market is overwhelmed with beautiful, cheap plants. The scent is strongly hallucinogenic, but genetically engineered to be toxic. Petra Wallace, a botanist and Julian Bailey, a scientist, detect an extraordinary plot created by the Kingdom of Plants to eliminate mankind. They have to unravel the plot by all the means at their disposal.

Available at all online bookstores

CHAPTER ONE

It's not right; I'm not right; nothing's right!

Sandy-haired, standard issue, five foot tall and fit as a weasel. What could possibly go wrong with Anthony Bailey? And why should it upset a ten-year-old boy in a class of only twenty pupils at the local primary school? But Anthony was not a happy bunny. He stared at the numbers and the numbers stared back, mocking him. It should be so simple. He was sweating and she was laughing at him. He hated Maureen; well, not really hated, because that wasn't fair. Just that he knew he was better at mathematics than she was but today, it was all going wrong.

Anna Prothero, the form mistress, looked at her watch and checked it with the wall clock. *What a relief,* she thought. *I can go home and have a snooze before I have to pick tomatoes, lettuce, and my tasty new rocket leaves for supper.*

It was a warm afternoon and Anna saw the drooping eyes of those who had finished writing. She leant down and picked up the old brass bell salvaged from a sunken fishing vessel. The deafening noise in the enclosed space cheered everyone up.

Anthony shrugged his shoulders and winced with the pain. *Why do they hurt so much? Anyway, saved by the bell! Time to go home. Thank God – if there really is one – and how do you thank something or someone that nobody knows anything about? But Mum is giving a late lecture at the university and Dad is in America. Oh! That's right. I'm going home with Auntie Lucy, to play football with Jeremy. Little bro',*

1

Sam too. I hope he'll be okay. He gets upset easily. But Paul is the same age and they can cheer each other up.

Lucy Radcliffe drove up on time and the two Bailey brothers scampered over the gravel to take their flying leap into the back seats of the car. Anthony missed his footing and crashed to the floor; he struggled onto the seat, his head spinning.

"Sorry, Auntie Lucy, hope I haven't made a mess of your car. Last time I did that, I had some funny virus and bled all over the seat."

"Don't worry, Anthony, as long as you're not hurt, and you can score goals; Jeremy has a new football and he wants to see how good you and Sam are. And my *dear* husband has at last repaired the net; not very well, but good enough."

Lucy made sure the boys' safety belts were fastened. One belt was badly twisted. "Bloody Brian." She said softly, but she was flustered and spoke too fast as she drove off.

"Your mum will be picking all of you up sharp after breakfast tomorrow, so none of your late-night chatter please."

She drove half a mile, through the village of Pensfield Kingsley. The sign read, Pensfield. One might have thought Pensfield Kingsley such a lovely name for a rural village in the north east of England that it deserved its full title, but the new regulations on signs were so frugally tight that the village had lost its 'Kingsley'.

Lucy drove a little further and parked in the drive of her 1950s boring house. Five minutes later the four boys were attacking Jeremy's new football. Sam scored the first goal, but Anthony was not doing well. He was tired, sweaty and not looking forward to his supper.

Lucy came into the garden and called out, "Come in, lads! Baked beans on toast with jelly to follow."

Jeremy kicked the ball just as Anthony turned towards the house. It hit him on the left-hand side, just above the rim of his pelvis.

"Ow! You bugger!"

"Sorry, Ant, I didn't mean it to hurt, just a thump. Friends?"

"Don't be silly, of course, we are. It's just …" he hesitated. "I don't feel good today. And I couldn't do the maths and that awful girl could do it easily."

"You mean Maureen?"

"You guessed! But it's not only that. I've been hit by thousands of footballs, but that one really hurt and made me feel bad, and a bit sick."

Anthony turned to Lucy. "I'm so sorry, Auntie Lucy , I only want a tiny supper, then can I go to bed?"

"Of course, you can, Ant," she said reaching her hand out to touch the boy's forehead. He wasn't feverish. "Sorry you don't feel up to scratch. Never mind, you'll be all right in the morning. Please, and both of you can call me Lucy."

"Lucy!" shouted Anthony and Sam.

"That's better."

*

It was almost half past eight in the morning. The phone rang and the automatic surgery system informed the caller that they would not have to wait more than a minute. The nursing sister, Sonia Makepeace, heard the demanding bell and glanced at the clock. *Thirty seconds to go. Just time to hang up my coat, have a quick glance in the mirror and a comb of the hair. Not bad, considering.*

She breathed deeply and picked up the phone, "Sonia here, just! Can I help?"

"Power station here; Arthur Honeywell. Hello, Sonia, sorry to ring so early but I'm afraid one of our nurses is off sick. I know it's short notice, but can we borrow one of your spare girls for a few days? Would it be possible to ask Lucy? She helped us out two years ago. Everyone liked her and she suggested a few changes which helped us to pass the latest inspection by those nosey so-and-sos from the big city. I know she has a family, but in your civilised village community I'm sure she must have an emergency baby-sitter. We also know she's not scared stiff by a miniscule dose of radio what-nots."

"Not sure Lucy would like to be called a 'spare girl', but she is a first class nurse. I'll give her a ring. She knows you pay well, and she probably could do with the cash."

Sonia replaced the phone with a deep sigh. *I could do with the cash myself.*

She looked in the mirror again and was pleased with the reflection. Shaking her head, her beautiful auburn hair flashed in the morning sun. Sitting down she picked the receiver off its stand and dialled a number.

"Lucy? It's Sonia from the surgery. Sorry to ring so early, but I've just had a call from the power station. They're short of a nurse for a few days or so, they didn't say for how long, I expect they probably don't know yet. Can Brian spare you for evening meals and bedtimes? I know he's pretty good with children, but can he cook?"

Lucy laughed with relief at the simple request. "Oh, Brian's an excellent cook – for a man. If they need me so badly, I can start right away. Brian's having a few days off again, what's new!"

A thought ran through her head, 'He's off seeing his lady friend in France. So, that'll be keeping him busy!' Instead she said, "Actually, it's better when he's out of the way, and my neighbour and sister are always happy to step in for me. My sister's boys, Anthony and Sam, are staying with us now.

They're both at the local school with my two. They love the company of my two and say they want to stay with us for ever."

"What a great little bunch of kids, bless them. Sorry to push you, but I get the impression the power station people want you for this evening's shift. You'll need to come into the surgery before you head off. We'll send a cab for you in the afternoon, okay?"

"That's fine by me. Come to think of it, I wonder if Roderick is creeping up the pecking order. He should be something to do with the control room by now."

"And who's Roderick?" Sonia asked with a teasing tone.

"Ah, just an old flame of mine."

"Come off it, Lucy, don't let your hormones carry you away from the straight and narrow. Remember you're a respectable married woman with two children, Parish Councillor and the best fund raiser in the WI."

"God! That sounds really boring." Lucy licked her lips as she resurrected distant and very pleasant memories.

Ending the call she shouted up the stairs to get the boys motivated for their day. When they were finally up and properly dressed she managed the various cereals and toast for their breakfast, but Anthony still didn't want to eat much.

"Are you okay, Anthony?"

The boy's answer was cut off by the doorbell.

Lucy opened the door to her sister, Petra.

"Hi, listen, I have a short-notice fill-in at the power station. Can you cover?"

"How long for?"

"Today, well this evening and tonight. Not sure if that'll be it or it might last a few nights. The money is really good, Pet?" Lucy said with a small smile that she hoped would win her case.

"Yeah. Sure. No problem," Petra said walking through to the kitchen.

"Morning, boys. Were you all well behaved last night? What did you have for supper?"

Jeremy replied, "Most of us had a big supper but Anthony hardly ate anything. And he's a bit low this morning, not quite his normal cheerful self." He turned to his cousin, "You feeling any better, Ant? You had a miserable breakfast."

Anthony shook his head. "Not really, and my wee smells horrible, like rotten apples."

Petra put her arms round her son's shoulders. "What's the problem, Ant?"

"I think I'm good enough, Mum. It's like…" he hesitated "…it's like being dull. Sort of not quite being switched on; like a flickering light." He thought for a few seconds. "I like that! A flickering light. On and off, as if I haven't been plugged in properly, so I'm on and off."

"See how you go, Ant. I'll be at home most of the day and your teacher's a very sensible woman. I've known her for years, I'm sure she'll keep an eye on you. I'll have a word with her."

Ushering the boys into a semblance of order, Petra gave Lucy a peck on the cheek and left for the school run.

*

They arrived at the school gates, recently repainted with the proud Pensfield Kingsley Primary School logo of bright red letters on a gold background. The headmaster, Tom Mayhew, was in the middle of the playground, chatting to Anthony's teacher, Anna Prothero, as Petra walked up.

"Good morning, Petra. Taxi duty again! You could be employed, you know. Might be more interesting than lecturing about nasty plants."

"Thanks a million, Tom, you're too kind. Can I have a word with Anna?" The headmaster wandered off to talk to other arriving parents and Anna stepped closer.

"Jeremy told me that Anthony's not on top form today. He describes himself as a light bulb going on and off."

"Don't you worry about Anthony, I'll keep an eye on him and if I'm worried we'll give you a ring."

Anna started to walk towards the classroom, then turned and walked back to where the headmaster was talking to other parents. "Tom, Anthony isn't the only child not on top form. Sorry to interrupt, but I overheard your conversation with Sally and Jo. I could add three more to the list after phone calls this morning, both boys and girls are affected. I hope it's not the school meals that are poisoning them."

Tom took Anna's suggestion to heart. "They always say they love the food." He pointed to the other pupils. "They look fine to me."

The school bell rang, loud and clear.

Anna gestured to the four boys to come with her. "Come on, Anthony, Sam, Jeremy, and Paul."

*

Break time came and went, and Anthony was not a happy lad. He was used to being top of the maths lesson, but things were not going according to plan. There was a tremendous buzzing in his ears, and he was finding it hard to hear the teacher. His head felt muddled, he knew he wasn't coping with the problems fed to him, and that girl Maureen was beating him every time. In despair, Anthony raised his hand and Anna came over to his desk.

"What is it, Anthony, what's going wrong? You don't seem up to scratch today."

"Sorry, Miss, I don't feel well. I'm all fuzzy, a bit sweaty, and a bit stupid."

"You're telling me you are," said Maureen.

"Oh, you shut up," snapped Anthony.

"Anthony!" Anna said. More gently she added, "Your mum said this morning that she felt you weren't quite right, but she couldn't pinpoint anything wrong. Go and sit in classroom three and the headmaster will decide what we shall do. Actually, change of plan; knock on his study door on the way. Tell him what's wrong."

Anthony left the classroom, walked the short distance to the door of the headmaster's study, and knocked loudly.

"Come in, come in. Hello, Anthony, I'm not deaf, you know. What's the problem? Sit down and tell me all about it. I could do with a break from filling in forms."

"Sorry, sir, Mrs Prothero told me to knock on your door. I didn't mean to knock so loudly. I don't seem to hear so well with all the sort of buzzing in my ears… and I just don't feel well. I was, sort of, not quite right yesterday. Then when my cousin Jeremy accidentally kicked his football into my hip, it really hurt. It shouldn't have hurt at all, and it went on hurting. I told Mum when she came to collect us this morning. We were staying with Aunt Lucy overnight. But she had an urgent call to go to the power station. Mum said I would feel better as the day went on. Then about break time I just felt really bad, all sweaty and dizzy, and…" The words had tumbled out and he'd finished with a sob.

"It's not like you to have anything wrong with you. I tell you what, let's have a go with my new thermometer. Let's see if just touching your ear will tell us if you're hot or cold."

Anthony felt better with the calm words of the headmaster and he was intrigued by the new gadget. His ear was touched and they both looked at the dial.

"Hmm, a little over a hundred degrees in old money – that's Fahrenheit to you. Now, let's see if it works in my ear. You have a go."

Anthony gently placed the gadget onto the headmaster's ear. They both looked at the reading; 98.4.

"Well, Anthony, at least I don't have a raised temperature." They both laughed. "Are the rest of your family alright at home? You said you were staying with your Aunt's family last night; are they alright, no coughs or colds? No bird flu or swine flu or other strange flu mutations?"

"Not as far as I know, sir, but—" Anthony tried to remember "—Mummy told me that another school was a bit short of players for the Saturday match with three of them falling ill at the weekend. She also said that other mothers were saying they had sick children, and nobody seemed to know what was wrong with them."

"That's interesting. I'll ring your mother and she can arrange for you to be collected and taken to your doctor. I assume you're with Doctor Liu?" Tom asked, knowing most of the village and surrounding districts fell under the GPs care.

"Yes, sir."

"Did you know he knows all about the types of Spitfires in the Second World War?"

Anthony perked up. "Yes, Sir. But he reckons I know as much as he does."

"Nothing would surprise me, Anthony." Tom said, already knowing about the young lad's love of aircraft.

CHAPTER TWO

The taxi arrived for Lucy at 3pm and after the short journey to the surgery she was met at the door by the surgery porter, Jack Oates, a pugnacious, irritating little man whose rugby muscle was turning to blubber, giving him the appearance of spherical ball, was determined to make himself heard. His rugby days were long gone and there was little to occupy his simple mind except beer, skittles and an overwhelming desire to be belligerent. He was under the impression that he had been employed to keep order in the surgery complex, but was increasingly finding that most of the occupants were ignoring his instructions.

He only had two years to go before he could hear the words "pensioned off" His daydreaming was interrupted by the urgent chime of the front door. He smiled as he looked through the window and said, "Come in, Lucy. Hope you don't mind but I've a hot cup of coffee here, so you'll be alright seeing yourself in. You've been here before. Is that alright?"

"Thanks, Jack, I know the way."

Lucy climbed the stairs and entered the main office space of the surgery to find the staff sampling the coffee machine. Doctor Liu, the younger of the two, was a native of Hong Kong. He was strict, but loved by all and was also an expert with the coffee machine. The older doctor, Charles Canning, stood up and held out a hand in greeting.

"Kind of you for coming at such short notice, Lucy. You did help us out a couple of years ago. Apparently, the problem at the power station is that one of their resident nurses has been taken ill and they need you for this evening's shift. I hope your husband can look after the children."

"I'm afraid he's away for now, but my sister will step in to help. I must say, I like the sound of the evening and night shift. The pay was jolly good last time."

"Great! I know you've done it before but I'm afraid you'll have to have a quick tour of the areas under your umbrella – regulations, of course. It might give you a sort of warning of the accidents that could happen. We can give you help, if you need it. There's always someone on call at the surgery and here's a list of numbers you might need to ring," he said, handing over a printed sheet. "The burns unit at the local hospital on our side of city is excellent and any accidents in the region of the cooling inlets are covered by the lifeboat service, bless them, so you don't have to swim."

"That's a relief; the North Sea at this time of year is a bit too cold for me. When do I start? Sonia gave me the impression it was pretty urgent."

"Right away. You might have noticed another taxi as you came in. I've asked the Senior Scientist at the power station, Roderick Simmonds, to meet you on your arrival and show you around."

"That's OK with me. Thank you."

This could be interesting, meeting an old flame in the bowels of an atomic power station. I wonder how he's aged, and how he'll be able to cope with a respectable married woman? I wonder; could be fun – or more?

Once she had completed the necessary temporary contract paperwork at the surgery, she left in another taxi and was driven towards the coast, through the scattered village of Brockbridge

11

Farm, arriving at a strangely shaped building surrounded by a fortified enclosure in front of the nuclear power station. The gates had immediately swung open; she was obviously expected. The taxi drove straight in and Lucy was met by a security guard with a beaming smile. "Very kind of you to come at such short notice, Lucy. You were a breath of fresh air last time you were here. How long ago was that?"

"Nearly two years," she answered.

"Wow, time flies. Our Super, Rod Simmonds, is going to give you the induction tour himself. Seems you are indeed special. He's usually much too senior for that sort of thing, but he says he used to know you from years back."

Didn't he just!

Rod arrived after a few minutes. He shook her hand and she leant in to give him a peck on the cheek. Lucy's instant thought was that he smelt the same. She remembered his not unpleasant smell from their shared history.

"How nice to see you, Rod. Long-time no see. I hear you're going to show me around, that's nice. I was here for a few days a couple of years ago, but never saw you back then. I can't believe it's changed that much."

Roderick smiled and she watched his gaze traverse her body. He took a deep breath and said, "Lucy, it's really lovely to see you. There's been a lot of water under the bridge in the last ten years or so. I'd like to tell you about it, some other time, perhaps. I heard you were married with two boys. Lucky man, Brian," he added, as if an afterthought.

Roderick turned away, waved for her to follow and continued, "We'll do the quick standard tour and then I'll suggest a circuit for you to do twice a shift as a routine, which ends up at my little cubby-hole at the end of the control room." He handed over the bundle of clothes he'd been carrying. "You have to wear the hard hat and this protective coat; it may not look it, but it is quite clean. Oh and of course," he said, fishing a flat card within a heavy plastic coating from his pocket. "You need to wear this radiation monitor. Not that you're allowed anywhere near the danger zones in case of accidents, but everyone has to wear one. So no one feels left out."

"Sounds great, Rod, let's go. I don't remember having to do a full induction before. And on that, where were you two years ago? That last time I came to do a locum."

Roderick thought for a minute or two. "Yeah, regulations update. Everyone working on the medical side gets 'the tour' nowadays, so you can be familiar with what type of injuries we might have."

"Fair enough," she said following behind and slipping on the protective coat before clipping on the radiation monitor to the outer pocket.

Rod was still talking. "As for me, I think I was in America and then Japan, on an accident investigation and mitigation course. We went to the old Three Mile Island site and studied what had happened out there. Then we were whisked off to Fukushima, in Japan, but that was useless. The whole area was so hot, we didn't have a hope of investigating anything. Now I'm back in the UK. I suppose it's a pretty routine job, but it does have a certain degree of responsibility. And it has the advantage of being able to ask a lovely girl to come and help us."

She couldn't see his face as he delivered the last line but thought, he's nicer than he was; kinder, softer. Not the self-confident, abrasive man I used to know. What a change. I wonder if he has a family? Perhaps he finally chose from the string of girlfriends he used to have in the old days. *Concentrate, old girl, live in the present, forget the past … perhaps! I feel uncertain. Oh well, you never know.*

"Let's start the induction, Lucy. We're supposed to do it bottom up, so to speak." Roderick laughed as his voice caught a sound of uncertainty. He guided her across to a smaller building and held open a door leading to a set of steps. "Down these stairs. Be careful, they're a bit slippery."

"Okay, and where does this lead to," she said, stepping gingerly and making sure she had a firm grip of the handrail.

"We're on our way to what's called the 'circulating water pump house'. From your perspective, problems here are mainly to do with condensed steam which makes the floor wet. Workers that go down regularly are supposed to wear non-slip footwear, but even then the occasional mishap occurs and the result is yet another sprained ankle. Nothing serious yet, but there's always the first. It is a bit stuffy, but there's nothing dangerous in the air. Just be careful not to slip on the odd dead fish. No, I'm joking!" He said when he saw her wrinkled nose.

Her foot slid forward and Roderick put his hand round her waist to help her. He was gentle, and she liked his touch. She put a hand on his to keep its reassurance.

"Ugh! Is a wet floor the only hazard?"

"And buckets full of jellyfish. When they come up the estuary, they can make one hell of a mess of the intakes. We send divers down to clean the devils out. They don't smell, the jellyfish, not the divers, but they make an awful, slimy mess."

"Now you're reminding me of something. I read in some magazine about mussels blocking up the cooling water intake and being hard-stuck on. The writer indicated they could do a lot of damage. Not heard of jellyfish before, though. Where do they come from?"

"You've being doing your homework?"

"Not really, but having a nuclear power station close to where I live makes me take an interest."

"Well, whatever the reason, well done Lucy! We think the jellyfish have moved into this area because the sea is just that bit warmer. One result of the fashionable climate warming our outlet valves add to the area. Come on," he said stepping over to a low opening.

"These are the cable tunnels. As you can see, they're quite narrow, and workers have to do a confined-space training course before they're allowed in. That said, if anyone ever gets into a bad way down there it would be difficult to extract them. On no account should you or anyone else go in to attempt to rescue them."

"What would we do?" Lucy asked gazing along the tunnel.

"Call for help on the special phones we supply. They're only for use in the station, by the way, but they work anywhere in the complex.

"Now for the basement. You'll need to wear your protective gloves when you're down here," he said.

Lucy fished the ones he'd given her out of her pocket.

"The floor's often oily and makes even the least clumsy people slip."

"Good job I've been here before," Lucy said.

"Why's that?"

"Because no one at the surgery or any of the information from the power station mentioned about boots and trousers. I knew I had to wear them, but imagine if I'd turned up in my usual shoes and a skirt?"

He stopped and turned to face her. "Yeah. That would have been terrible." He gave her a cheeky grin. "I always quite liked you in a skirt." He smiled, turned, and led the way up the stairs to the main corridor, muttering to himself. Lucy thought she heard him say, "Or out of it..." Thankfully, with his back turned, he failed to see the rising flush on Lucy's cheek .

"Not far now. Up one more flight of stairs and we're back to square one."

At the top of the stairs and through another heavy door, the corridor opened out into an expansive space and their voices sounded hollow.

"This floor is mainly offices. Most are usually empty, but we don't want to release them to the administrators. There are so many of them and all they do is fill in forms and file loads of rubbish into locked drawers. As if they had any value to anybody who wanted to pinch them. Especially as they usually lose the keys."

He stopped outside an open door with the notice, Surgery, above it. "Well, Lucy, this is your empire now. Apparently the staff prefer your door to be always open, it's what makes it welcome. You're quite lucky to have an outside window, so you can have a glimpse of the real world."

She entered her empire and looked through to the slightly darkening early evening sky. "It'll be dark, Rod. Not much to see."

"Even on the night shift there's plenty of light outside with people coming and going the whole time. You might remember from your last visit, one part of your job is to give the weekly first-aid lecture which includes CPR. Don't worry, you can use Jane's notes."

"Jane?"

"The woman you're filling in for."

"Right. And who am I teaching?"

"A lecture hall half full of sleeping people. They'll have heard it all before, but the regulations say it must be done on a regular basis. Sorry about that, Lucy." He pointed further down the corridor. "The main control room is just round the corner which is my little bit of the empire. I usually sit in a cubby-hole at the far end. Come and see it?"

"Sure," she said.

Roderick escorted Lucy into the control room, past almost-silent workers seated by the central console staring at computer screens. One or two of them were muttering, but the screens failed to answer back. In front of them the entire wall of the control room was a mass of dials and lights. Three bigger dials were headed with the names of the three nearest villages: Pensfield, Daleshott and Wedmore. Every now and then, one of the workers would grunt, lean forward and write something on a pad of paper. They all looked engrossed in their work and after the initial glance, took no notice of the couple walking past behind them.

Lucy and Roderick entered his tiny office at the far end of the control room. Again, the walls were speckled with yet more dials with tiny, almost inscrutable writing below them. There was one comfortable armchair in front of a desk on which sat three brightly coloured knobs, all that would be within easy reach of whoever sat in the armchair.

The central button looked like what she imagined one of her boys would have designed if asked to think of what is in a nuclear power station. "That big red one is dramatic looking, Rod. What's it supposed to do?"

"I'm supposed to press it if the two dials in the middle go five percent above baseline. Not too difficult; they give out a pinging noise that wakes me up. It's to do with air pressure in the main reactor chamber. If it goes too high, I release a tiny amount to the atmosphere. The trouble is that the admin people insist a siren is also activated."

"You leak radioactivity to the outside?"

17

"Oh Lord no! There is a maze of detectors that scream at us if radioactivity is detected on its journey to the outside world. No, it's just high-pressure, but otherwise boring old plain air."

"So you're in charge of all the safety?" she asked.

"Not on my own. If anything goes wrong I can summon a wide range of people who can sort out problems within minutes. The other coloured buttons do something almost useful. They aren't vital, but they sometimes make noises to keep me awake. The night shift can be tedious. We can opt for music, but the sound system is awful, and I tend to read or write silly stories. You might have thought the opposite would happen, but they turn up the lights at night. It's subdued during the day and the increase at night is supposed to keep us from falling asleep. It usually works well, apart from Christmas."

He sounded bored with his job, Lucy thought. Which was both sad and a bit of a worry. She tried to cheer him a little, "Nice little room, Rod. And you've got your own coffee machine. That's a luxury! And it's good that if you are in charge of even some safety there's nowhere to lie down for forty winks!"

"No way! That's it then. So you'll be okay the evening and night shift?"

"Of course I don't mind. You lot pay well and there's always someone prepared to baby-sit. I can call on neighbours or my sister, Petra."

"She will look after your boys?"

"Yeah and she has her own kids. In fact, we have twin beds for her sons, Anthony and Sam at my place. Anthony's ten and Sam's nine. They're lovely, all four make a good pack and they're brilliant at football. I'm sure they'd love to come and see all this. Apart from Sam, he's more interested in wild things."

"Not allowed I'm afraid. No children permitted into this part of the building. You can imagine a school visit with the kids giving in to natural temptation and fiddling with the dials."

"Oh well. I've really enjoyed your showing me around. I'll have to come and sound you out in your little cubby-hole, as you call it." She laughed and looked at Roderick's back as he fiddled with the coffee machine.

Still athletic and gorgeous with those piercing blue eyes, slightly mournful mouth, and mind as sharp as a razor. He never mentioned a wife or family; perhaps there isn't one. I used to think he was a cocky little bugger, but he seems to have softened with time. Is he calmer? Perhaps a little sad; difficult to tell. We'll have to find out. There's always tomorrow night...

Back at her surgery base, Lucy was met by a small, agitated man, identified by a very impressive label on the front of his jacket: 'Arthur Honeywell; Deputy Manager, Control Room'.

"Sorry to barge into your surgery, Lucy, but I have bad news for you. I'm afraid it's Jane, that's the nurse you're standing in for."

"Yes, I've heard her name. What's wrong?"

"She's not at all well and we've been told she'll be in bed for at least a week. She's had another attack of the dizzies. She often gets them, but this time it sounds a bit more serious. Do you mind doing the night shift for the whole week?"

"Oh that's terrible," Lucy said and managed to keep her voice sincere whilst thinking how great it would be to get a whole week of power station nightshift pay. She frowned to show her sadness at poor Jane, but Arthur misinterpreted her expression.

"I can probably scrounge you a bit more overtime if you have to pay for anything at home, babysitters and the like."

Lucy supressed her smile. "Oh that's kind and yes, Arthur, don't worry, I can do the whole week for you. No problem."

"Oh, thank you, Lucy. It is so difficult to find people as well qualified as you are at a moment's notice." He reached out to shake her hand before bustling off back down the corridor.

Lucy looked round her tiny empire and was pleased to find a coffee machine as good as Roderick's. She sat in Jane's chair, made herself a cup of coffee and tried to interpret Jane's doodles on the ink pad. There were a few drawings that implied an attempt at artistry but showed only boredom. She took off the outside protective coat Roderick had given her and hung it on Jane's hook. Opening a few drawers she finally found the clean white surgery coats. Transferring the radiation monitor onto it she shrugged into what was a bit of a tight fit and however much she moved her shoulders around, Lucy had difficulty doing up the buttons.

Looks as if I'm a trifle more top heavy than Jane. Breath in, old girl; I'm buggered if I have to try on the outsize coats.

Lucy was about to open one of Jane's old novels when there was a gentle tap on her door.

A woman called Rosemary, with a sore thumb. Lucy diagnosed the patient had a touch of RSI, probably been pressing too many buttons, and gave her two paracetamol tablets.

After an hour she got up to make the first of her 'rounds'.

*

The diminutive Doctor Liu, stood up and held out his hand. "Petra, how nice to see you; I was just speaking to your sister earlier. And Anthony, this is unusual. How is my mathematical genius? And where is the only original type six Spitfire kept?"

"New York, in a museum, Doctor."

"Well remembered. Now, tell me why you're here. I gather your mother thought things were not quite right this morning, but I expect you both gambled that you would get better as the day went on. What was the first thing you noticed that might give us a clue?"

"Yesterday, when I had a pee it had a funny smell, like rotten apples. Then later in the day I had a pain in my left side, round the back a bit, and I was sort of dizzy with an odd whistling in my ears which wouldn't stop. Then today, I just felt ill and told my teacher Mrs Prothero that I didn't feel well."

"Your wee smells of apples ... you're not a secret cider drinker, by any chance?" Doctor Liu smiled and raised an eyebrow.

"One of my uncles was a cider drinker. I tried it once, but I didn't like the stuff he was drinking. It made my tummy sore and I had a terrible headache afterwards."

Doctor Liu, Petra and Anthony were laughing as the nurse came into the examination room.

"What's the joke?" she asked.

Doctor Liu answered, "We have established that Anthony is not going to become a cider addict."

"That's a relief," she said.

Petra asked, "Do we have any clues as to what's wrong with Ant?"

Looking to the nurse, Doctor Liu said, "We can wind up the system to get going on a urine sample and some other tests, so we're not relying on simple guesswork." He turned back to Petra. "I don't suppose it's any consolation, but Anthony is not the only one with a pain in the side and a temperature. This week we've had several children with a similar picture, all within a fifteen-mile radius. The presumption was that there was an odd germ floating about causing these cases. But the geographical spacing is odd, and it's difficult to work out how transfer has taken place from one family to another. How do you feel at the moment, Anthony?"

"The pain in my side is almost gone and I feel kind of better. Do you think it might have anything to do with Mummy's peculiar plants?"

Doctor Liu looked over at Petra. Or more properly, Professor Petra Bailey, a specialist in botany. "Do you bring your work home, Petra?"

Petra shook her head.

Doctor Liu thought for several minutes. "I didn't imagine you did. On a philosophical note, I don't believe there are fundamental barriers between the extraordinary number of types of living organisms. In my home country we have been studying nature for thousands of years and constantly come up with strange answers. Don't dismiss anything."

He stood up and went to the window. At last, he turned with a smile. "We'll have to see. Remember the old saying, common things occur commonly."

*

The night was beginning to drag and the main problems Lucy was encountering on her wanderings were people suffering from intense boredom and, she sensed, an underlying anxiety.

It's as if all these workers are simply waiting for a disaster to happen. Is it because they are worried this whole extraordinary complex of buildings is suddenly going to erupt like Chernobyl and there would be nothing left except a huge hole in the ground? How can I contribute to alleviate the boredom and their anxiousness? Music? Writing? Reading? We need original ideas. I wonder if Roderick can help. That's a good excuse to go and visit him. A bit thin, but it'll have to do.

Lucy finished her latest walkabout at the main control room where Roderick was explaining a problem to one of the technicians. The dials twittered back and forth without anyone seeming to worry too much. Roderick finished his lecture and swept Lucy towards his office.

"Coffee time, Lucy? Let me treat you. Milk? I can make you one of those frothed up ones, cappuccino. I always have black, as you know, or used to know."

It was good coffee and the frothing machine worked well. She perched on the edge of the desk in front of Roderick's chair, enjoying the slightly flirtatious thrill she felt, knowing he was looking at her. Wearing jeans or not, she knew her legs had always held his attention.

They reminisced about the past, sharing a laugh and a joke at some of the dafter things they used to get up to. After a while, Roderick said, "Do you still love to dance, Lucy?"

"Oh, I do, but it's been such a long time; Brian's not keen."

Roderick stood and held his hand out towards her.

"Here?" she said, looking around the tiny space.

"Ah, c'mon, a small shuffle for old times' sake," he said, his arm still extended.

She held her position, a smirk playing on her face. "We're at work Rod."

"All work and no play," he said.

She stood and took his hand, "Makes Rod a dull boy?"

Laughing, he moved her a foot away from the desk, held her close, swayed her gently and looked deeply into her eyes. Then, with a flourish better executed when they were both younger, he lowered her into a backbend. Lucy felt her balance go and reached out automatically. Her hand fell directly onto the red button ... Immediately a muffled siren started to complain.

Roderick jerked back, scowling. "Bugger! That'll start the bells ringing." He roughly pulled Lucy away from the desk. "Ever so sorry, Lucy. You'd better scarper through the back door." He quickly guided her towards a small door at the back of his office, pointed to the left and closed the door behind her.

Lucy found herself in a gloomy corridor that she hadn't seen before. She was flustered, angry, and feeling hot.

"Miserable devil! How dare he chuck me out like that. I can't believe his bloody red button is that important. And we were getting on pretty well after all those lost years."

After a few minutes she found the correct corridor, made her way back to her surgery and sulked into Jane's seat. Lifting one of the dog-eared novels of the side cupboard she had barely finished the first chapter when there was a knock at the open door.

A weasely-looking man poked his head into the room.

"Come in. How can I help you?"

"Sorry to intrude, Miss. My name is Gavin, Gavin Thomas, and my job is to try and predict the weather, Miss. I was up top just now. Sorry, on the roof of the building, above the main reactor area, when I just didn't feel well. Not really supposed to be there – that's reserved for terrorists!" He laughed. "Sorry about that, it's not that funny, everyone's petrified about the dreaded terrorist threat. Anyway, it's all quite safe, you understand, covered in thick wire netting. I was checking one of my monitors – with permission, you understand. But for some reason, I felt dizzy. I was so dizzy, I could have fallen over the railings. They're much too high, of course, so I couldn't have fallen. I was near one of the air vents and there was a funny smell coming from one of them – rather like rough cider that's gone off a bit. I should know, I drink a lot of it."

He laughed. "Thought you ought to know, in case anyone else has the same thing. Not the cider, the dizziness."

"Thank you, Gavin. Gavin Thomas, you said?" The man nodded. "And how are you feeling now?"

"Fine, miss. Fine. I just thought you should know, we have to, are meant to, you know, report, any… all of… you know?"

He gabbled, tongue-tied and Lucy wondered if he'd only come along to get a look at the new nurse.

"Well, I'll note it down, Gavin. As you say it might help others if they have the same thing. Do you get dizzy when you are up at height?"

"Sometimes, miss."

"Have you tried any seasickness pills for your dizziness? I can bring you some tomorrow if you like. Otherwise, you should go to your general practitioner."

"I'm all right now, thank you, Miss. I only came to warn you if anyone else had the same thing."

"Thank you, Gavin. Warning noted."

She transferred the notes of Gavin and the earlier Rosemary onto the official cards.

I wonder, that fellow who had the dizzy spell on the roof? He said he was near an air vent. I wonder if that had some connection with Rod's precious red button?

CHAPTER THREE

Four weeks later.

Petra came into her husband's study looking worried.

"Jules, I know you must be jet-lagged and I understand that you are probably wanting to crawl into bed, but we need to talk about Anthony."

Julian Bailey frowned and set his briefcase down. His trip back from the States had been long and tedious, as was the way with trans-Atlantic flights, but the look of concern on his wife's face made him focus. He sat in the chair behind his desk.

"I've had a phone call from Doctor Liu. He told me that they're now thinking that Anthony has some peculiar disease of his kidneys. Apparently seven more pupils in Anthony's class have presented with similar symptoms. They haven't given the disease a name yet but they're all off sick. Can you put your thinking cap on and think of your family for a change?"

"My dear Petra—"

"Don't you 'my dear' me," she said cutting him off. "I'm the youngest Professor of Botany in the west, although it's more like the Wild West now. Anyway, please concentrate on this. Our son has a peculiar disease of his kidneys and nobody can give it a name, nor do they know what to do about it. There are other cases in Anthony's class. To cap it all, Doctor Liu tells me there are at least a dozen more cases from round and about, all in children. And that's just his practice. He's phoned around to other surgeries and he's quite certain there must be a lot more dotted around the county."

"Sorry, Pet, I'll start again." Julian shifted in his chair and tried to look serious. "Back to the beginning. Surely you don't think the Kingdom of Plants, all those crazy primeval giants, have simply reared their ugly heads yet again. That was nine years ago. We incinerated all the peculiar Buddleias that frightened you at the railway station. And that weirdo who was selling them has vanished. He was clever, though, to identify the mutation so quickly. He should have been incinerated as well, instead of having all his money pinched and exporting him and his friends to some God-forsaken country."

"No way! The Greens would instantly have adopted him as their next martyr."

"Hmm, perhaps." Julian thought for a while. "How is Anthony now?"

"Ant is feeling very low; slight fever and a dull ache in the kidney areas that is not helped by any pain pills that we've tried."

"Tell me the whole story."

"The best place to make sure the story is correct, I suggest, would be the headmaster's study at the school. I've made a few calls to some others, including Anthony's teacher, Anna. I think we need her husband, Van. He's got a fantastic brain and he could do with putting his thinking cap on instead of obsessively keeping fit and inventing awful devastating explosives. And, the doctor from the surgery, Doctor Liu. He has a startling way of thinking laterally. I've arranged it for tomorrow morning."

*

"I like your study, Headmaster, very comfortable and plenty of room. How do you like life in the frozen north?"

"I love it here, Petra. I came from a ghastly suburb in the south-east of the country with the promise that I could resurrect this school from the doldrums. Three classrooms with no life in them. Then you may remember that my lovely wife, Sarah, was dying from an unusual disease. She rallied for a while, but the bloody thing caught up with her. There was always a hope she might recover. But you all are the nicest bunch of people I have ever come across – kind and sympathetic and damned clever. I came out of the doldrums feeling a helluva sight better, don't you think?"

Tom grabbed Julian's hand and shook it hard. There were tears of gratitude in Tom's eyes, but he managed to choke down his emotions and regain control. Petra reacted by putting her arms round Tom's chest and giving him a great hug. He laughed and said, "You must have been reading that lovely article in the *New Scientist* that extolled the virtue of the hug as against those futile pecks on the cheek."

Tom straightened up and took a deep breath. "You asked about my study. I insisted on a big room that could take twenty people at a time. I find I need room to manoeuvre and mix up the various factions so that they can fight it out before I have to intervene!"

They all laughed.

"Ladies and gentlemen, welcome to you all, please make yourselves comfortable, there are plenty of chairs. Petra and Julian, I'm glad that you asked Anthony to join us. Anna, thank you for asking Van. For those who haven't met her, this is Carole Price, the school secretary," Tom said indicating the woman standing next to his desk. "I've asked her to take minutes as I think we shall want this on the record. Ah, I can see Doctor Liu's car. That's good, we shall have a full house. Petra, would you mind being chairperson? We need someone in authority, and you are a professor. Come and sit in my chair. Carole will clear the mess in front of you."

Petra settled herself into the headmaster's ample armchair. "First off, do we have a six-inch to the mile map of the surrounding area and somewhere to attach it so everyone can see?"

Carole and Anna disappeared and by the time they returned with a rolled-up map, a wooden easel with board, the group had been joined by Dr Liu.

"Thank you," Petra said to Anna and Carole. "Now we need to map all the cases with the dates they became ill. I have details of over twenty cases from my discussions with the school. As far as we know, Anthony was the first case around a month ago and the bulk of the others were identified by you, Doctor Liu, and other general practitioners around that time."

Petra and Julian spent the next ten minutes attaching stickers to the map with the dates when the children became ill. They were interrupted by a gentle knock on the door.

"Come in!" Tom had a powerful voice.

The door opened slowly, and a woman appeared with her blank-faced offspring. "Sorry to barge in, Headmaster. I thought Lucy Radcliffe would be here for Ben's extra lesson. She's very good with him and there are tremendous signs of improvement; his autism is much less than it was. She must have been held up. I'll wait in the hall." She looked round the packed office. "Sorry, sorry to interrupt the meeting."

She retreated with her son, shutting the door quietly behind her.

"That dear lady is one of the cleaners at the school." Tom nodded his head. "Charmaine Bradley is her name and her son, Ben, for your information, is an autistic child. He's the first we've had in this school. He's only nine and is just beginning to use words properly and react to people. Your sister Lucy,

Petra is doing a fantastic job. There's so much potential in that child that we haven't got near to discovering, yet. When you give him a problem, he sticks to it like a limpet. Now, Petra back to you."

"Can any of you see a pattern in all these cases? Jules, this is more in your line; Ministry of Defence, and all that."

"I can't immediately see a pattern but, logically, there should be one." He studied the map and shook his head. "Just a minute! Perhaps we're all missing a trick. Carole, can you ask Charmaine and her son Ben to come back; we need him. The autistic brain does sometimes have some wonderful facility with this sort of problem."

Carole shepherded in Ben and his mother, followed by Lucy who had just arrived. After some shuffling about there was room for the extra three to sit comfortably at the front of the group. Ben immediately stood up, came forward and stared at the board. He turned and looked straight at Anna. "What lesson is this, please, Miss?"

Anna looked at Julian who simply nodded his head and took up the baton.

"Ben, this is an odd sort of game. We must find out the origin of all these little stickers. Perhaps their relationship to each, where they all started from; does that make sense? They all have dates attached to them. Have a go, see if you can find an answer."

Tom coughed. "Sorry folks, we have to treat this a bit more seriously. Ben, this is a map of where all the sick children from this school and other schools round here come from. Some of them are more ill than others and these stickers show where they live. So far, nobody in this room has managed to see a pattern. That's why we need your help. Can you see a pattern?

There's no hurry but we really do need you to solve the problem."

Ben looked around the group of people. He appeared to know most of them. Then he stood up and with an intensity that was stifling, circled the area round the headmaster's desk. He gently touched the telephone, the neat line of pens and pencils, and then moved on to other items. He touched the coffee machine, the hat stand, and the headmaster's bookshelves. Finally, he seemed satisfied with his analysis of the state of the headmaster's study and sat down in his chair, only to get up again after ten seconds.

Ben approached the map with its mass of dots. He stayed quite still for a full five minutes. No one had interrupted Ben's manoeuvres and his audience remained silent, waiting. Ben continued to stare at the board. His concentration was total, and the audience were forced to remain silent for another three minutes; then he stood back from the board and thought for a while before approaching the board again. There was the hint of a frown on his forehead. He did this three times, each time standing quite still. Suddenly Ben erupted, snatched a black marker and rushed to the board. He drew line after line until the board looked like a Picasso drawing. Then he stood back and viewed the mess he had made. A twitch of a smile, he seemed to like it. Finally, he drew, very carefully, a circle round the nuclear power station.

Julian laughed and Ben looked worried. Lucy whispered to Julian, "Ben doesn't like being laughed at."

"What's the joke, Jules? You've upset Ben." Anna put her arms round Ben. He squeezed his eyes and started for the door, but Anna held him back. "Sorry, Ben, I didn't mean to grab you. Commander Bailey is very pleased with what you have done; he said you would be brilliant. Isn't that right, Julian?"

"It crossed my mind that visual patterns are sometimes solved by the autistics of this world. I laughed because it was well done. Very well done, Ben!"

Julian stood up and went to the board. "Well, I never! This is fractal logic taken to extremes. He's right, you know. Ben, you are a miracle worker, we could easily have spent weeks trying to work out the answer. Well done, lad, you are a magician!"

Ben summoned a weak smile which grew as he saw Lucy, Anna, and his mother all smiling.

"Lucy, you've done locum nursing duties at the power station, perhaps you ought to ferret around and sort something out. What are you thinking, Van?"

"I'm thinking that we should investigate wind speeds and directions for the days up to a month ago, or perhaps a bit longer. Lucy, do the power station guys keep such records? And, if they do, can we get at them easily?"

"Their tame weatherman came to my surgery as a patient. His name is Gavin Thomas. He said he had been up on the roof—"

"What!" Julian roared. "The roof is strictly out of bounds except to the top security people. Just think, if a helicopter with terrorists landed on the roof, they could do one hell of a lot of damage. What was he doing there and why wasn't he picked up?"

"I can't answer that," said a miserable Lucy. "It was during my first evening shift. He came to me, but he wasn't really ill. He came, I suppose, to warn me. He said he'd been on the roof to get some fresh air. He had the excuse that one of his monitors didn't seem to be working properly. He had to walk near an air vent and that was when he felt dizzy. Oh yes, he said there was an odd smell coming from the vent."

"That's interesting," said Julian. "Very interesting. Make sure you note that down, Carole."

"Every word is noted, Commander Bailey." Carole sounded offended.

"Lucy, can you get hold of your Gavin Thomas and find out if he or someone else can let us have a look at the weather records? Then we should study the structure of the power station and find out more about the air vents on the roof and other places. Van, can you use your advisory position on the UK Nuclear Regulation scene to get permission, as soon as possible."

"I certainly can. We'll have permission tomorrow at eight o'clock in the morning. How many can come with me? We'll need passports to show at the gates and preferably driving licences. Petra, Julian, Lucy, and I; four minds should be enough."

"I'll pick everyone up between seven and half past," said Julian.

As they were about to leave the school grounds Julian stopped. "Before I forget; as we were winding up the meeting, Anthony asked me what we were looking for. I didn't confess that we had no idea, complete blank so far. So, I chickened out and told him we would have to play it by ear."

The next day as Julian drove to the power station, he asked his passengers, "Anyone got any suggestions what we are supposed to be looking for?"

Van answered first. "The obvious one is detection of the escape of radioactivity. But I see the records daily. They're all checked on a regular basis in London and they couldn't be lower, almost below background, if that's possible. You can't cheat on those results as they are instantly transmitted by automatic machinery. So, as far as humanly possible, they must be fool proof. It's a continuous process and you can't cheat. I suppose the automatic systems can go wrong; anything can go wrong. Petra, any thoughts?"

"I can't think of anything, looks as if we are going to have to rely on Jules' ear. Your turn, Lucy."

"Gavin's strange comment worries me. I'm sure he said there was a funny smell coming from the air vent on the roof. We ought to investigate that. Apart from that problem, I've no idea, sorry Julian."

"Well, we've arrived. Don't forget to show passports at the gate. Oh, they're already rising. We must be expected. Who is the funny little man in the glass box? Van, do you know him?"

"His name is Martin Orme. He's the health and safety officer. Pompous little fart. He doesn't like me, I've overruled him several times and I have carte blanche to go anywhere except the really dangerous areas; you have to have special protective clothing for those."

Julian parked the car and Van went back to the little man. "Good morning, Martin. I see you have hard hats and dosimeters at the ready, well done." He turned to the others. "These are mandatory. Try them. I think you'll find the hard hats are quite comfortable, but not so good for the hair styles."

"Good morning, sir. I have strict orders to assist you in any way. If you come with me, I will introduce you to the senior scientist, Doctor Roderick Simmonds. He will take you to the areas you would probably like to see."

Martin guided the visitors to Roderick's office.

Roderick appeared. "Welcome, folks. Shall we set the scene in my office? It's nearly coffee time. Then I'll take you on a whistle-stop tour of parts of the complex that I think may be of interest. Hello, Lucy. Lucy helped us out for a whole week of nights last month."

Van frowned, but he said nothing.

"Is there anyone you particularly would like to talk to?"

"Only one person. We'll need to have a word with your weatherman, Gavin Thomas. Hopefully, he should have all the recordings of wind speed and direction, rainfall and so on for the last three months."

"I'm afraid Gavin has gone off sick. He phoned this morning and he's full of apologies. But he did leave me with a great sheaf of recordings. They're transmitted wirelessly from half a dozen monitors dotted throughout the whole complex. They should give you a reliable picture of wind speed and direction. Have a look. I've also got records of precipitation. Pretty boring – it's been unusually dry for the last couple of months."

They spent some time poring over Gavin's charts and records of rainfall.

"Interesting weather," said Julian. "It looks as if it has been set fair for the whole of the last three months, clearly blowing in the direction of the school and the surrounding areas. Nothing too violent, but steady. Ideal for sailing, of course." The others laughed, knowing that Julian spent every possible free minute on his yacht.

Roderick stood up. "Let's have a go at the tour. Please keep your hard hats on the whole time. Some of the pipes in the corridors are set a bit too low, and we don't want any sore heads."

As they walked through the complex, Roderick repeatedly explained that the monitoring for radioactive leaks was as accurate as was humanly possible.

"This is the last flight of stairs that lead to the roof. Gavin and the safety officer are the only ones with access, but every visit to the whole of the roof area must be documented. Van, I gather you have permission from the Regulator to visit the roof as long as I'm there. Well, I have the keys, so I have to be there."

Lucy grabbed Petra's arm. "Petra, hold onto your skirt."

Petra laughed. "Thanks for the warning."

Roderick opened the double armoured doors and they went out into the sunshine. "Enjoy the view folks, and the breath of fresh air. How about the view, Petra? I saw some of your paintings in the fete at the village hall. The hills to the west take on the most beautiful colours in autumn evenings. Then the sea on the east side – you can just see it in the distance – it can be really wild in winter."

"You're right, Roderick. This would be a splendid place for an artist's studio. In this weather, I could sit here and paint for days."

"Lovely idea, but the security people would be unhappy. Sorry about that, Lucy, you haven't been up here before?"

"You're right about that, Rod. It's a pity Gavin isn't here. He could point out which air vent had the peculiar smell which made him go all dizzy."

"It must have been this one, next to one of his monitors. There's nothing coming out of it right now – the vent, I mean – so there's not much to smell."

Van took a deep breath of the bright morning air. "Well, Roderick, we've had a very interesting tour. Maybe not so helpful as far as our patients go, but reassuring, nonetheless. We'll be on our way and leave you in peace. That all right, Julian?"

"Actually, I have two questions for Roderick."

"Fire away, Julian."

"Firstly, what is the nature of Gavin's illness? And secondly, the air that sometimes comes out of this vent, where does it come from?"

"I can find out more about Gavin by ringing his home. We go fishing together so he won't mind. As far as the origin of the air expelled through this vent, I shall have to ask the engineering department. As soon as I have the answers to both of those questions, I'll give the school a ring. I gather you meet there in Tom Mayhew's study."

*

"Who's for another slightly dry sandwich? Carole made them a while ago and unfortunately you took rather longer than I expected this morning. Come on! Don't look so gloomy, I'm sure something useful came out of your tour."

Tom looked at Petra, expecting a comment.

"A whole lot of negatives, as far as radioactivity goes. But Julian asked two questions right at the end of our visit and Roderick Simmonds will be phoning us as soon as he can."

Tom turned to Anthony. "Come on, young man, you're usually boiling over with questions, have you anything to add?"

"Mr Mayhew, I would like to know what was the peculiar smell that the weatherman said he smelt from that thing on the roof. He said it sort of made him feel dizzy."

"Thank you, Anthony. I don't think anyone has asked that. Why are you interested?"

"Because when I first got ill, my wee smelt of apples and my friends who have the same thing say the same as me. I'm sure it's important, Dad. And another thing, my – our – dog growls at people when they get ill, and sometimes before they get ill. It's as if she knows they're going to get ill. Well, she growled at my friends before they became ill. I'm sure it's important."

The phone rang and Tom turned on the loudspeaker. "Good afternoon, Doctor Simmonds. Headmaster here, do you have any news for us?"

"Two very interesting pieces of news. The most important is that Gavin stayed at home because he noticed that there was blood in his urine. He's been to Doctor Liu who is arranging for a scan and a biopsy this afternoon. Gavin was quite happy with my telling you this and Doctor Liu has said he will keep you in the loop.

"The second piece of news is very odd. The vent on the roof receives air from three sources. Two of them are concerned with routine regular air changes in storerooms, but the third is straight from my office at the end of the control room. It connects directly to the emergency pressure release button on my desk. Whoever is on duty is warned by a bleeping noise that the air pressure in the main reactor chamber is five percent above the arbitrary limit set by the Regulator. The red button is pressed to release excessive air.

"It's a very simple system. The air is stored to make sure there's no release of radioactivity and, when given the automatic signal, it's discharged through what we might as well call Gavin's vent. Not a very complimentary term but we all know what we're talking about. Well, that's it so far. I hope it helps."

"Very many thanks, Doctor Simmonds. That has been most helpful. I hope you won't mind if we need to come back to you."

"Any time, Headmaster. I will phone again as soon as I get more news from Gavin."

"I've thought of something else. When you speak to Gavin could you ask him what was the peculiar smell that he thought was coming out of the air vent? You may laugh, but it's not a silly question. There's a chance it might be a clue. It was Anthony's idea. Thank you again, Roderick, goodbye."

CHAPTER FOUR

"Petra, this is Doctor Liu speaking. Is it all right with you to ask the hospital to biopsy Anthony's kidney?"

"Of course it is. Anything to get a proper diagnosis, then we might be able to find something that helps all your patients."

"You're ahead of me, Petra. I'm also asking the parents of six other children if they are prepared to agree to the biopsy. You will know the pros and cons of the procedure. There may be a slight bleed into the urine but that should be all. We do need a diagnosis and, so far, we've come up against a brick wall. There is an additional worry that if all these cases are caused by an infectious agent, we may be spreading whatever is causing it throughout Europe. The school football team have just returned from a, happily, very successful tour of five European countries. They won all but one of the matches."

"Well done school. Who is the sports master who teaches them football?"

Doctor Liu laughed. "You must be joking, Petra. The headmaster does, he's done it for two years. He used to be the stand-in for the county coach when he was living down south."

"Thanks for ringing, Doctor Liu. Julian did think you could be asking for a biopsy sooner or later. We both agree it might help to get a diagnosis. Carry on, Doctor Liu. Now, Julian has a request. You can probably guess what it is."

"I guess he might be going to ask to see the slides and perhaps use some of his magic machinery at his research laboratory? If so, I'm sure it can be arranged. I take it you will explain to Anthony that we do really need to have the biopsy done, mainly to get a proper diagnosis, but also to see if we can get a clue to the right treatment."

*

An unhappy Anthony looked at the plate of food in front of him. The thought of eating any of it even one mouthful, was not on. "Sorry, Mum, I can't. Sorry, it looks so good but there's no appetite in me."

Petra came around behind Anthony and put her arms round his shoulders as he cried. "Never mind, darling. What can I get you instead?"

"I'm so thirsty, Mum. All I want is a whole jug of water. Then I don't seem to be able to pee properly, it's all burning and horrid. Can they do anything else to help? My friends are all the same as me."

"Doctor Liu phoned today and asked if you, and the others, could have what's called a kidney biopsy. They do this in hospital. It takes about three minutes and the small piece of tissue they take can then be looked at and analysed to see what is going on."

"I suppose I have got two of them … will they leave much of the other kidney?"

"What they call the biopsy is about a millionth of the volume of the kidney so there is plenty left, and kidneys grow pretty fast. Tomorrow morning, us seven mothers will all go in convoy to the city hospital, and we will all be back here for lunch. There's no breathing in anaesthetic, just a little needle prick round the back and a slight amount of pushing, that's all. Dad is also going to have a look with his magic machinery to see what's going on."

"Dad will find something, I'm sure of that. Can I email the others?"

Petra laughed at the idea, relieved at the loving confidence of their son. "Of course, you can, darling."

*

The return journey was hysterically cheerful. It had been decided to hire a minibus and they were all together. The children had all stood up to the procedure well and were proud that they had been so brave. Mothers were mostly relieved that, at last, something was being done to determine what was the matter with their children. They had each been given the precious tiny pieces of tissue, well protected in small polycarbonate containers. As they approached Pensfield, Petra collected the samples and she and Anthony waved the minibus goodbye.

"I have the slides, Jules, and the tiniest pieces of tissue. There's enough for electron microscopy but I'm not sure if there's enough to do any genetic work."

Julian looked at the meagre offering. "Don't worry, Pet, there's plenty there. I only need a few hairs-worth of DNA to produce a reasonable genetic screen. I'd like to start as soon as possible. There should be a few technicians around this time of day – if not, I'll start the sequencing myself."

Julian went to retrieve his car keys from his gardening trousers and set off in a cloud of dust to the hills behind the village. The road wound in a zigzag, up through a patch of woodland to a relatively flat area next to a small plastic-reinforced grass airfield. A single-engine aeroplane owned by Bill MacIver, a local farmer, rested beside the airfield, warm inside its hanger. Fifty yards from the airfield, partly hidden by a line of low-cut trees, was a grey single-story building. There were no clues to explain the function of the building, which emphasised the secrecy surrounding it.

The entire compound was Julian's baby, inherited from his time working for MI6. It was mostly used to sort out the effects, good or bad, of genetic engineering. The four scientists who worked in the building were flown in every morning by helicopter, so they had little to do with the surrounding villages.

Julian drove up to the main gate which opened when he flashed a sensor with the entry code. He parked at the front of the building as a white-coated scientist appeared. Julian handed the scientist the samples from the children's kidneys.

"Urgent sequencing please, Martin. Look particularly for anomalies, animal or vegetable. Quick as you can!" They keyed through two armoured doors and entered the main, brightly lit laboratory area that was filled with machinery, some of which made odd noises and flashed coloured lights.

"Nice clean specimens, Jules. We should have at least two of them ready by tomorrow morning. May I ask if any of the subjects have a surname?"

"You may. This one is Anthony Bailey. Anthony is our eldest son."

*

The next day, Julian returned triumphant. "Hello, Pet. Thanks to your wonderful Doctor Liu we have samples from the other cases. We have two full screens this morning. Martin has excelled himself, and the rest will be ready by this evening as long as we don't run out of reagents. And at last Liu has learnt where my lab is. I can't believe it's much of a secret in this day and age with drones buzzing all over the place.

"Anyway, as far as the slides go, under ordinary microscopy all of them show the same picture, with some very odd dots, but under the electron microscope the dots look as if they have a peculiar structure. I've brought prints to show you and see if you can recognise them as some weird sort of organism. The quick and simple genetic screens also look rather odd. Here, have a look."

Julian took photographs from his briefcase and they studied them for a while.

"What do you think, Pet?"

"Jules, I would like a friend of Doctor Liu's, a professor of microbiology at one of the universities in Beijing, to see these photos. I've got my suspicions, but we should ask him. He's staying with Doctor Liu today and I could take them over. In the meantime, you can puzzle over the peculiar genetic screens in your briefcase."

"I could also do with advice from the professor from Beijing. We can go together."

*

The door was opened by a smiling Doctor Liu. "Welcome, both of you. Can I first offer you both tea or coffee?"

"We both prefer coffee, thanks. Jules has his black."

"Excellent. May I introduce an old friend of my family, Professor Dola Tan Yi. Yi, this is Professor Petra Bailey, a botanist, and Commander Julian Bailey, who works for the Ministry of Defence and has his own high-tech laboratory somewhere in the hills above the village. They have something to show you, a puzzle for you, my friend!"

The gnarled white-haired old gentleman, probably in his eighties, smiled at them and bowed as much as his rigid back would allow. "I would be very pleased to help you. Liu has told me the story of the pupils who are suffering from a kidney disease of unknown cause. Let me first see the photographs of the microscope sections and after that, the picture revealed by the electron microscope."

Julian handed Yi the photographs and they waited while he spent some time studying them with a large lens.

"Your little black dots under the ordinary microscope enlarge under your electron microscopy to resemble something I have seen before. They are indeed organisms and, if I must give them a name based on their visual appearance, I would plump for members of the Archaea. Several palaeontologists have suggested that they were some of the first inhabitants of this planet, together with bacteria and viruses. They have a characteristic genetic picture, but they are extremely variable and can swap great chunks of their genetic code with a wide range of organisms. Your organisms seem to have characteristic stringy bits attached to them. Do you have the printouts of the genetics of the abnormal kidneys?"

Yi looked up. "Now this is very strange. I have just been reading, can't remember in which journal particularly, about these organisms. Off the coast of Japan, using a submersible, they scraped up some mud from around a hydrothermal vent at the bottom of the ocean. They eventually isolated DNA from an unknown organism, finally identified as an Archaean. Now parts of the DNA in your printouts resemble that of multicellular organisms – in other words, from the kidneys of the children. But there are sequences that are more likely to be from whole Archaean's. Well, the plot thickens.

"Now, the guy from the submersible suggested the peculiar stringy extensions from the organism could act like a fishing net and trap bacteria; for good. He further suggested the trapped bacteria might, with a few kicks from an evolutionary process, become powerhouses. In other words, the bacteria could become the mitochondria which drive many of the processes in the cells of multicellular organisms, like you and me.

"The reason they are not generally thought to be the cause of illness in humans is that nobody has looked. That's not *quite* true – about thirty years ago there was a microbiologist who was investigating a peculiar ulcer on the leg of a fisherman. He isolated Archaean organisms, but he was shot down by others who suggested that they were superficial contaminants.

"These are very interesting pictures and, if it is possible, a concentration of the little black dots might reveal a recognisable organism. However, you must remember the science of the Archaea is in its infancy. Viruses have been identified that attack Archaea and so they, the Archaea, have the protective mechanisms which we have used in the CRISPR technology that will protect them from attack. It is a vast subject, and I would be interested to see how far you get in your investigation."

Yi looked up at the ceiling. "I am told that the French have some expertise in the field of the Achaeans. One thing about that group of organisms is that many of them are extraordinarily resistant to stress, and many of them have delightfully been called extremophiles. Some can survive at very high temperatures, exposure to high levels of radioactivity, or extremely acid conditions."

Petra and Julian exchanged glances but said nothing.

"They can be isolated from places like the hot springs in the Yellowstone National Park, the hot rims of the volcanoes in Kamchatka, Russia and miles under the sea from the surroundings of volcanic vents, as I told you earlier. You may not believe this, but these organisms produce strangely shaped, highly acid globules when they are in some high sulphur environments like old volcanic caves. They have been called snottites, for the obvious reason that they look just like humans with a bad cold!

"Culturing has to be done, bearing in mind their origin. For instance, one might have to use a highly acid medium or the whole process may have to be undertaken in the absence of oxygen or in great heat. You seem to be concerned with radioactivity, but I would not suggest you try to culture in that environment."

The professor laughed and his listeners laughed with him. "If you succeed in finding the genetic code of the organisms within the kidneys of your patients, you may be in the position to detect an anomaly, a mutant part of the genetic code that is the cause of their illness. I can see a lot of work ahead and would be very interested in the outcome. I wish you well."

Petra took a deep breath. "Thank you, Professor, I think Jules and I have a mountain of thinking to do. You've already given us an interesting list of leads to go on. And thank you, Doctor Liu, for the introduction. I love your story about the snottites."

They drove back to the now regular meeting in the headmaster's study. Julian started the discussion. "This calls for a marked rethink. Firstly, we are going to have to have another go at the vent in the roof of the power station, although I really can't see what bearing it has to the red button in Roderick's office."

"I'm afraid I can," said Lucy, blushing furiously. "It must have been around that time, say, a month ago, that I was asked to do locum nurse duty for a week at the power station. You see, Roderick used to be an old flame of mine, years ago.

"He took me round the power station, and we landed up in his cubby-hole. We were reminiscing and mucking about a bit.

Recalling how we used to dance and I over balanced. I put my hand on that blessed red button and all hell broke loose."

"The dreaded red button now takes on a greater significance," said Tom. "We are going to have to ask for another visit. I don't think they will be pleased. Julian, what excuse can we use this time?"

"That's easy. No attempt has been made to look for anything apart from radioactivity, so a tight piece of sterile muslin or filter material at the same time as someone pressing the red button should do the trick. We would have to wipe the outside rim of the vent first, of course, and try and keep the whole operation as clean as possible. Van, can you get another permission from London to go on the roof?"

"No problem, I'm sure I can. And, hopefully, we can sample the vent as soon as possible. The weather's fine tomorrow so tomorrow morning would be a good time."

CHAPTER FIVE

Van had the bit between his teeth. "Well folks! Here we are again. On the trail of the mysterious ancient germs. Let's hope this is the last attempt by Gaia to get rid of us all. I would predict that James Lovelock would give you an elaborate explanation of that statement. What say you, Julian?"

"Don't you be so sure, Van. Petra will tell you that this so-called solid earth will have the last say in any debate about the future of *Homo sapiens*. With our destruction of the environment and the absurd global warming, we're on a hiding to nothing. Listen to the children in the streets – they are right about the politicians doing mighty little except when it affects their take-home pay. We're burning up the planet and, apart from all the natural - more like unnatural – disasters, mankind will end up with, I suppose you might like to call the remains of us *'Homo derelictus'*. At the very least we might be able to help a few young children from suffering. Sorry, but I believe we're walking, slowly but surely, towards something very bad indeed."

The usually ever-cheerful and thoughtful Julian was descending into a deep gloom.

"Come off it, Julian. If we – well, you – can fully identify this microbe, you can use all the kit in your laboratory to neutralise it."

"Don't you be so sure, Van. Live in the present, our first problem is the obnoxious Martin Orme. Here he comes."

"Back again, I see. Well, sir, do you have written permission this time?"

Van said nothing but showed the gate man the required paperwork.

"I have asked Doctor Simmonds to accompany you for the second time. I must warn you, he's not pleased at all, but he has the Geiger counters which he will hand to you on your way to the roof. Hard hats for you all, please."

"This is a bloody obsession," said Julian when they were out of earshot.

They could see Roderick approaching. "At least our so-called displeased guide has a smile on his face. Good morning, Roderick. Kind of you to assist us again."

"No problem. I have Geiger counters to reassure you about my main concern, but I wish you well with your searching for mysterious ancient germs. To save your legs we could take the lift to the penultimate floor and then you only have to climb one flight of stairs. That must be better than six."

A bright draught of fresh country air met them as they opened the final armoured door to the roof. Petra took a deep breath. "I suppose we should be wearing masks, although they're pretty useless. Fantastic view, Roderick. The colour of those hills!"

"As you say, Petra, the colours are beautiful. It's a shame it's all so dangerous. Well, here we are on the roof and it's another lovely day, perfect for the artist. Did you bring your paints and easel with you, Petra?"

"Afraid not, Roderick. Nice idea though. My only equipment is a sterile cloth and surgical spirit to clean Gavin's orifice. I hope he doesn't mind me calling it that."

"Who have you delegated to depress the dreaded red button?"

"I thought Lucy might like to. After all, she's done it before!"

"That's not funny. But at least I know where it is. There's nothing coming out of the vent now, Petra, so when you're ready I'll disappear. Just remember, this vent also comes from a couple of storerooms."

Petra smiled and concentrated on the job in hand. "Give it five minutes while I clean the surroundings and we wait for the radioactivity check. In the meanwhile, we'll be sunbathing in the fresh air."

Roderick followed Lucy down the stairs and along corridors until they were in his office. "We could resurrect the original pressing of the button, Lucy."

She smiled at him. "Twenty years too late, Rod. And I'm grown up now. But, some other time."

"Of course, some other time. The story of my life – too little and too late. Just one kiss?"

She gave him a quick peck on the cheek, breathed deeply and stroked his face. Roderick leant round behind Lucy and pressed the red button.

"That's to show you I still—" She was cut short by the siren wailing.

Petra waited until the siren went off, and then applied the cloth to the vent through which a moderate amount of air was being discharged. After ten minutes the air flow was dwindling, and she used sterile forceps to remove the cloth and place it into a sterile box. "I hope that reveals something. There is a slight grey stain of the material so we may be in luck, Jules."

"Give me the box and I can be in the laboratory in the twinkling of an eye."

"Not too fast, old son, we want you back in one piece," warned Van. "And we have to pick up Lucy on the way so that she can escape from the clutches of her old flame."

*

Julian sounded excited. "A great mass of them, Pet. On the surface they all look the same, but I bet it's a mixed culture. I'll try growing them on but at the same time do a genetic scan of a sweep from the surface of the cloth. Electron microscopy shows they are Archaea, most likely classifiable as *Lokiarcheota*. They were first found near Loki's castle at the bottom of the Arctic Ocean near a hydrothermal vent, just as we were told by Professor Yi. Anyway, there was no sign of present day bacteria or the viruses that we could use to attack the archaea, but ultrasonic might reveal some. We're far more likely to find viruses that attack Archaea in the spume from the seaside. We need a good storm and a trip to the nearest lighthouse. How about Porthcawl in South Wales? We often see that lighthouse at the end of the pier with waves breaking over it on the television weather programmes. If there's a big storm we might need some serious waterproofs. Then we can play golf afterwards… perhaps not so sensible in a storm. Nice clubhouse. The only snag is it's three hundred miles away."

"Plenty of stormy weather in the North Sea, Jules. At least we now have something to go on. Perhaps if we can identify a mutant gene there might be something we can attack or modify or even eliminate with CRISPR."

"Remind me what that fashionable acronym stands for. It sounds almost edible."

"I keep on telling you. Clustered Regularly Interspersed Short Palindromic Repeats. There, now you must try to remember it. Discovered around the beginning of this millennium by several people, especially a brilliant biochemist called Doudna in America. I can lend you her book, *A Crack in Creation,* if you ever have time to read it. When will your genetic screen be ready?"

"You can have the preliminary gene-screen this evening, then you can get going on your crisp packet. I fancy a trip to the seaside. You'd better tell Van and wind him up so he can put a bomb under his scientists. Just remember we have a very sick son, together with several of his friends. And there are between ten and twenty sick children in other villages. They're all beginning to slip away and there isn't much time.

"We need to compare the genetic make-up of the wild Archaea which I'm sure we can get from a reference laboratory, the isolates from the dirty filter, and the strange bits of DNA from the patients. I have computer programs which can detect differences quickly, especially mutations of sections of genetic code."

CHAPTER SIX

"Just as well I'm in charge of this unruly mob." The headmaster sounded angry, but there was a smile. "Anna, your job is to find a couple more easels in the art department. They often hide them in the cupboard on the far left, especially if they are more clapped out than normal. We can use the white boards to write anything new as it occurs to any of us; we don't want to rely on memory. Right, Julian, what have you brought all the way from your laboratory in the hills? I expect you will have to enlighten us with very simple language."

"We have produced miles of genetic printout with billions of letters to digest. Happily, we also have the machinery to scan, digest and spit out the anomalies. Well, they have all been read and the anomalies are not too many. There is one major anomaly that is present in the Archaea from the vent on the roof of the power station that is also present in our patients, but absent in the codes from the reference laboratories. It's a short piece of genetic code that I hope we will be able to either eliminate or change using Petra's crisp packet.

"There's also another major anomaly which I hope is not relevant to our patients as they don't appear to have it. I suggest that we forget that for the moment and concentrate on the obvious one."

"Thank you, Julian, so what are the next steps to deal with the anomalous gene?"

"Petra and Van have been wound up to persuade their laboratories to concoct mechanisms to eliminate these genes. It has never been attempted before in a human – child or adult – so we will have to obtain special permission from the Regulator. In our case it shouldn't be too difficult as, so far, the cases are uniquely local. Permission from the parents will, of course, be needed, especially if we are forced to do it intravenously. The patients will have to be treated very slowly and very carefully and some of them, perhaps all, may have tremendous reactions. We have to expect that, and close observation will be vital."

"When will this strange treatment be available?"

"Three or four days' time, with luck."

"Good heavens above, that's quick. I wonder what Anthony thinks about it?"

"He's at home, feeling sorry for himself. I'll give him a ring after the meeting. No; he should have time to think about it. I'll ask him this evening."

*

"So that's it, Ant. We should have a sort of curative medicine to make you and the others better in a few days' time. How does that grab you?"

"I'm glad something has been found and you can do something about it. But I don't like the idea of sticking foreign stuff into my blood. Why can't I have it as a powder or a sort of mist? You know, what Uncle Brian blows into his mouth when he gets an asthma attack?"

Petra thought for a while. "I think that's a very good idea. After all, it's how the little beast got into you in the first place, so perhaps it is the best method of attack. Good thinking, Ant."

"I'm not just a pretty face, you know!"

"You seem to be looking on the bright side, that's good. Now, Dad's in a wandering mood so I'll have to send him a text."

"Why don't you blow the medicine into the classroom so all my ill friends can be treated at the same time?"

"We don't want to waste it. There are quite a lot of children who haven't been ill, and it would be a waste to treat them as well. But we should remember that. If it comes to the crunch, it may be needed."

*

Three days later, Anthony felt like the star of the show. Doctor Liu, Petra, Julian and Van were all wearing masks while listening intently as a white-coated scientist from the laboratory showed them a small box of screw-topped bottles. Mothers and the rest of the affected pupils were waiting in the corridor.

With a flourish, Julian produced his up-market machine to squirt the liquid into the mouths of the patients.

"Hang on, Jules, that's mine!" said Petra. "I last used it to prevent black spot on my roses. You'll have to buy me a new one."

"Yes, dear. They cost less than two pounds, and it was the only machine I could find to do the job. Brian's atomiser for his asthma is all sealed. Let's see if it will do the trick." Julian poured a little cloudy liquid into the atomiser.

"Open wide, Anthony – no, better than that."

Anthony opened his mouth as wide as he could.

"Now, Anthony, when I say 'bingo' I want you to breathe in as deeply as you can. OK?" Anthony nodded his head. "The only thing you might notice will be an odd taste in your mouth, nothing nasty. Ready? Bingo!"

Anthony took a deep breath and received a squirt of the liquid. Immediately he coughed out most of the liquid.

"Try again and don't cough for at least a minute."

This time Anthony kept the spray down. "Does that mean I won't get black spot, Mum, like your roses?"

"Try and be serious, darling. This is going to make you better. Hopefully it will mend the damage to your kidneys."

"That should do the trick. I'll keep some in reserve, in case we have to do this again in a week's time," said Julian.

"That's it, Anthony," said Doctor Liu. "Not very dramatic – you're not going to see stars in ten minutes. In fact, you may not notice anything at all, but you might develop a slight fever in the next few days."

"As long as my kidneys stop hurting and people stop saying I'm a cider addict, I don't care about anything else."

Petra turned to Julian. "That reminds me, Roderick phoned and told us that the peculiar smell experienced by Gavin on the roof was similar to rotting apples." Julian smiled to show he had registered the news but said nothing.

"Thank you, all. Well, that worked well, now for the others. We'll take Anthony home now and hope that his kidney pain disappears, and he doesn't smell like a cider farm. Tom, is it alright to treat the children from the other schools here? Then all the documentation is in one place."

The headmaster nodded his head, pleased with the simple nature of the treatment.

*

A cry in the middle of the night; Petra leapt out of bed and ran to Anthony's room. He was sitting up in bed, bathed in sweat with his eyes wide open. She put her arms round him.

"Did you have a horrid dream, Ant? Dad thought you might have dreams related to this little beastie."

Anthony was now fully awake. "Thanks, Mum. I was dreaming I was going to fall into one of those boiling springs they have in the park in America. I suppose that's where the little beast came from originally. I didn't believe it, so I made myself wake up. I feel a bit, sort of, hot, but I'm alright now. Thanks, Mum. Good night. I'll be alright in the morning."

Petra had reached the door of Anthony's bedroom when he spoke again. "Mum, there was something else that was very odd. It was as if there was something or someone looking at all of us and testing how to get rid of us. I'm not sure if it was meant to be frightening, but it was very weird. I suppose I was sort of frightened, but I didn't know what I was frightened of."

"Leave it till the morning, darling. Try to sleep now."

Julian was struggling to wake up. "How is he? If he's got a temperature, that is all to the good. It shows some sort of fighting reaction is going on. His kidneys will be a bit swollen, but they'll recover. They should be as good as new in a month."

"Let's hope so. I don't fancy the thought of taking Ant to hospital in this weather – have you heard the wind? This must be the tail of an Atlantic hurricane. Perhaps this is the end of the kidney cases and we can all relax."

"I wouldn't bet on it, Pet. Remember, we found two major anomalies in the genetic code of the Archaean and, so far, we have no idea what damage the other one is cooking up."

"There was something else Ant said as I was leaving the room. Something about all of us are due for the chop and he and his mates were part of an experiment. I suppose it was simply a function of a nightmare. At least, I hope so."

*

Two weeks later, Petra picked up the telephone. "Hello, Doctor Liu." She listened for two minutes. "Tomorrow morning, you said. That's OK with me. I can bring four of them and I expect Lucy can bring the other four. Is this the final sign-off? What a relief. Let's hope the whole thing is over." She replaced the phone and shouted to Julian, "Jules, Doctor Liu wants to have a final sign-off at his surgery tomorrow morning."

*

Eight healthy children waited for the doctor to give his verdict on their health. Doctor Liu came into the room and his smile made them all relax. "Well, girls and boys, I can find nothing wrong with any of you. So, you are all dismissed and just in time for Petra and Lucy to take you back to school for the afternoon lessons. Anthony, what's the problem?"

"Sir, can we all have the afternoon off, please? There's something wrong with today. We all feel the same. We all woke up with the same idea. It may be something to do with the awful hot wind that seems to come out nowhere. It made us all feel sick. That's why we were all so silent when you first came into the room. We are all very grateful for the news that you can find nothing wrong with us, but there's something that is not quite comfortable today and we just want to go home, and ..." He tailed off.

"I'll have to ask the headmaster, but I'm sure he will say it's OK. Off you go then, Petra and Lucy will be back in a few minutes and take you all home."

CHAPTER SEVEN

There was a knock on the door of the headmaster's study.

"Come in!" He waited and called again, but nobody entered. He got up from his chair and opened the door to find Anna crouched down and weeping silently. He gently led her into the study and sat her down, snatching a paper handkerchief from the box to dab her eyes, and waited for the storm to pass.

"Not like you, Anna, tell me all."

"Oh, Tom, there's something terribly wrong with my class. I can't control them. I felt there was something wrong as soon as I started this morning. There were so few of them, what with the absence of those who are ill with the strange kidney disease. The air was stifling, which is all wrong for this time of year, so I opened the windows. But the fresh air wasn't fresh at all. It smelt fusty and odd to me. And the children complained about it. So, I closed the windows again. The more I think about it, the more peculiar that air was. It was as if it was dark air, if you know what I mean – the air had something evil that hated us. The smell was most odd. The sort of smell you think comes from spraying the fields with fermenting cow dung, but worse.

"Then one of the girls started to scream. So, I went to her and she was pointing to her hands which were a sort of grey colour and changing quite fast. Then awful black hairs started sprouting from her hands. The other pupils crowded round and two of them said the same thing was happening to them. They showed their hands to me and it was true. It was a nightmare."

59

Anna's voice rose and she covered her face. The headmaster had to bend down to her level to hear her voice.

"Things got worse, and I knew I was losing control. I shouted to everyone to sit down, but they were milling around making very odd, noises, like animals. Then they stopped looking at me or taking any notice of anything I said. I was shouting quite loud by then, but they were grabbing at each other and not making any sense."

Anna had to stop and blow her nose.

"I saw they were all changing colour and the snatching at clothing got worse until there were piles of dirty clothes on the floor. They were taking off their own clothes, not just from each other. The only child not affected was Ben – he was sitting in the corner, just watching. His face was impassive, as if he was watching a play and the whole action was for his benefit. The grunting got worse and the children started fighting and breaking up things. Anything! Chairs, desks, even tearing up the books and pulling down the blinds and trampling on them. I tried to stop some of them, but they ignored me and pushed me away. They were incredibly strong and there was nothing I could do.

"And the children's skin had this odd colour, sort of dark grey. But the grey became darker and darker until they were all covered in masses of black hair and they had no clothes on at all. When they had taken all their clothes off the children didn't have normal pale pink skin. They were covered in masses of black hair, grabbing at each other and fighting, pulling off great lumps of the awful hair. And they were making peculiar grunting noises all the time. Two of them completely smashed up a desk – I know I'm going to be blamed. I don't mind paying for a desk, but I don't understand what's going on. Oh, Headmaster, I don't understand. And why is it only my classroom; first I had the children with rotting kidneys and now this?"

"Anna, what you're saying doesn't make any sort of sense to me, it's weird. Come with me, I'll help you back to your classroom."

"No! Please, don't. I need my husband. Van is strong enough to control them. I can't do anything. They pushed me out of the classroom, out of the door, and it was all I could do to shut the door on them. That's why I was crying outside your study."

"Don't worry, Anna, Van should be on his way for a meeting in a few minutes' time. Stay here in my study while I go and see the problem for myself."

The headmaster walked the short distance to the classroom and peered through the clear glass window in the door. "Oh my God! Van, we sure do need you," he muttered as he returned to his study a very, very worried man.

"Tea is the great cure all, Anna. I suggest we make a pot and try to get our thoughts together."

The headmaster stood up. "Here he is, I can hear his car on the gravel."

They heard the car door shut and Van's athletic steps along the corridor.

As Van entered the study, he hesitated. "Good morning, folks. Do I detect an air of something very wrong? Tom, anything I can do to help?"

"You certainly can, Van. Come with me and have a look through the door of Anna's classroom."

As they walked down the corridor, they could hear the strange animal noises and the breaking of furniture. They only had to glance through the window of the classroom door to see the mayhem inside.

"What do you make of that, Van? About half an hour ago I heard a knock on my study door and Anna was crying outside in the passage, distraught, not knowing what to do. She said the class was completely out of control; fighting, breaking up the desks, and then they threw her out. Oh yes, they were all grunting in a disgusting manner."

Van watched the chaos in the classroom for a full two minutes before he spoke. "Did Anna say anything about the hairs on the children's hands and the odd way they progressed? Colloquially it used to be called 'knuckle walking'. Headmaster, I am afraid we have a very serious problem indeed. Can we get Petra, Julian, and Lucy here as soon as possible? Did you see Ben sitting quietly in the corner, minding his own business? He appears to be safe now, but I don't give him much of a chance if they turn on him."

Petra, Julian and Lucy appeared quickly, with Anthony in tow, and were taken to look through the door of the classroom. Back in the headmaster's study, another pot of fresh tea was required. They were gloomy, looking to the headmaster to start the discussion about what on earth was going on.

"Van, you took some time looking at the riot before you made a comment. Did you come to any conclusion?"

"The instant growth of a mass of black hair on the hands of the pupils and the knuckle walking set my hair on end. It is a very long time since I read Darwin's brilliant *Origin of Species* but in the back of my mind there is a sentence from the book that did not quite ring true. He raised the hare that, in his opinion, it would be most unlikely that evolution might, given unusual circumstances, go into reverse. The children have discarded most, if not all, of their clothing and reverted to an extremely primitive type of animal resembling the prehominids of several million years ago."

He stopped and looked at his audience to see if they had taken in the importance of his statement before he continued. "Sadly, I have to point out that the children now resemble members of the ape family. They are not even hominids – they are pre-hominids. *Homo sapiens* have not progressed on their knuckles for the last two million years. I'm afraid they have gone back five, perhaps ten, million years. Oh, dear. This is very hard to believe. And I don't think it's going to get better." Van, the calm, huge man, bowed his head in disbelief.

Anna came over and put her arms round his broad shoulders. "My darling, if anyone can solve this, you can."

Van kissed her and wiped his eyes. "All of us have one hell of a battle on our hands. Julian, what on earth do you think has gone wrong? And so incredibly fast."

"Van, off the cuff, I suspect this is related to the second mutant element that we found in the screens of DNA. That element was streets bigger than the solitary mutation that we appear to have defeated. And I must say, I have a feeling that this is too deliberate and weird to be chance. Something or somebody is trying to get rid of the whole of *Homo sapiens*, and this latest attack is far more devastating. I'm sure we all noticed Ben sitting quite alone in the corner. I'm not convinced the mutants were simply ignoring him. Perhaps because he appeared not to be frightened, they were either fearful of him or respected him. All the same, we should try and get him out of there. How do we do that, Petra?"

"We tempt them with something edible towards one end of the classroom. While they are all at that end, it should give us a chance to quickly snatch Ben. I suggest a bag of fruit and vegetables – raw, of course. Headmaster, can we open the rear door and then lock it from the outside?"

Tom Mayhew, for once out of his depth, nodded.

"Good. Now we need a snatcher. Van, you're the strongest and fittest. Is that alright with you?"

"I suppose I would be the best person to act as the Ben snatcher. It doesn't take much effort to chuck in a bag of fruit; that's nice and quick. An incidental thought, Julian, and more in your field – how about the idea that I might be able to snatch some of the hair that they are so busy pulling off each other? That might show us evidence of the second mutation."

Julian nodded. "Good idea. You'd better be quick. I know how strong you are but looking at how destructive they are, you wouldn't stand a chance against the whole lot of them. They're already attacking each other, and I suspect we may well find that some of them will be injured by the time we sort this mess out, if we ever do. Well, Tom, what next? Fruit and veg?"

"Carole, I give you the task to extract a box of fruit and veg from the kitchens. Tell them – I've no idea – I'm sure you can think of something. Say it's urgent."

Carole returned with a large box of mixed fruit. "I bought these from the reject box in the kitchen. What can we give them to drink, Headmaster?"

"That's difficult. They've smashed the water dispensing bottle and most of the water has already been licked up from the floor. Let's concentrate on getting Ben out, then we can reappraise the situation. Van, you get ready to snatch Ben and I'll slip this box of fruit through the fire exit. I'm not sure I can lock it from the outside, that's against the safety regulations. But if one of them works out how to use the escape handle, they'll be in the playground in seconds. They only have to lean hard on it."

Through the window of the classroom door they watched as the fire door slowly opened and the box of fruit was quietly inserted. The door was slammed shut to attract the children's attention. There was a rush to the box as they fought for the fruit, leaving a clear area round Ben.

"Van, go!" shouted Julian. Van pulled the door open and quickly snatched a tangle of hair in one hand and the surprised Ben in the other. Van slipped on the wet floor, frantically looking towards Julian who was standing in the doorway. "Catch!" he shouted as he threw Ben towards Julian. One of the mutants heard the shout, turned, and caught hold of Van's ankle.

"Let me go, you bastard!" Van shouted; but this alerted the other mutants who began to approach, looking as if they wanted to join the fight. Van picked up a broken chair leg and hit the arm of the animal. He heard the bone break, but the hand still grasped his ankle. "Julian, pull me out, then slam the door." Julian grabbed Van's arm, pulled him through the doorway and slammed the door shut, cutting off the mangled remains of the animal's forearm.

Petra screamed. "Oh my God, this is horrible. Its hand is still twitching." They watched the hand very slowly lose all its hair and begin to look like a seriously damaged child's hand. The hand then disintegrated before their eyes, leaving only a tiny pile of brown dust. "I don't believe this; there's nothing left. Just dust, but, Jules?"

"I can guess what you're thinking, Pet. If all that hair can be shed so quickly, then there's a clue to tempt us that we can cure it. Goodness knows how we can persuade that lot as individuals to gently inhale a magic gene destroyer. Anthony, you're full of ideas – what can we do now?"

"It would be very wasteful, but you could use some sort of spray gun and do the whole lot at once. I suggested that before, but it didn't seem to be practical at the time."

"Good idea, but all the laboratories in the country would have to work flat out to produce that sort of volume."

The headmaster returned. "Are you in one piece, Van? I saw you being dragged back; and the result. Where did that come from?" He pointed to the little pile of dust.

"The child's hand just disintegrated." Tom went white and swallowed hard, but he kept control. "Ben, are you alright?"

Ben looked at the group and calmly said, "I'm good, thank you. Why did you take me away from my friends? They need me, and their hands are ever so soft. I want to go back into the classroom and finish the lesson. Then I can look after them and take them away to a nice place where they will be safe. They won't last long, you know, it's not fair." He stood up and went to open the handle of the classroom door. "No! Let me!" he cried in frustration as he was pulled back.

Anna opened her arms, but Ben shrank away from her cuddle.

"What can I do?" She pleaded, "I can't let him go back in there; he wouldn't last a second if they turned on him. And what is Ben talking about when he says he can take them to a safe place? Petra, what shall I do?"

"It *is* a hellish gamble but why don't we take Ben at his word? Let us imagine he is the new pied piper of Hamlyn? He has obviously already decided where he wants to take them. If he's thinking of the hills and the woods, that's alright; in their present state that would be ideal. I suspect his last statement is correct and they're not going to last very long. If you take a bunch of *Homo sapiens* into the woods, they will start to construct buildings for weather protection. You have had enough of that in those dreadful television programmes. But these are no longer *Homo sapiens* – they are so damaged, they should be called *Homo derelictus*. And they're not coming back. I'll give his mother a ring."

Van found he was still clutching the mass of hair. He handed it to Julian. "This should reveal the anomaly, rather a matted bloody mess but there's plenty of DNA for you to be going on with. I agree with Petra. It is a gamble to let Ben lead what are now animals to a better place for them. He obviously has them in the palm of his hand. I suppose we could have assumed that by the way they left him alone in the corner, and he seems quite happy with the idea of heading them to some sort of freedom. Our problem will be to identify where Ben will take them. They're so strong, it would be stupid to expect anyone to follow them on foot. A drone is the obvious choice. Headmaster, does the school have access to one?"

"We don't have any of those machines but there are several parents who have them. The local farmers might be the best bet. They use them to see how their crops are doing."

Van glanced into the classroom. "They're a lot quieter now, must be all that fruit. Before we go ahead, has anybody thought to warn the hill rangers and the parents of these creatures? That's the saddest bit."

The phone rang and the headmaster picked it up. His face darkened and beads of sweat formed on his brow. After a few minutes he replaced the handset.

"That's about the worst news—" He looked at the others in the study with tears in his eyes. "I'm sorry to have to tell you, but we are not the only ones with weirdly changed children. That was the Council chief administrator for schools. He told me almost all schools in his catchment area are affected. Two teachers have been killed and the army have been called in to calm down a riot in one of the secondary schools. There have been shootings." He broke down in tears.

Ben came over to the headmaster's chair and placed his hand on the weeping man's arm. "Let me—" The sentence was unfinished, but the request was obvious to everyone. "I can help the other schools, if you like. I know the hills. That's right, Miss?" He looked at Anna as if wishing her to back him up.

"Ben's right, Headmaster. He used to disappear for hours and returned quite tired. Then he would draw extraordinarily accurate pictures of where he had been. He must have made friends with the ponies on the hills, and he knows where the deer go to get away from tourists. That's true, Ben, isn't it?"

"I know the hills," with a twitch of a smile.

CHAPTER EIGHT

"All right, Ben, we're relying on you and I am sure the other schools will be very grateful for your help. Van, how are we going to organise our own evacuation with the least trouble?"

"Tom, you have the key to the fire door so we can open it from the outside. Ben will be with you and he will have to show himself to the animals and, using his magic, he will lead them out and up to the hills. I expect he's already worked out where to take them. He probably knows the hills like the back of his hand. I would hazard a guess he has in mind a derelict barn with a spring as a water supply. Any other ideas, Petra?"

"Feeding them all, assuming all the schools in the neighbourhood will be joining our lot, is going to be a major problem. It's going to need a lorry load of fruit daily. Perhaps dropping food from a helicopter is the answer, from a safety point of view. What else, Jules?"

"If Ben can work his magic, it might give us time to work out how we are going to cure our children before evolution has reversed too far into the distant past. I was going to wait until this evening, but I might as well tell you now, Anthony's kidneys have recovered completely as have those of his friends. They feel fine and one of them even said it was all a terrible dream. But this reverse evolution is quite a different problem and is happening at an astonishing speed. I'm only guessing, but I strongly suspect that all those children in Anna's class have been affected by the second mutation, and they don't stand a chance. Happily, Ben seems to be immune. It's not up to us to question why."

Julian picked up the mass of hair snatched by Van. "This, I hope, may confirm my suspicion. If it doesn't, then we're hopelessly lost, in the dark without even a hope of a torch. If it does help us, we can try to correct the altered gene, even multiple genes; but it takes time and must be done carefully and possibly individually. That's our real problem. I'm afraid Ben's comment that he doesn't think they will last long, sadly, is most likely to turn out to be true and we will indeed be faced with *Homo derelictus*. If adults go the same way as these children, *Homo sapiens* will cease to exist. On that dismal note, which, I fear, may well turn out to be true, I shall disappear and give my technical staff a huge amount of work. See you tomorrow, folks."

"What is it, Ben?" The headmaster turned to the little boy who had been tugging at his sleeve.

"Headmaster, can I start, please? My friends are not happy and sort of noisy."

The animals in the classroom were fighting again and breaking up more of the furniture. There was a lot of blood, mostly from the severed arm of the animal that had attacked Van.

Van glanced into the classroom. "Interesting, they don't use any of the chair legs in their fighting, just fighting with their hands and feet. Tom, I believe Ben will be quite safe. Shall we begin? So, you will take Ben to the outside of the fire door, and then open the door. Then you can come back here to see his friends follow Ben. Ben, you'll be the hero of the hour."

The little boy looked at Van with a twitch of a smile. He said nothing and followed the headmaster.

The fire door was cracked open and a completely calm Ben opened the door fully and stood still while the animals came towards him. One of them put out a paw and, very gently, touched Ben's face. Ben turned and walked towards the back gate of the school playground, across the road and onto the path leading to the hills. All but three of the animals followed Ben and they were quickly lost to sight.

"What's wrong with these?" Petra quietly opened the classroom door, tiptoed in and gingerly touched one of the animals lying on the floor. "He's dead! And I think the other two are as well. I'm not surprised about the one with the lost arm as he's bled a huge amount, but why these two, Van? They're quite cold!"

"Just a guess, but perhaps the reversal has been too quick for them. Maybe they've lost some metabolic systems that we have developed over the last two million years and their machinery has clogged up. There's a scientific term for you to digest!" He looked towards the hills. "I wonder if Ben's prediction is happening faster than even he hinted at? Look closely at these two dead ones."

"Oh my God! They're shrinking!" Petra touched one of the dead apes. The body of the animal collapsed inside the coating of black hairs. She screamed. "Jules, I can't believe – they're disintegrating into – nothing."

Julian held her tight. "It's Ben we need to worry about, my darling. These are well past salvaging."

"So, if we were brave enough to follow him, we might find bodies falling by the wayside. That means anything your lab is doing will be much too late."

"Afraid so, Pet. I'm off to the lab."

Only two hours later, Petra's mobile rang, and she glanced at the screen. "Talk of the devil! What's happened, Jules?"

"I've found the major mutation in the DNA of the blood-soaked hair but there seems to be a much bigger invasion. It could be that the whole of the Archaean organism has invaded them. The only way of getting around that problem is to attack it directly with a virus. It looks as if we're forced to make a trip to the seaside. How about tomorrow? The forecast is for fine weather but a very high wind. There should be plenty of sea spray around our coastline."

"Lovely idea, Jules. We could all meet there with our wet suits and sterile bottles. We'll need to make sure Van is coming. Was there something else, Jules?"

"Unfortunately, there is. We've had a dozen phone calls from colleagues across the Continent. They're having the same problem and they're blaming our football team for spreading it. But geographically that suggestion doesn't stand up, as most of the calls come from places that our team didn't visit. On the other hand, they are near power stations, not just nuclear ones, any old power station – coal, gas, you name it. Oh, and they have had a fair number of adults affected. I'm afraid in some countries, the politicians have ordered the troops to shoot the apes as they aren't able to control them. A bit drastic, but inevitable. What a mess!"

CHAPTER NINE

Three cold, miserable people desperately held onto the balustrade at the base of the lighthouse, waiting to capture the spume from the big wave.

"Jules!" Petra had to shout. "I have to confess, this is not my idea of fun. How many viruses are there supposed to be in all this froth?"

"About a billion in every cubic centimetre. There are bound to be a few that we can use. Takes time to grow them, of course, and to get enough to treat more than one or two people might well take weeks. I don't think my lab could cope with all that work without massive extra funding. Would your organisation offer to help, Van?"

"Let's see if your technicians can isolate the right sort of viruses first. Hang on, I've been counting, and the next wave should be the eleventh since the last big one. That's what the story books say is the cycle. Well, I – hang on folks, here is the big one – hold on!"

An enormous wave erupted from the boiling sea as if it had been requested. The sea wall shook as the wave hit the side of the cob and exploded vertically. Three shaking hands held out ridiculously small containers to collect tiny amounts of the froth. Containers were closed tight, and the three pathetic, cold humans huddled together as the sea tried to sweep them into the path of the next wave. It sank down as if it was storing up the energy to have another go at trapping the three. A tiny window of very damp calm gave them the opportunity to escape another drenching.

"Now!" shouted Van. He grabbed Petra's and Julian's hands and pulled them back along the cob. "Another fifty yards, that's all." Eventually they reached the doors of the lifeboat station where they were met by a fully-kitted lifeboat sailor holding a pair of powerful binoculars.

"Just as well you told us what you were doing," said the sailor. "We were about to get the lifeboat ready when you came back. I hope you succeeded in your strange mission. By the way, what exactly were you trying to do? From here you looked like three witches casting a spell on the ocean."

Julian laughed and became serious. "What we are hoping to do is to find viruses in the spume of the exploding wave. We hope to use those viruses to kill off the very primitive organisms which are attacking human beings in a particularly nasty way. So, you see, we are not completely mad, and we don't deal in witches – we haven't done that for a couple of hundred years.

"But I can understand how people get swept off the cob; that wave hit the wall with one hell of a bang. All that energy must be dissipated somewhere. The cob wall shook tremendously and if we hadn't been holding on tight, we could easily have been sucked into the sea. How often do people find themselves in the sea? That would be a difficult call out. How often does that happen?"

"Three or four times a year, I'm afraid. But it takes a while to launch the boat and by the time we get there they have already been bashed onto the sea wall, so they usually don't survive."

The sailor heaved an unhappy sigh at the all too frequent memories. "Anyway, you're alright so we can stand down. I'm sure we can offer you a coffee or tea while you get changed into dry clothes and escape with your samples."

Surrounded by culture plates, tubes, and whirring, sparkling machinery, Julian saw his mobile phone was blinking. He frowned. "How the hell did that get past the blocking system?" He picked up the tiresome instrument. "Hello, Headmaster, you must be very persuasive to be able to ring me. What can I do for you?"

Julian listened for one minute. "Both of them? I'm in the lab at the moment. I'll ring you back in half an hour."

He finished looking down the electron microscope, gave instructions to the technician, took off his laboratory coat, and walked to his office. He sat for five minutes and finally picked up his phone.

"Sorry to cut you off, Tom; I'm in my office now and sitting quietly. Tell me again."

"Julian, I had a call from a neighbour of the parents of one of our children who has died. This lady said she had heard banging coming from the house next door. She went over and as she got to the front door, the banging got worse. So, she went home and this time she and her husband returned and tried the door. They found it was unlocked. But just as they opened the door, the parents rushed out, knocking them over. Both the mother and father were like animals and covered in black hair. And they were walking in a—" Tom choked, breathed deeply, and continued. "They were walking in a peculiar manner with their bunched hands on the ground. Then they rushed off in the direction of the hills. They were going in the same direction as Ben was leading the ape-children. There was nobody to direct these two adults, they simply seemed to know where to go. I'm just worried about the parents of all the other children that we have lost." Tom coughed and couldn't continue.

"That's a pretty sad thought, but I can understand your concern. I think we need reinforcements from the big city. I know just the right person and I'll get hold of him as soon as I come back to the school. Leave that to me. Goodbye, Tom."

"Is that Lord Ogilvie's office? Good! Will you tell Q that I need his help as soon as possible – I should have phoned earlier but we thought we were under control. This is Julian Bailey, by the way, you may remember me?"

"He will be in this office in five minutes, and I promise I will tie him to his chair until he rings you. Yes, I remember you very well and Lord Ogilvie speaks very highly of you. Don't worry, Julian, I'm on a mission!"

"Julian, how nice to hear from you after, how long is it, five years, perhaps twice that? How can I help? There have been very strange rumours of peculiar happenings in your neck of the woods. Tell me all and I'll see if I can help."

"Thanks for ringing, Q. It all started with about half a dozen boys, my son amongst them, developing an unusual disturbance of their kidney function. But there were many more cases in other schools near us, so the total number was around fifty. To cut a long story short, a few of the children had a renal biopsy and under the electron microscope were peculiar large elements within some of the kidney cells. We basically ignored those. But, the genetic screens from all the biopsied children showed elements that probably came from very primitive organisms and there was one gene which we identified as a definite mutation. Well, we managed to correct the altered gene that was affecting all of them and they're fine now.

"We had more than a strong suspicion that the active agent came from a growth of an unidentified agent squirting out from the ventilation orifices on the roof of a local nuclear power station. In retrospect, we should have taken more notice of the strange dots from the biopsies of the kidneys of one or two boys.

"Sorry if this sounds muddled, but with the help of an old Chinese professor who happened to be staying with our general practitioner we identified the invading agent as a mixture of Archaean organisms. Until now these organisms were not thought to cause disease in humans, but they seem to have inserted the mutant gene in all these children. We used a CRISPR to correct the mischievous gene and all the children are now cured.

"So far, so good, and we all began to relax. But suddenly, all the remaining children in the class that the original sick children came from grew extremely hairy and degenerated to ape-like creatures. This happened in all the schools and the change was incredibly quick. Over a period of less than five minutes we were left with degenerate animals which resemble what would have lived at least two million years before *Homo sapiens* came on the scene. It was horrendous to watch it happening in front of our eyes. The only unaffected child was an autistic child, loved by the entire school.

"Wonderfully, this little boy offered to lead all the animals, that had been children, up into the hills. He was quite insistent and wouldn't take no for an answer. We accepted his offer, which was fantastic. He also collected children of about the same age from other schools and presumably they are now all together on the hills. There is, of course, now a huge logistical problem to feed and water them. On the other hand, Ben, the autistic child, says quite clearly that in his opinion none of the animals will survive. I suspect he's right."

Julian had to pause to catch his breath before he was able to continue.

"But the latest disaster is that adults are also being affected. Both parents of one of the mutant children were seen to discard all their clothing and appeared covered in masses of black hair. They have also disappeared up into the hills without needing to be led. They were knuckle walking like apes, and—"

"Julian, if it were anyone else but you, I would put the phone down and assume it was a scam. Right, old son, what would you like me to do? I will help all I can, and I can tell you I have a hell of a lot of under the counter power these days. I expect this call is being listened to by a whole host of ridiculously obsessed people of various nationalities, but I am past caring. How can I help, old son? Tell me all."

"I've told you all I can at the moment, but I'm sure we need you on site."

"My goodness! As I understand it, you originally thought the hairy apes had been created from the second mutation produced by the Archaea?"

"Correct; but now I have actually grown Archaea from the bloody mass of hair snatched by Van from one of the mutants in the classroom. You must appreciate that no amount of gene correction will make any difference. The differences between hominids and the apes have less to do with genetic sequences and more to do with how the genes are switched on and off; the whole process is incredibly complicated. Evolution teaches genes to do new tricks, so maybe this is an unlearning process and there is damn-all we can do about it. It has even been suggested that somehow the Archaean organisms have managed to rocket evolution into reverse.

"No, it seems our only line of attack is directly by killing the Archaea with natural viruses. My next job is to try to identify viruses from the natural environment to attack the Archaea. I have ten or so under study at the moment, but this takes time. We now have a gigantic problem. How on earth are we going to be able to tempt a full-grown gorilla to take its medicine?"

"Don't you worry, Jules, I'll catch the first train. No, I won't, I'll use one of the pool drivers and be on your doorstep as soon as possible."

Julian heard his old friend shout to his secretary to cancel everything before the phone went dead.

CHAPTER TEN

"Tom, I have asked Lord Quentin Ogilvie to come and give us a hand. He is a very old friend and likes to be called 'Q'. Gives him a sense of mystery, I guess. But he is very adept at altering the direction of the wheels of power. You'll like him,"

Tom laughed. "Don't you worry, Julian. Quentin! Well, I'm damned – I knew him well. I was at school with him many years ago. He always seemed to be on cloud nine, but he was amazing at getting us out of trouble when we had done something particularly stupid. Well, I never! I hope he's given up that disgusting pipe-smoking habit."

"He'll be here in the next hour, maybe three hours."

A shower of gravel by the front of the school heralded the arrival of the Lord Quentin. He came in almost at the double. "Bloody traffic, no wonder people hate driving. Anyway, I'm here. Good to see you Julian, and Petra."

"And well, I never! Haven't seen you, Tom, since, when? School days? Put on a bit of weight, perhaps, but still that mop of curly hair and bright eyes. Let's hope the brain cells are as slick as they were at school. Good to see you."

They welcomed each other with open arms.

"Tea or coffee, Q? Or can I get you something stronger?"

"Coffee, please, a little milk and no sugar. Thank you, Tom. If you were going to offer me a biscuit, I'd better wash my hands, especially with my scientist friend watching every move.

And, I nearly forgot, a very large whisky and a small amount of water."

Quentin returned, washed and refreshed, and they sat down to relax over the coffee and whisky.

"I've been mulling over what you told me on the phone, Julian. This strange reversion, I suppose you might call it, to the pre-hominid stage of evolution. I have some further dismal news. I'm sorry to have to tell you all that calls from the Continent have indicated that the same situation is happening over there. There seem to be at least ten European countries that are similarly affected. And the bulk of the cases are relatively near nuclear installations or even gas-powered power stations. The puzzle is that there are several outbreaks that are as far away from power stations as you can get. We are now left with the hint that the condition may be human to human spread, although I find that hard to believe.

"I had a curious thought on the way down. Your original cases, Julian. They were quite different. It sounds as if they were what could be called 'a shot across the bows' – a simple wakeup call, almost a try-on. What do you think, Petra, get your imagination into first gear, like you used to do? Get your thinking cap on."

Petra looked startled. "That would imply there had to be a sentient being with a determination to rid the planet of *Homo sapiens*. Well, we know it's been tried before and failed, so let's hope it is going to fail again. There are seven and a half thousand million of us so there's a very long way to go. That's not funny, by the way, but you can see my thinking. I remember, the night after we treated Anthony and his friends, he had a weird dream which had elements that suggested a deliberate destruction of *Homo sapiens*.

"We know the Archaea are susceptible to a wide range of viruses. Naturally they also have a complex armament of protective mechanisms. Logically, we need to have a huge range of viruses to fight for us. We can always be tempted to do another trip to the seaside and increase our collection of new viruses simply with a view to increase our firepower. How are your new babies growing, Jules?"

"I fail to imagine how the first forms of primitive life can be called sentient. But you never know what might be motivating them. The viruses are growing very well, thank you. I reckon in a week's time I should have half a dozen raring to go and destroy any number of Archaea. So far so good, Tom. Any better thoughts?"

"How are we going to see if they're safe to use in derelict humans? I have a feeling that if they're going to be any use at all, they'll have to be administered at the first sign of things going wrong. In other words, we must wait for the first sign of hairy hands, and we must, somehow, apply the viruses. Any ideas how we are going to do that? Intravenous injection would be impossible in an angry derelict ex-human. We have seen first-hand that the derelicts are, for a short while, as strong as giant apes. Perhaps an aerosol might work. Didn't Anthony suggest that, Petra?"

"Trial and error, Tom. But just think, squirting an aerosol would be incredibly wasteful of Jules' valuable viruses. We need a very early case to experiment on. And don't forget we should really ask for permission from the appropriate authorities. Can we ask you, Q, to move mountains?"

Quentin laughed and then instantly became serious. "If I were in your position, I would write a general request to use your viruses on the usual experimental animal. Poor old mice would do, I suppose. It's doubtful that they would suffer any peculiar effect as long as they don't turn into apes. Now that would be interesting!

"It could be that a particular human case might be in the vicinity and we can then assess the effect on him or her. Sounds devious, I know, but I can't think of anything better. I can give you permission to do that. With the enormous number of humans being destroyed, there is a problem with timing which we will have to overcome.

"I understand from friends in high places that any age can be affected. Even babies as young as a few months are changing into baby gorilla-like animals; and that can happen in a few minutes. Also advanced geriatrics are going the same way, and just as fast. The crippled and those with Alzheimer's die on the spot."

Quentin stopped and took a deep draught of his whisky. "I suppose that could be thought of as a blessed relief."

"Relief for the carers as well," remarked Petra. "As long as they are not affected the same way."

Van, out of breath, came into Tom's study. "Come to report on the state of the hills. I was up early, so I thought I would walk up to the top and see what was going on. I ran most of the way back – too old to run uphill anymore. I saw thousands of the poor things on the hills. I even saw two huge apes capture a fully-grown deer. Then ten or more of them just tore it to pieces and ate the raw meat. It was a horrendous, primitive sight. I took Sheba with me and she growled when a young ape came near us. The little thing didn't like the sound of Sheba growling and moved away to join the group of adult apes. It tried to get some of the meat, but the big ones pushed it away. It tried again, making very odd noises. You couldn't call it speech. Two of the big apes turned on the little one and simply tore it to pieces and ate it. There was nothing I could do to stop it. We're too late for all of them." He finished sorrowfully.

There was quiet in Tom's study, and Van noticed Quentin.

"Hello, I'm Van; my hobby is explosives."

"Quentin, Q to friends. I was in tanks. We would have made a good combination."

"Well, Q, what do you make of our problems?"

"In my opinion, Van, for all those on the hills, we are, indeed, too late. But what are we going to do about them? All those thousands of mutated people, I fear, are going to die. They will die of cold, starvation or disease. I'm afraid it's back to the Dark Ages and there is absolutely nothing we can do. Just a minute – Petra, you told me that the original class of children simply disintegrated into dust – perhaps that will happen to those on the hills."

Julian broke the silence. "We do need a fresh case. How, the hell are we going to find one? How is Gavin, by the way? Petra, you were going to see him."

"Happily, Gavin is well; his kidneys are now working perfectly. And he has no hair on his hands – well, not yet, anyway. I said I would call and see him at the power station this afternoon. I'll give you a ring if I find anything wrong with anybody there. I think Lucy is doing another locum nursing job so we can go together. Maybe her old flame Roderick will be there."

Roderick was sitting in the gatehouse, a picture of bored misery. He cheered up at the sound of Petra's car, and came out and opened the car door.

"Welcome back, we're a bit short of staff with so many going off sick or becoming another casualty to the beastly little germs. Those of us still standing have to do penance on the gate roster. Thankfully, so far, I seem to be immune from that horror. Hello, Lucy, thanks for coming at such short notice, again. You both know your way around so you're on your own – I'm stuck here until the afternoon shift. Gavin is in his own little cubby-hole. Don't forget the hard hats! They're supposed to be cleaned between use but, I'm afraid, that's gone by the wayside. If you catch someone else's dandruff, you can blame it on me. I've got a roll of kitchen paper, if you fancy it, to protect your hair. I can even twiddle the corners to make you look like real tourists."

"We'll make do without the kitchen roll, thanks, Rod."

The two women walked through the swing doors and made their way to Gavin's bolt hole. They found an empty room with its walls covered in brightly coloured charts. A hot cup of coffee was the only sign of occupation.

"We seem to have missed Gavin, Lucy. Do you think he's on the roof?"

"Maybe. Now we've cured him he's probably sniffing at the vent that's the cause of the trouble."

"I thought the boss had said absolutely nobody was to go on the roof?"

"Remember, Gavin has all the keys to the top doors, and he's bound to be tempted to have another sniff. I can hear him coming along the corridor. He's got a good singing voice; happy little fellow."

Gavin entered. "Hello, this is a nice surprise. Lucy, Doctor Simmonds is doing his stint on the gate. Could you have a good look at him as you go out? There's something not quite right. I can't put my finger on it, but he was very short with me this morning. Not like him at all, he's always been so nice and cheerful. He seemed vacant, miles away. Anyway, you should check him over as you leave."

Petra frowned and noticed Lucy was seriously worried. "We came to see how you're keeping, Gavin. You sounded pretty good coming along the passage. Smooth tenor voice are you in a choir? There's a lovely group of barber-shop singers starting up in the next village, and they've booked our tithe barn next month. Have you got any questions, Lucy?"

"Only personal ones for Gavin. I'll see you later in the surgery, Gavin, and we can do your blood pressure and test your urine. That's about all. Thanks for the comment about Roderick – he was all there as we came in, but you never know with this bug. Have you been up on the roof lately?"

"I had to go up there yesterday as one of my sensors was playing up. You might like to know that smelly vent has been sealed off and the stale air is sent through an incinerator at over a thousand degrees. Nothing can survive that sort of temperature. Got to go now; I'm fine but the guy who stands in for me has gone off sick. Help yourself to coffee, if you've got time."

As they approached the gate, Petra stopped and sniffed. "Smell, Lucy, that strange smell, like badly made cider. It's all around us and it's getting stronger as we get nearer the gate. Where is Roderick?"

They approached and found Roderick with his head in his hands, still seated as they had left him, but with gloom oozing from his crouched body. "Lucy!" Petra had no chance to say anything more as Lucy opened the door and held Roderick's drooping shoulders.

Roderick made a moaning noise and tried to smile. Lucy turned to Petra and pointed to Roderick's hands. A faint greying of the skin was happening in front of their eyes.

Petra screamed, "Lucy! Into the car with him and back to the school. Jules should still be there. Quick! You drive; I'll phone."

"Petra, he's trying to help and making mumbling noises. Oh, Rod! Please keep going. We're going to cure you. Julian has a magic virus to get rid of the little beast. You drive, Petra, fast as you can; I can look after him in the back."

They arrived at the door of the school in a cloud of dust and Van came out to open the car doors.

"Van! Van! We need help."

Van lifted Roderick out of the car like a sack of potatoes, carried him into the hall and laid him on a pile of cushions. "Julian, come and help, we've got our first patient."

Julian appeared with a vial of clear fluid and the garden atomiser. "This'll have to do, it's fairly clean. Sit him up and make him comfortable. He's still mostly human. Roderick, can you hear me? I want you to drink a glass of water. The water's alright, it's from the school dispenser."

For a moment Roderick's eyes cleared. He tried to smile. "Beer ... Lucy ... How—"

Julian looked at Lucy. "He's still on our wavelength. Any hope of a beer in this place?"

"I've a can in my backpack. Let me find it."

Roderick's hands, darkening by the minute, grasped the can and he drank greedily.

"That went down well," said Julian. "Now, Rod, I want you to open your mouth as wide as possible and take two deep breaths, then breathe out and wait for me to shout, 'Breathe'. At that moment breathe in as much as you can – fill your lungs right to the bottom. Are you with me?"

Roderick nodded and took the two deep breaths while Julian poured the contents of the vial into the atomiser.

"Breathe!" At Julian's shout, Roderick opened his mouth wide and took a deep breath while Julian pumped the atomiser as deep inside Roderick's mouth as he could. "Now I am going to squirt the rest up your nose, one nostril at a time. Are you still with me?"

Roderick's eyes cleared for a moment. "That feels good. Beer?"

Julian nodded to Petra. "There's a case in the boot of our car. I'm sure we can spare a couple of cans."

Petra went to the car to retrieve more beer. She returned with six cans. "I thought we could all do with a lift. Jules, if there's just a tiny amount of the virus suspension left in the vial, why not spread it on Roderick's hands?"

"Brilliant! Nothing lost if it doesn't work."

One drop to each hand was enough. As they applied it, the dark grey vanished instantly, and Roderick's hands returned to normal. He brought his hands up to his face and for a full minute he studied them. Tears followed, pouring onto his restored hands. He looked at his saviours and smiled. "Thank you, all of you. I felt as if I was being taken to another world, like a sort of waking dream, but quite horrid, and frightening. Everything was happening as fast as lightning. I was being dragged down into a great pit. It was all dark and horrid. But then you pulled me back. Why is it so bloody quick? Van, you seem to know the some of the reasons for this sort of thing?"

Van sat down next to the recovering patient. "Whatever, or perhaps even whoever, is controlling the attack on *Homo sapiens* must be in a hurry. We can't blame it. After all, we are destroying the earth at an extraordinary speed. The climate is warming and changing. There are extremes in every direction. We are dumping plastics into the ocean at a terrifying rate and poisoning the earth with horrible chemicals. I suggest that Gaia, to give the earth a name, is fighting back and is desperate to either eliminate *Homo sapiens* or, at the very least, eliminate the vast majority – over ninety-five percent – of us. Gaia's last line of attack is using the most primitive form of life.

"I wonder what James Lovelock thinks of it all. He's the man who coined the term Gaia to represent the sentient earth. He's still alive at over a hundred years old, and as bright as a button. Well, we've saved a few boys and a weatherman and, assuming your improvement continues, one normal adult. It's a start! Only just over seven and a half thousand million members of the race of *Homo sapiens* to go. Not a hope in hell."

Van shrugged his shoulders.

CHAPTER ELEVEN

The next day, Julian returned from his laboratory with twenty precious vials of newly grown viruses. He carefully stored them in the refrigerator in the school kitchen attaching a note to each vial – *Only to be used under strict instruction from Commander Bailey*. He was closing the door of the refrigerator when Doctor Liu appeared.

"Julian, do you think we can use the school as a sort of first-aid post? I'm sure we could borrow camp beds from people in the village and give immediate treatment. I've sounded out the headmaster and he agrees with the idea."

"It might help, certainly. The trouble is, as we know, we have to treat people at an extraordinarily early stage to have any hope of success."

"How about emailing everyone in the village and warning them. Or running around in a van broadcasting far and wide?"

"It might work. I gather from Lucy ten more adults in her road have mutated and gone up to join the mass of people on the hills. The little devil seems to attack whole families, adults and children. How does it do it? Makes no sense."

"I gather when they get to the hills, they don't last long. What kills them? They do age incredibly quickly and they can't all die fighting. How on earth can we organise a proper post-mortem? Actually, what's the point of doing one?"

"Then we're back to the same old problem, how are we going to recognise those in the earliest stages, Liu? Roderick, for instance?"

"Something that Anthony said right at the beginning. I know! His dog only growled at the children who were going to be ill. We need Anthony and his dog. Is he at school today?"

"Tom is taking Anthony's class right now. I'll see if I can extract our little wizard from under the eagle eye of the head teacher."

Julian identified the classroom and knocked on the door.

"Come in! Who is it this time? Oh, it's you, Julian – I suppose you want to snatch your son. You can tell him the origin of the word 'algebra'. I have been hard at it to persuade this lot that sciences, especially mathematics, were saved from extinction by predominantly Arab scholars in the twelfth to fifteenth centuries. We tend to forget that."

"Well, Headmaster, how about Musa al-Khwarizmi, one of the greatest of the Arabic mathematicians, although he did confess that he had gained a great deal of knowledge from India. He publicised the modern numbering system from the original Indian writing; and for the first time in Western mathematics, he included a zero. He was probably the greatest occupant of the House of Wisdom under the aegis of al-Mamun. Born about 786, he -."

"Thank you, dear boy. I see young Anthony has a lot to learn. Anthony! you are needed at the first-aid post. I suspect you may be continuing the lesson about the origins of mathematics."

"Dad, what do you really need me for?"

"Doctor Liu remembers that you told him that Sheba growled at the children who were going to develop diseased kidneys. She seemed to be able to detect a change well before there was any clinical signs of illness. We may have thought it amusing at the time, but Liu points out that Sheba could be hugely valuable in early diagnosis. She could be our canine detective. We could give her a space to sniff out cases at the entrance to the first-aid post. If you were worried about her, you could come and bed down here as well. What do you think of that?"

"That's fine by me. I've read that some animals, especially dogs, are sort of experts at finding cases of cancer and some brain things. Anna told me dogs have a thousand times the number of cells to do with smelling than we have. If Sheba is going to be outside our home care, I must warn whoever will be looking after her that she does like her biscuits in the morning. I can bring her bedding and her favourite toys. And … and she must have a good walk before she lies down for the night. Anyway, if I can't be here all the time, who will be looking after her? Van seems to be pretty good with animals."

Van had been listening to the conversation. "Don't you worry, Anthony. If you trust me, I'll look after Sheba. I promise to take her for long walks in the evening and give her the biscuits."

Van turned to the others. "Young Anthony is very attached to Sheba. What sort of a dog is she, Julian?"

"Sheba is a fully-grown Alsatian and permanently hungry. We trust you to remember that she needs a good walk every evening. And, Van, the biscuits will disappear in seconds."

"I could do with a long walk in the evenings myself, but I mustn't have biscuits." Van patted his stomach and muttered, "Losing battle, I'm afraid, Anthony."

CHAPTER TWELVE

The next morning Anthony appeared with Sheba, her basket, a very old blanket and a dog bowl. Petra carried in a large box of food and biscuits.

"Where is Sheba going to live, Ant?" asked Carole.

"I thought we should put her by the main entrance, then if she senses someone is sort of wrong, she can growl before they get too far into the building, and we can rush in with the treatment, Mum's black spot and all." The headmaster appeared. "Sir, I hope Sheba is going to be paid the minimum wage?"

"I shall have to ask the school accountant about that!" he laughed. "This is an interesting experiment. If it's any help, I have at last extracted permission from the education authorities to have an animal on the premises. I originally asked for a pair of guinea pigs for the biology group. They didn't believe a word of what I told them, but I'm not bothered by that. Good idea placing Sheba by the entrance. Perhaps when that's locked at night, we could move her somewhere warmer."

"Sir—?"

"You don't seem too keen on my idea, Anthony, why is that?"

"I am, sort of, puzzled about locking the door. If people get ill so quickly, it could happen at any time of the day or night."

"That is a very good point, Anthony. And, since this is now the first-aid centre there will always have to be someone on duty. So, perhaps, there's no point in locking the entrance door. Well done, young man. I read somewhere that there are dogs that can identify people who are going to develop parkinsonism, often years before there is any change clinically, wonderful animals. And someone told me that in a part of Africa they have trained rats to recognise cases of tuberculosis. They get the children to breathe into a bag and then expose the rats to the children's breath. I'm not sure how the rats are supposed to say the diagnosis."

Two worried people appeared during the night, but Sheba failed to take any interest, so they were sent home. Van had been on duty all night and heard a car on the entrance to the school. He glanced out of the window, recognised the headmaster's secretary's car, and returned to his book.

"Good morning, Carole, we've had a quiet night."

Van put his hand down to stroke Sheba and immediately paused. "Hang on a minute; Sheba's ruff is standing up, and she's as tense as a bowstring."

The dog approached Carole and emitted a soft growl.

"What on earth—?" Carole looked shocked and staggered towards a chair. Van caught her before she collapsed. "Oh, thank you, Van. I did feel a bit funny this morning. You don't think I might be—? We were planning to go away together for the weekend."

Van produced his mobile phone and dialled a recorded number. "Julian, a high level of suspicion according to Sheba. Carole came in this morning, not feeling particularly well. She's collapsed." He listened for a minute. "Hands are normal at the moment, but you'd better come over right away."

Julian appeared with the atomiser and a fresh vial of virus, with an anxious Petra and Anthony in tow. Doctor Liu had also been called; he immediately started to examined Carole. "Unusual temperature and slow pulse – more the picture of typhoid, but it can't be that. Van, did you say Carole's hands were normal half an hour ago? Well, look at them now."

Van looked in disbelief at Carole's hands. They were already becoming a light grey. "We'd better get those rings off pretty quick, in case her fingers start to swell." He started to remove the rings.

Anthony watched the struggle. "I'll get some olive oil from the kitchen. Try spit, Van." Van smiled and did as he was told.

"You are a clever devil, Anthony. Over to you, Julian." Petra helped Carole get comfortable on one of the camp beds while Julian poured the contents of the precious vial into the atomiser.

"At least we know our so-called treatment didn't harm Roderick and he seems to have recovered completely. Carole! Can you hear me? I want to get this stuff down to the bottom of your lungs. You don't have to say anything, just nod your head twice and look at me at the same time. Well done! Now open wide."

Carole did as she was told, and Julian squirted in the contents of the vial deep into Carole's throat. She coughed twice and settled back on the camp bed. Julian straightened up and smeared the remaining liquid on the backs of Carole's hands.

Half an hour later, Carole's eyes opened, and she tried to get up. "There's the post to be opened. Oh, Headmaster; oh Tom, I'm so sorry."

Petra put her arms round Carole's shoulders. "Tom's not here yet, and – Doctor's orders – you're not moving anywhere until Doctor Liu has had a thorough look at you. Don't cry, just try and believe you're getting better. It's a few days before the weekend."

"Why did you say that?"

"When you arrived, and you became ill you said—" A glance from Van stopped Petra from saying any more about Carole's weekend. "—Sorry, I was confused. Everything seems to happen so quickly, I get muddled. Ah, here's the headmaster just driven up. Van, you'd better tell him about our hopefully cured second case."

Van went outside and returned with a shocked Tom Mayhew who immediately knelt beside Carole, kissed her and whispered in her ear. He straightened up. "Julian, I now have a great deal to thank you all for. Not forgetting the wonderful Sheba.

"I guess you all will be putting two and two together and making a very big number. Please keep it to yourselves for the present, if you don't mind, thank you." Tom smiled at Anthony. "Well, Ant, I presume we have Sheba to thank for saving Carole?" Anthony nodded. "What a wonderful animal, it must be about my turn to take her for a walk. Van you can go and have a well-earned rest."

"I'd rather come with you. I had an idea we might explore the hills and hopefully identify, from a distance, the place or places chosen by Ben to take the damaged ones."

"Fine by me. Weather forecast is good, and I could do with some decent exercise."

CHAPTER THIRTEEN

It was a warm spring day with a light breeze, ideal for walking with a friendly dog on the hills. Tom and Van said nothing for the first half an hour. They stopped and sat on a fallen tree halfway up the comb.

Tom started to open up. "Carole's husband has been doing the dirt on her for years. She came to me one day and poured her heart out. She is a very attractive woman and my wife, as you know, died two years ago, so you can imagine the rest. Thank you for coming out to the car and warning me; that was very kind."

"Petra must have twigged and sent me out, good timing. Just as well, perhaps. It must have been something Carole said to Petra, something about a weekend?"

"We've been planning this for weeks. There aren't any children around, they're all too old to bother, anyway. And Carole's husband is somewhere abroad with his latest mistress. She must have been frightened out of her wits. Fancy being caught out by a primitive organism!"

Tom laughed, relaxed, happy to be talking, unwinding years of tension. "Don't know why I'm telling you all this, Van. It must sound so superficial when we're surrounded by death and destruction. I reckon, so far, over a third of the village inhabitants must be dead or dying. Whole households are empty, discarded clothing everywhere." He gave a deep sigh and was consoled by Sheba's wet nose.

"Come on, Tom, cheer up. Carole's in the land of the living and it's only a few days from the planned weekend. Time now for us to find the hiding place of all those damaged *Homo derelictus,* as we're now calling them. I wonder if we should have brought Ben with us, but perhaps he wanted to keep his little secrets to himself. He must have collected well over a thousand people up here; surely they can't all be dead."

"We've sat for long enough. I'm getting the flat-arse syndrome. Where has that wonderful dog gone?"

"Last time I saw her she was nosing about in the bushes behind us. There she is, come on, old girl. What's the matter now, Sheba – have you found something suspicious or are you agitating us to keep moving?"

They only had to walk twenty yards to find the bodies. Two adult hairy creatures were locked in a final embrace; they were very, very dead, and quite cold. Van touched the arm of the larger of the two and a mass of black hair came away in his hand. He let it fall to the ground.

"Strange; it's almost as if they died months ago, but that's not possible. There's something humbling about these two. An awful lot of people think animals have a simple mental life. But there are some who believe the higher animals experience the same emotions as humans. Higher in the sense that they are more advanced in the tree of evolution. I realise these two are reverted humans but, in their present state, they can still love and die loving. Sadly, the bodies are disintegrating much too fast; going back to the earth, from whence they came. That sounds sombre. I'm inclined to leave them alone – they may be still here when we're on our way back, but we just don't know how fast they decompose after they die. Well done, Sheba. Come on Tom, we haven't reached the top of the hill yet. And we still haven't found where the great mass of damaged people ends up."

They were about to give up the search after two hours of strenuous walking along the high ridge of the hill when Sheba's hackles rose. She stopped and crept towards a ledge covered with a great mass of impenetrable briers.

"What now, my canine Sherlock Holmes; more disintegrating bodies? There must be something that worries her over this lip. But I don't fancy pushing my way through these healthy natural defences. Tom, give me a hand up to the lowest branches of that huge oak tree. I can shin up halfway and see into the secret valley."

"You be careful, Van. You're a big man and I wouldn't have a hope in hell of carrying you back to base; and I doubt if there's much of a mobile signal up here. Can you see anything? Sheba must think there's something suspicious. Please come down, Van." Van descended, making a lot of noise, and they waited quietly to see if they had been detected.

"Horrendous, quite horrendous and difficult to describe. There are the remains of an old barn or some sort of simple dwelling and a dirty pond fed, presumably, by a mountain spring. But the whole area is covered in the dead." Van took a deep breath before he was able to continue. "I hope nobody makes the effort to find this place because it is pretty obvious that the one or two still moving are into cannibalism. Some of the bones lying about are from big animals like deer or hill pony but I'm afraid there are quite a number of broken human bones. Goodness knows why they haven't disintegrated. Perhaps if the bones are broken before death, some sort of weird post mortem activity fails to take place."

Tom shook his head in disbelief. "I had a nasty thought we would find something like that. How on earth are we going to tell the rest of the village."

"No good comes of hiding the truth, Tom. For years, I have been hiding the truth from myself, but the reality of modern warfare and the advances of science have destroyed what religion I ever had. Let's go back to that welcoming tree we sat on a couple of hours ago. I feel an urge to have my unwinding, just as you did, and talk to a friend. Come on! At least it's downhill. I'm willing to bet those bodies behind our seat won't be there."

They reached the fallen tree and sat down.

"Thank goodness, Van. It's a damn sight quicker downhill. I could do with a rest. Where are those bodies? You reckoned they wouldn't be there. Let's have a look."

Sheba helped with the searching but there was no sign of the bodies.

"You were right. But how could they vanish so completely? They weren't worth scavenging and there aren't any animals big enough to scavenge. All I can see is a great mass of hairs, there are far more than the few that came off in your hands. As you said, dust to dust – back to the earth."

Tom spread the thin grass with his shoe. "With a little imagination, this earth is a little darker than the surrounding area. There are a few black hairs further away and some odd white things that could be the remains of teeth, but no actual bones."

He shrugged his shoulders and put his arm round Van's shoulders. "Now you can open your heart and tell me all about your inner problems."

"Very difficult to talk about such a fundamental change of life plan. I'm not going to pretend I'm on the road to Damascus or anything like that. I suppose the problem, a very big one, arose early in life. Coming from a family which was so closely related to the Church of England, I suppose I drifted into reading religion as a subject at university. I should have twigged much earlier that every, or almost every, discussion about the fundamentals of religion eventually had to rely on that one word, faith. In other words, the whole edifice, the whole power structure was based on a myth. The myth being that the belief that there was a supernatural world somewhere "out there" which was ruled by an omniscient creature called God who, from time to time, made his, or her, or its, thoughts known in our world. If this was ever questioned, the questioner was shot down by the bullets of this one word – faith. The power structure and exclusion zone round the whole edifice of the Church at the present time is extraordinary and highly politicised. It was also, for thousands of years, and still is, ruthless and cruel to anyone who questioned the status quo. It just happened that one day, I stopped believing and I feel much better for it. The only remnant is a pleasant hope that I shall be at one with my deceased loved ones when I die. There, you have it in a nutshell."

"I understand everything you've said. It is a very big fundamental nutshell. Is it too flippant to try to determine whether religion is good or bad for humanity? There seem to be so many differing viewpoints. Should religion be seen to be "good" because it inspired beautiful art and buildings, when at the same time religious zealots encouraged torturing and murdering people of different beliefs and cultures? Or, can one say that it has encouraged society to grow and flourish? So, perhaps, there is one question only. Why is it that mankind seems to have a need for some sort of belief that can be summed up in the word religion? Is it the need as a social glue to bring groups of people together? Or is it an excuse for tribal warfare?"

"There's a lot to be said for that. Social glue is a very useful phenomenon. The problem surely arises when perfectly sane people begin to question parts of the New Testament. I'm not talking about the Old Testament which is unbelievably savage and primitive. There are parts of the New Testament which are wonderfully humane, but not all of it. And, remember, most of the items in the Bible were written way after the event, often hundreds of years. Hindsight is a very convenient facility to forget or forge actual events. You'd better read the latest offering by Richard Dawkins."

"Oh well, back to the present. What are we going to tell our little group? That's the difficult one. I wonder if Sheba will growl if we are economical with the truth?"

"She's much too tactful to do anything like that. Come on, it's getting dark. Let's go. I'm hungry, and I expect Sheba is too. She needs her biscuits."

CHAPTER FOURTEEN

The tired and hungry trio arrived back to the welcoming smell of frying bacon, eggs and, oh bliss, fried bread!

Petra had taken charge of the cooking. "Sit down, boys! Before you tell us anything, get this lot down and open a beer or two. By the way, Q is on his way down from the big city. He sounds rather serious, but he couldn't talk much on the phone. Something about an international meeting to be held right here, in this little village. Do you think he reckons it's all our fault as the first cases were identified here? Sorry, I shouldn't talk shop until you've finished. Tom, I'm sure you'd like to know that the lovely Carole is looking well and sleeping peacefully on one of the beds in the second classroom."

"Thank you, Petra. In fact, thank all of you. I must go and see her. Van will tell you what we found at the top of the hill. Thinking of my wandering years ago as a teenager, I remember camping around this area and walking for miles all over the hills. I remember the place that we found was called the secret valley as it was so difficult to get to and it wasn't specified by name on any Ordnance Survey map; strange that!"

"Well, Van, tell us all. Hang on! That must be Q, actually driving himself."

Lucy went out to the new arrival and returned with a distraught old gentleman, not his usual self.

"Sorry I'm late. There's a lot of rioting in the midlands, and I fear I must have hit a few wild ones. Van, Lucy says you and Tom have been exploring the hills to identify where all the *Homo derelictus* have been taken."

"Only the original batches of children were actually taken into the hills. All the rest, which means mainly adults starting with those from the same households as the derelict children, simply gravitated in that direction. I must warn you, there are very few left. We found the valley very difficult to identify. Tom tells us it was always whispered as the 'secret valley'. For an unknown reason, it was never marked on the Ordnance Survey maps. I doubt they would be interested now, but it might be worth asking at some future time. That oak tree that I climbed must be at least a thousand years old. It could last for another thousand, I reckon. Three of the side branches are resting on the ground; that will protect the main trunk from the winds up there.

"Anyway, we were forewarned as we approached the valley by this wonderful dog. I managed to climb the oak tree and caught a glimpse of the hidden part of the valley. There is the wreck of an old farmhouse and what, from a distance, looks like a reasonable water supply. But there were very few creatures alive up there." Van choked with the memory and took a deep draught of beer.

"There are numerous bones scattered around, some of them are obviously animal; deer, hill pony or sheep. But the majority are human. You can read into that whatever you want, but as far as I am concerned, it is evidence of cannibalism." He had to pause to allow the horrendous news to be digested.

"Something else you should know. When we were way up the valley, there was a convenient fallen trunk, so we sat down to discuss life in general. Sheba was having none of it and insisted we go a few yards into the forest. There we found a sad couple of adult derelicts in a very close embrace. They were both dead and, on the face of it, had been dead for some time. The bodies were disintegrating in front of our eyes. I only had to touch the hair and it came away in great handfuls. Incidentally, when we returned to the same spot on our way back, the only evidence there had ever been a couple of bodies was a slight darkening of the earth and a fair number of black hairs. Now, there are no scavengers in the area and the only conclusion is that disintegration, once it started, must have occurred at an incredible speed. All I could see were hairs, like the hairs that had come off the animals when I touched the bodies when we first saw them. I don't know what you make of that, but I thought I had to mention it."

Petra stepped into the silent breach. "Q, can I make you a bacon sandwich? You look all in after that horrendous drive."

"Petra, I would simply love a bacon sandwich. I haven't had one for years. Van, that's a very sad story, but I'm not in the least surprised. Stories from all around the world are beamed to us and they all tell us the same. People of any age are reverting to ape-like animals. And they all reckon that the cause is those infernal primitive organisms, the Archaea. Like you, the people who phoned – and I am talking about the experts in China, the United States, and all over Europe – they all are incriminating machines that have, what we always assumed to be, a lethal level of radioactivity or simply great heat or pressure. One guy who was piloting a submersible to a ridiculous depth was infected from a strange creature he salvaged. It sprayed him with disgusting fluid and within a week he was dead with the same clinical progression as your cases.

"I will get to the point of my rushed visit today. They – in other words, the experts in other countries – are amazed that you have saved anyone. I told them about your damp and very dangerous experiments at the seaside and they simply didn't believe that you could isolate such a series of viruses from sea froth. So, I am going to surprise you with the thought that the international scene is hoping to hold a cosy get together to learn your secrets and, frankly, ask you what the hell they are going to do. Julian, what do you have to say to that?"

"Where is this cosy little get together going to be held? That is, if we agree to it."

"You sound wary of the idea. Here, of course. Van, what do you think of the idea?"

"I think the idea is splendid. There is an enormous tithe barn within the village boundary which would be ideal. But before we rush into the idea we should think of the logistics. Bearing in mind the problems you had getting here, how are they going to arrive? Most of the international collection of experts – the microbiological mafia – will think they are much too important to come to a meeting in a tiny little village in the middle of nowhere. How many are you expecting? At the very least, a few army tents and latrines may help. And getting here in a reasonable time could be tricky. There is a tiny, privately owned grass runway further up the hill, but there are no lights and it would only be able to take small planes. It is in use to ferry in scientists that work in Julian's laboratory. How many people might we be expecting?"

"Not less than a few hundred, mainly scientists and politicians. What's the problem, Julian?"

"Not the scientists. It's the idea of asking politicians. They'll be disastrous. They'll only be thinking of their own jobs and their own cash flow. Lucy, you look agitated. Give us your views."

"Thanks, Jules. If it is agreed to hold such a big meeting here, how are we going to persuade all these important, or should I say self-important, people to do a series of simplistic manoeuvres without talking down to them? I believe we need just one person with the gift of the gab to persuade everyone to do the same thing. And we need you, Jules, to teach the world how to produce a mammoth amount of your wonderful viruses. As far as the logistics of treating millions of people – I haven't the faintest idea. Somehow, we must be able to treat the whole world. You think I'm serious? I suppose I am. To start with, it was meant to be a joke. And who is going to be able to produce such a lot of virus? Q, ideas from on high, please."

"Well, that's alright for the UK. While I was in the big city, I heard that we had been officially informed by the Chief Scientist that this extraordinary reversal of the evolutionary process has affected the whole world. There's not a single country free of it. I told him that we had cured a few people who were in the very early stages. He leapt at the carrot and said firmly that this village is the ideal place to hold such a conference. Incidentally, your nice Doctor Liu has a great friend at one of the universities in Beijing and kindly suggested that he gave me a ring. He sounds very sensible; his name is Professor Yi. Interestingly, apparently 'yi' is an ancient Confucian thought process that includes the inspiration to have correct behaviour as well as good deeds. My ex-teacher wife collects these useful snippets of knowledge. Very clever and, from time to time, quite useful.

"Anyway, back to the present. I'm sorry to report that the whole of London, or the bits I have seen of it, is one big disaster area with streets littered with the debris of the remains of fighting apes, or ape-like creatures. Most of them die very quickly and some revert to even more primitive creatures. A few, very few, of them seem to live a bit longer. The result is that they do more damage to the infrastructure. There's also one hell of a mess in India and the rest of the Far East.

"As for the Far East – that's another disaster, mostly self-inflicted. Great swathes of forest are on fire, most of which have been started deliberately by greedy farmers. One weird result is that the humanoid apes are deliberately walking into the flames. The black hairs, of course, vanish in a puff of smoke and flame. Then they collapse and lie there until there is nothing left. There are tens of thousands of them and they are walking to their death as if pulled by a magnet. In London, a lot of them drown in the ponds in the royal parks – thousands of them – and they just disappear.

"As for the European countries, most of the social structures have broken down with overall mortality in the region of ninety to ninety-five percent. Essential services are beginning to suffer. The big cities appear to have some electricity, but this is fluctuating wildly. The automatic systems are coping now, but they won't last for ever. Water is the main problem as the survivors try to flush away the remnants of the collapse of their local civilisation. Food is also running short with residual population fighting amongst themselves for what food is available, with some people stockpiling ridiculous amounts.

"I was able to discuss the disaster with a number of scientists and they are intrigued by what you chaps have managed to achieve just in this small village. They are especially interested in your ability to cure people. How to translate this ability to attempt to cure, or at least protect, the survivors throughout the world is a major problem. Some countries, like China, India, and three European countries are offering laboratory facilities to grow huge amounts of viruses. But the remains of the World Health Organisation have so few staff left they have no idea what to do.

"There you are! It looks as if we're back to the usual band of brothers, this little roomful and perhaps a few others to find the worldwide answer. Hello, Anthony, sorry, I didn't see you hiding behind your dad. You were about to put your hand up a moment ago. What's on your mind?"

CHAPTER FIFTEEN

Anthony blushed and began to sweat.

"Um! Sir, Lord Quentin."

Lord Quentin Ogilvie laughed and put his hand out to Anthony to come and stand in front of them all.

"Now, Anthony, you've heard everyone else call me Q – why don't you do the same? After all, you are the famous one, having been the first person in the world to be cured. Now, tell us your analysis of the secret of success."

"Um, Q. So, I'm remembering that Grandpa was a farmer, and a long while ago, he was, sort of, worried that one of his crops was being messed about by a swarm of some funny sort of beetle. One day he phoned up the ministry people and they came to see us, and they were quite helpful. They said they knew of an African farmer who had a plane that could carry a huge tank of stuff that would kill beetles. He would fly low over the crop and squirt this stuff out through lots of holes in the back of the wings of the plane. At least, I think that was what he said. Then he asked Grandpa if he knew anyone who had a plane that could do that."

Anthony paused.

"Go on! I think you might just be on to something really clever."

"Thank you, er, Q. Well, Grandpa did have a friend who had a little plane and they both made an old oil drum into a big tank which they filled with poison against the beetles. I

110

remember, they tried to lift it into the plane and Grandpa hurt his back, so we had to get the neighbours to help. The man managed to get his plane to take off and because there was a leak in the tank the poison all dribbled out of the bottom of the plane. I don't remember if it killed the beetles, but the family all smelt of the poison for days."

Julian joined in the general laughter. "I remember that, and I can tell you all that the beetles were seriously frightened. But they had vanished by the next day. Can't say whether they were dead or frightened away. Crop spraying! Of course, you clever old thing, Ant. That's the answer. There must be hundreds of small planes with spraying holes in their wings throughout the world. The limiting factor now will be the ability of the various national and private laboratories to produce enormous amounts of mixed viruses that, hopefully, will kill off all these Archaea that seem to be determined to eliminate poor old *Homo sapiens*. We simply must work out how can this little group of people persuade the rulers of the world to switch their energies to a single objective? Then, to cap it all, to squirt the whole lot over the entire world surface. Well, Q, any comments?"

"Let's wait until we have all the representatives of the most powerful countries of the world sitting in your beautiful old tithe barn. I have seen it, by the way, and it strikes me as the most ideal venue to have such a meeting. The invitations have been sent and we'll have to wait to see if there's an enthusiastic response. There is, of course, the possibility that too many countries will simply not reply and the whole idea will be a dead duck. But, hopefully, enough will come and we can persuade them that this is the only approach that's possible. I'm hopeful that we can persuade China, Russia, and the United States to be the main participants. They should be able to persuade most of the smaller nations to agree to have a swarm of tiny planes spraying a cloud of strange viruses all over them. Doctor Liu, do you have any thoughts on the subject?"

Doctor Liu stood up and came to the front of the group. "I have phoned Professor Yi in Beijing and we spent a long time wondering what we can do about our entire race dying in such a peculiar way. He is on his way here now. He was coming to stay last year but couldn't for some reason that I forget. Anyway, he'll be here very soon.

"It reminds me of the original arguments concerning the Origin of Species. I wonder what the good bishop would have thought when presented with our problem? To be faced with the ancient historical actuality on present day terms would, I'm certain, have been too much for him to take on board.

"On a slightly different tack, I fear you will come up against huge pressure from the self-styled do-gooders of the world, particularly the American religious right who will say that what is happening is the will of their god and there is nothing we should do about it. Now if, and it is a big if, enough virus can be produced to spray on large populations, the first country to agree to do the spraying will have a tremendous advantage in that the salvaged population will be ahead of all the others. That is all I have to say right now."

Quentin smiled and nodded his old head. "You should have been a politician, Liu. Nothing like a little pressure to make people sit up and take notice. I like it! We'll have to see how many nations, particularly the powerful ones, care to send representatives to our beautiful barn. Then we have the problem of finding somewhere for them to stay and how to feed them. That's going to be quite a worry, looking after them.

"Anthony, you have that look on your face as if a profound statement is on the front of your tongue. Come on, out with it; we're all listening."

Anthony stood up. "We were talking last night and we came up with an idea between us. Sol found out that the father of one of our friends in the school works in television. I think he said the man was a cameraman and so he should have some up-to-date equipment in his house. We could try and persuade him to record the whole of the meeting, or conference, or whatever you want to call it. If it all works, his film would be a valuable record of what went on. I'm not talking about the money – it would be the start of a new history of us. A few people have taken pictures with their phones of the mutants but they're not up to professional standard, and these silly phones don't last very long anyway, so all the visual memories will be lost."

Quentin smiled. "Well there's a job for you and Sol. Go find your cameraman. Let's hope he is still in the land of the living. You know, if you three continue to come up with bright ideas, you want to be careful; we might ask you to take over the running of the village when this is all over. Here he comes."

Sol appeared and was brought into the idea. He laughed. "Come on, Ant, Ben, we have to go cameraman hunting."

CHAPTER SIXTEEN

It was a warm sunny day and two heads were deep in thought in the headmaster's study.

"How many pupils have we lost so far, Carole? If we lose many more, we'll lose central funding for everyone else but you and me. I reckon not more than ten boys and girls turned up for school yesterday. And that begs the question as to how many of their parents are alive? What a disaster! Three of my neighbours, another complete household, have suddenly degenerated and rushed off into the hills. The only, still rather depressing, upside is that there should be plenty of empty houses to put up the visitors from other countries. Do we have any right to investigate the whole village and see where we stand? At least two thirds of the houses are empty."

"We did have a peculiar email from the education authorities. It was difficult to understand, but I have interpreted it to mean that we can do anything we like. I suspect, Tom, that they have no idea what to do, just as we haven't the faintest idea how many village people are still alive. And, let's face it, why should the authorities have any better ideas? We must already have lost three quarters of the village, probably more. Everything in the village has been cancelled, even church services. Congregations are only made up of tiny groups of very frightened people. Typical – if you are scared out of your wits with nowhere to go for advice, ask a totally unknown quantity, like God. Big deal!

"One casualty has been the organisation that I started a few years ago. We called ourselves the village visiting group. We used to visit all the new families in the village, send cards to the bereaved and congratulations to families when they had babies. We also visited the lonely. We originally had a close relationship with the local church, but that folded when they tried to take over the whole thing. Then we got a new vicar and things were improving. But our system is now so overwhelmed we've had to give up. Perhaps we might start again when it's all over. Depends on how many of us are left."

Tom put his arms round Carole and she looked up for the healing kiss.

"Tom, do you think Q has had any sensible instructions from London? They must have been hit just as hard there. I'm not sure it is London any more. There's a rumour that parliament has moved to Reading where the mortality is quite a bit less."

"Large cities are such complicated places. I can predict most of the essential functions will have collapsed, which will lead to the next stage, which is rioting. I guess Q must have experienced the start of the disintegration. He was fast asleep on one of the camp beds an hour ago. I think it's my turn to walk Sheba and Q was out for the count. I'm going to wake him up with black coffee and a large brandy. Carole, darling, where did we hide that bottle?"

Carole laughed, "Don't worry, Tom, I'm sure I can find it. We could all do with a dose." She left the room to search for the wandering brandy. She returned with the precious bottle and Van in tow.

"Tom, that is most kind of you. And it's good brandy, where did you get it?"

"A grateful parent presented it to me years ago and it lay forgotten in the back of the school cleaning cupboard. Spanish, Carlos Primera; it should be good. I tried it before I brought your glass. I thought we should at least make sure it is the best medicine for the moment.

"Ah, here's the Bailey family. They should have some idea how we are going to look after the swarms of important people we're expecting. I also want to know how Julian's virus cultures are going. I forgot to tell you last night that London has said that we have explicit permission to find houses that have no living occupants. We also are encouraged to make such houses habitable for visitors and use any foods available to feed them. There's memory for you, I knew there was something I had to pass on. Come in, Julian, Petra and Anthony; I suspect we're all in need of a shot of brandy; Sam, you can have a sniff of Anthony's. We've been discussing how to accommodate and feed our international visitors. Any helpful ideas would be welcome, Julian."

"Sir!" Anthony held up his hand. "Are there any policemen left? Or at least people who, sort of, look important and, sort of, official. They could go around the whole village and knock on doors to see if they get an answer. If there's no answer, they could break down the door and clean out bodies, if there are any ..." His voice died away as the ideas took shape. "Sir, I don't know if we can. Oh dear, Mum – I don't like this drink, it's, sort of, burning."

"That's good, even more for us. Well, Petra, your turn. I do believe Anthony has the germ of a good idea. Can anyone think of a suitable uniform that would look impressive and not too frightening?"

"Fire brigade uniform is pretty impressive, especially those wonderful brass hats. It could be fun wearing one, although perhaps they might be a bit big for us. There's a shortage of petrol and diesel so the searchers will have to go on foot."

Tom held up his hands in horror. "Sorry to butt in, but that is an unfortunate choice of word, searchers. They are well described in a book written by Walter George Bell, first published in 1924 called *The Great Plague in London 1665*. He writes that in the – almost – last outbreak of the Black Death, it was not the national or county or civic officers' duty to ascertain death; in fact, no man's job. It was a woman's job – that of the 'searchers of the dead'. They were all women who fulfilled this gruesome office. They were appointed by the parish from the paupers and paid a small fee. The collection of the statistics, you can imagine had little to do with accuracy. Sorry to interrupt; more useless information for you to use in crosswords or scrabble."

"Thank you, Tom, headmaster to the core!" Petra smiled tolerantly. "Well, with enough people in various striking uniforms we could cover the whole village in a couple of days. I would guess that at least half the houses have no occupants. It wouldn't be too difficult to make up beds and, with luck, get cooking facilities going. The water supply is still holding up in the village, thank goodness, so that's a relief. And when our international brigade appears, they're only going to be here for a couple of days; three at most. Jules, what do you think?"

"Feeding them all should not be such a problem. This is, after all, a country village and there are a couple of local farms still operating. Thinking sideways, it may be of some interest, but I have a feeling that the mortality amongst farming families is less than the general population. Perhaps they might have a minimal immunity to the Archaea and that protects them. If that turns out to be the case, then spraying the whole countryside may not be necessary. There's a thought for you,

Q. Carole, are a reasonable number of children from farming families still coming to school?"

"I hadn't thought about that, but you may be right. I certainly know of six children from a couple of local farms who were brought in yesterday. No, they weren't! They all came by bicycle as the farms were short of diesel and they needed that to power the milking machines. The electricity supply to some of the farms is failing because there's nobody to repair the broken power lines after the storm. They had to start up their emergency generators. I heard a rumour that our local power station is closing down. So many people are dead that there's a huge surplus of power and you can't store the excess. Shall I ring the local fire station about those uniforms? What do you think, Tom?"

"Good idea. If they haven't got enough spare uniforms, we could go to the dressing up boxes at home." His laughter fell on deaf ears. "We'd better get going and mobilise as many people as possible to find how many survivors there are left."

CHAPTER SEVENTEEN

"Can I help, Lucy? We've shut down the power station as the demand is so low it's becoming dangerous. It may sound strange, but you can't get rid of excess electricity, so the whole thing starts to heat up. Anyway, just for the time being, there are so many automatic systems in place that I'm not needed to be on site. I've brought Gavin along as well."

"Oh, Rod, yes; any help is gratefully received. How are you feeling?" *And you look so well, and as handsome as you were twenty years ago.*

"Thanks to Julian, I'm as well as I've ever been, and all the better for seeing you, Lucy!"

"Give over!" Lucy was feeling very hot and trying to disguise her fluttering heart. She shouted to Tom, "We need shorter trousers for Gavin! Hope you don't mind me saying that, Gavin?"

Gavin smiled but said nothing. He was simply grateful to be alive.

"Thirty people!" shouted Tom. "I've divided up the village into fifteen sections, that's two people for each section, preferably a man and a woman. We should be finished by nightfall. I'm afraid there will not be a fee – we are not exactly paupers. I suggest we meet back here at seven o'clock in the evening and compare notes. The school kitchens say they can rustle up enough food and drink for us all and I can probably persuade the local pub to give us a barrel of beer or cider. Well, that's all, now off you go. What is it, Anthony?"

"Please, sir, how do we get into houses if there is no answer to the door. Are we allowed to break windows?"

"Good point. There are a few stakes in the playground, and we could use those. But, as a last resort, I suppose we might have to break windows to gain entry. Is that all right with you, Q?"

"It does seem to be a rather rough and ready treatment of law and order, but we don't have an alternative. Thank you for raising it, Anthony. We'd better get going, Tom."

Determined pairs of searchers made their way along the deserted streets, dressed in brightly coloured pseudo-official uniforms and armed with wooden staves to beat in the front doors or windows of all the village houses. One street of thirty houses was enough to discourage the first pair. The effort and time involved to ring bells, break down doors and search houses was too disheartening. Julian and Petra had only found one deserted house out of the thirty that was habitable. All the rest were disgusting and not fit for the hoped-for distinguished visitors. They sat disconsolate on a wall by the little church.

"Pet, why don't we borrow beds from the army camp which is only a few miles away and put all our visitors in the church and village hall? This idea of smashing our way into people's private houses is not going to work. The owners could easily have gone on holiday or simply run away terrified to hide in some bolthole. They're going to be pretty upset when they return to find their home in a right old mess. I vote we go back to the school and see if the others have the same idea."

The searchers collected over the next hour in the school playground. Other couples had come to the same conclusion as Julian and Petra. So, general opinion favoured the accommodation of the hoped-for visitors in public buildings. Q announced that enough public money would be made available to reimburse any costs involved.

"Telephone connections with my office are becoming erratic, but I hope I understood them correctly. The main problem is going to be the supply of food and drink. I gather supermarket shelves are emptying mighty fast as the lorries can't get through and they're having enormous problems finding enough drivers. What other problems can you think of, Van?"

"We have to hope the water supply keeps up and the few remaining workers in the electricity companies keep the voltage up. I can't believe many survivors miss their television and I have to say, it is a relief to listen to the old wireless, as it used to be called. And I know Anna and Lucy have been window shopping in a big way. How did you get on, girls?"

"We borrowed bicycles to get to the next town. Interesting journey – there were a lot of cars just stuck in the middle of the road with nobody apparently in them. There was even one car with its engine still running. We opened a couple and—" Anna gagged as she remembered the horror. "In the driving seat of some of the cars was a heap of clothing with a small pile of dust and a lot of greasy black hairs. In the town itself there were very few people around and it was weirdly silent in the big shopping areas, but we did find a few useful things. There's lots of bedding, mainly camp beds and sleeping bags in a warehouse this side of town, but the main clothing department has burnt down. I expect that was deliberate. The place is a complete wreck as there was no attempt to stop the fire and it had spread to the buildings on either side before it burnt out. All rather depressing with so few people left to do anything useful. I'm sure a couple of lorry loads of borrowed bedding and camp beds would come in useful. Have I missed anything, Lucy?"

"I suppose if we were really desperate, we could plunder some empty houses, but it's all rather gruesome. Jules, do you think there's enough fuel to be able to use lorries to collect beds and bedding? Garages are mostly shut, and I don't fancy sucking diesel out of the forecourt tanks. I expect they're all locked, anyway."

"That shouldn't be a problem. Roderick seems to know a thing or two about locks. He had to when he was in charge of the power station, in case any of the staff went bananas. Isn't that so, Rod?"

"Correct, Julian – that was supposed to be a closely guarded secret." He laughed. "Three of us went on a lock-breaking course for precisely the reason you suggest. We thought it was a joke but one thing I do remember; our tutor told us the most useful tool was a jemmy. It was faster than a straight piece of steel and you didn't mess with the berserk employee when you caught him, or her. Oh yes, there were several wild women around in some of the power stations and they had to be under control. Don't you agree, Lucy?"

"I could name a few," said the blushing Lucy, hoping to change the subject. "When are all our important visitors supposed to be arriving? And how much time have we got to prepare for them? We don't even know how many are on their way. Q, do you have any idea on that score?"

"Invitations have been sent to around a hundred and fifty countries to send appropriate delegates. They are all from countries that have the capability to produce significant amounts of virus culture and might well have the necessary aircraft to deliver the virus as a fine spray to urban areas. If they all agree to cooperate – and, I assure you, that won't be easy –

if they can be persuaded to cooperate, then our job is done. It might seem to be a tall order, but at least we have to try." Quentin drew a very deep breath. He knew this was not going to be straightforward.

"If, as is usual, the delegates start to squabble and the arguments go on into the night, we'll have to abort the whole thing and just look after ourselves. There is the hope that since people are reverting and dying at such a rate that the horror of it all will persuade the whole world to come to some sort of agreement. There's always hope! Tom, as a schoolteacher, do you have a magic method to encourage delegates from far and wide to be persuaded to do something that is in everyone's interest, apart from their own?"

Tom looked surprised to be asked. He thought for a while before replying. "Worldwide agreement – you're joking. Remember the Paris conference on climate change. It's never happened before, but we are in an immediate situation that is getting worse every day, so there's a chance it might come off. Otherwise, if it doesn't, it's the end of *Homo sapiens* and, I suppose, climate warming. That's an interesting thought. Jules, you don't look convinced."

"I agree that the survival of *Homo sapiens* is on a knife edge. But the suggestion that it would be a good thing to solve the problem of climate warming may be a step too far. After all, the Holocene, our present warm period after the Ice Age, has lasted around ten thousand years and previous warm episodes have lasted about that time. Now, if the Holocene is coming to an end and potentially, we are lurching into another ice age, perhaps we need a dose of climate warming simply to keep the cold at bay. There's a thought for you."

"I take your point, Julian. Now back to the present. I'm sure we can rustle up a couple of lorries and a gallon or so of diesel to get hold of Anna's camp beds and bedding. Any ideas, Q?"

Quentin had been on the verge of falling asleep. For the last few nights, he had missed his comfortable bed in his flat in London, being brought tea with the daily newspaper and a breakfast cooked by a loving wife. He worried about her and all his friends in the big city. Life had been much simpler as a tank commander during the Second World War. He stretched and snapped back to the present.

"I would remind you all that there's a transport company on the edge of the village and, with the persuasive powers of our lady cyclists, I suggest we aim to beg, borrow or steal a couple of their trucks for a week or so. With luck there may also be a driver still alive. If there isn't, I can teach any of you to drive a large diesel engine machine, it should be easier than driving a tank.

"Don't talk to me about climate change, I'm bored to distraction by the subject and, anyway, I'm too old to be bothered. It's all very well, this obsession with worrying about the next generation. There won't be a next generation unless we pull our fingers out and get a bloody move on."

CHAPTER EIGHTEEN

Two more bicycles were found in the school playground, but they were both padlocked to the wire fence. "Here we are, folks!" Tom produced a heavy pair of bolt cutters.

"I had to get these because there were so many pupils who left their bicycles still padlocked to the fence. Quite ridiculous, they must have had more money than sense. Some of the bikes must have cost a fortune. There was even an electric one which had been abandoned by a rich foreigner – quite extraordinary. There you are, Van. Every primary school should have a pair of these."

It took the big man a few seconds to destroy the padlocks.

"There you are, four bikes, no obvious punctures, with only one tyre pump. On your way, then. You can stuff the bikes in the back of the truck with the beds and sleeping bags."

It was a beautiful sunny day with cotton wool clouds casting fleeting shadows before them. Four earnest cyclists: Anna, Van, Petra, and Lucy, set out on a mission. They began to relax as they used muscles ignored for months. After two miles they were stopped by a mass of crashed cars. Lucy was the first to dismount and investigate the vehicles.

"Van, unless we can identify a different route, we're going to have to move these, or at least some of them, to be able to get our trucks through. Apart from a few dents, I can't see anything wrong with any of these cars, so we could probably push them into the ditch. Petra, were these blocking the road yesterday?"

"I don't remember them, or perhaps we were on a different road. Sorry, I just don't remember. Did anyone bring a map of the area? No? Marvellous! I guess we were on a narrow country road yesterday. Let's carry on until we find the transport company. It can't be that far."

Round the next corner they were relieved to find the transport company with two brand new shining trucks on the forecourt. The office door was swinging on its hinges and Van shouted, "Anyone at home? Hello! Hello!" He entered the office and saw a board with several keys attached to the numbers of the vehicles. He took the whole board off the wall and went out to the forecourt.

"Now, let's see; I've got the keys to these two trucks. It all depends on how much fuel we have to play with. These organisations usually have their own pump hidden in the back."

He handed Petra one set of keys, climbed into the first truck and switched on the ignition. "Wow! We're in luck, a full tank. How's yours, Petra?

"I think this truck is full as well. They must have filled up before they died, or they might have your hidden tank somewhere." Petra frowned. "If there is an underground tank full of diesel, we could tell the local farmers to come and help themselves. At least that would mean they could keep their tractors and combines going for the rest of the year."

"Concentrate on the present, Petra. I suspect giant combines are a thing of the past. With such a tiny residual population, there will only be a minimum need for grain. Are we ready, folks? I'll go first so if there are any blockages, I'll have a go at pushing them out of the way. Don't follow too closely, I don't want to be bumped into from behind."

"Thanks a million! I've never driven a tank, but it can't be too difficult to drive a removal truck. They're always advertising for drivers – I expect they die of boredom. Are we going to leave the bicycles here or take them with us?"

"Take them with us. There's a map in my truck so we can find another way back to Pensfield to avoid that mass of cars."

A slow and steady journey with no obstructions landed the two trucks at the entrance of the warehouse, only to find the gates locked.

"Come on, Van, my classroom could have solved this. There must be a towrope on these trucks. The gates don't look particularly strong and we can surely pull them down."

"Bugger, I should have brought the bolt cutters. Looks as if you're right, Anna. Here's one under the driver's seat. It looks pretty strong, a proper nylon one. We just have to hope it doesn't snap and come back like a rocket to smash the windscreen."

"Pessimist; think positive, my dear husband. Easy does it."

Van tied the towrope to both the gates, then worked his way back to attach it to his truck. Gently he reversed the truck until the rope was taut. But, however much he tried to reverse further, the gates failed to respond.

"That's a bugger. We'll have to use a bit of momentum."

He slackened the rope and reversed hard so that it snapped tight. At the second attempt he felt the gates move, just a little.

"Third time lucky. Stand clear, girls." Van attacked again and with a satisfying tearing noise the gates and half the outside wall gave way and thundered onto the roadway in a cloud of exhaust fumes and burning clutch smoke. They cheered and both trucks drove into the compound and up to the warehouse doors.

"These aren't locked, thank goodness. Now to investigate our Aladdin's cave." They crept into the silent warehouse. There were ominous little piles of dust where they presumed the original workers had been, but they were becoming used to the signs of human disintegration. It took less than ten minutes to work out what they wanted.

"What's the verdict, Anna?" shouted Van.

"There's enough camping equipment to supply an entire army. I bet most of it was stolen. 'It fell off the back of a lorry, mi'lud.' Come on girls, we can pinch as much as we want. That's what Q said yesterday, or was it the day before?"

Three hours later, two heavily laden trucks reversed out of the warehouse forecourt and slowly made their way by empty country roads back to the school. They were met by a line of solemn faces, fronted by Tom who had obviously been chosen to break the news.

"Glad you're back; we were getting worried about you. Roderick will explain our gloomy welcome. Over to you Rod."

Roderick took a deep breath before he was able to speak. "Julian and I were scouting around the village when we came to your house, Lucy. We knocked on the door, but the only response was a very odd sound from inside. Well, we bashed the door down and found Brian and your two boys all going bad. They were covered in the usual hair and couldn't speak properly. We couldn't stop Brian rushing by us, and he lumbered off to the hills. But we managed to get the two boys into the back of the car and raced back here. It was quite a battle as they seemed to be so strong, but they were mainly fighting each other.

"When we got back here, Julian shot off to his lab and came back with a jar full of virus. Liu arrived and had to inject the boys who were struggling like mad. That calmed them down just enough to let us shout instructions to them. Eventually we managed to get them to inhale without too much fighting. It was a bloody close thing, but it worked. You'll find them sleeping in the next room. They've shed most of the hair and I hope the rest will fall out before the day is finished. I'm sorry about Brian, but we didn't have a hope in hell of controlling him. On the bright side, Liu says he is as sure as he can be that the boys will be fine tomorrow. I'll take you to them, but Liu says to let them wake up slowly and naturally. He predicts they won't remember a thing."

Roderick brought a shocked Lucy back to the group. "Can I get you a drink, Lucy?"

Without waiting for a reply, Tom placed a glass half-filled with amber-coloured liquid in Lucy's hand. She took a deep draught of the whisky, breathed deeply, and sat down. Very softly, she whispered, "Thank you both, you saved my two darlings. I don't know what else to say. Oh, dear!"

They let her cry her heart out. "Thank you," she repeated. "I don't suppose Brian will know much about what is happening to him. He was never very interested in strange happenings, and you can't get stranger than turning into an ape."

Most of the listeners failed to make sense of Lucy's wandering mind; but Roderick had his own interpretation of Lucy's words.

CHAPTER NINETEEN

Tom took charge of the unloading. "Fantastic! You lot have brought well over a hundred camp beds and goodness knows how many sleeping bags. Put the whole lot into the third classroom. Well done, girls and boy!" He laughed. "I gather Van is now an expert in destroying gates."

"Not a great attribute to place on my CV, Tom, but it was quite fun, and it worked. If I had all my home kit with me, I could have blown the gates open, a hobby of mine. One item that we should think of is how to provide enough loos and washing facilities. We don't have enough time to dig a 'long drop', and some ass is only going to fall in unless we're very careful. If all the representatives are male that solves one problem, particularly as most countries are not so secretive as we are with our ablutions. Anyway, if they're only going to be here for a couple of days perhaps it's not quite such an urgent problem. It's nice that the old Professor Yi is staying with Liu, so at least he's cared for."

Lucy appeared, radiant with happiness. "They're fine – both are asking to go fishing this afternoon. I can't believe it. It's just as you were saying, Rod, or was it you, Liu? They have absolutely no memory of the horror and near death they experienced. And they haven't asked after their father. I suppose that's not too surprising as they hardly ever saw him. He's just a distant memory already. Can I help with anything? How about making up a few meals for the visitors as they arrive? Tom, some of those huge catering pans in the school kitchen will be ideal for the job. What do you think, Petra?"

"Steady, old girl, calm down. Liu, come on doctor, what do you advise?"

"Lucy, I know what Petra is thinking. You would be best occupied tucked up in bed with a nice hot drink and a great slug of whisky. Tomorrow is another day, we haven't a clue when the visitors are going to arrive, and it'll be busy enough then. But for now, you need bringing down to earth. Bedtime! Tom, revert to being a teacher and tell Lucy what to do."

"He's quite right, Lucy. I can take your boys fishing and we can all have trout for supper. Bedtime now, and that's an order. Petra, you and Anna go and tuck her up. Carole will bring the hot drink and whisky."

"Julian, how goes the production line in viruses? Have you managed to rope in any of your ex-colleagues?"

"I'm afraid, Tom, there's a marked lack of enthusiasm for such repetitive work. I am now sounding out the main drug manufacturers who are much easier to deal with. Fortunately, the viruses all grow and multiply at a fantastic rate and the actual logistics are simple. Three of the big firms have promised me they can produce enough virus to cover the main centres of population within a week or so. And that is even with the shortage of workers. Anthony suggested one of the big cider companies. I telephoned North-East Cider Company and they were very enthusiastic. They reckoned they could produce enough mixed virus cultures to supply the whole country in one of their giant stainless steel vats. So that was good; it makes up for the peculiar smell that Anthony had in his original wee. Happily, none of the people I have talked to have asked to be paid.

"The supply of little planes could be a problem. It's a very strange thing, but the farming community, with vast numbers of people dying around them are still worried about spraying their crops so they have a better harvest next year. I can't get into their thick heads that if we're not successful in our worldwide project, there may not even be a next year – not for anyone.

"There's also another problem, which is rather important. I'm afraid the use of crop spraying planes was banned about thirty years ago. Unfortunately, even with the slightest breeze, the accuracy of the spread of the agents being spread often went haywire. They tried to switch to helicopters but the downdraught from those machines simply flattened the crops; so that was no good. Drones didn't exist then, but they can only carry a limited amount of fluid.

"There's also another problem in this country. We seem to have a huge number of suspended power lines and the authorities were naturally worried stiff by the number of accidents between low flying planes and high voltage cables. So that's a problem. There must be ways round this and I'm working on a range of them. We need a few canny pilots, for a start.

"I am now inclined to think that we will have to persuade Quentin to pull dozens of strings centrally and mobilise all the little private planes, with live pilots, of course, for this one-off spraying of centres of population. We must make the effort to save at least a twentieth of the population to be able to continue as a civilised country. Humans can breed ridiculously fast and if we start with three to four million people, we'll be up to ten or fifteen in no time at all. Just a word of warning. To get some help from history, we should all start by reading Malthus again and learning from the, when was it, eighteenth century? He wrote 'An Essay on the Principle of Population'. Worth a read, but not at the present time."

"Then the few that are left will have to get their heads together and resurrect the routine systems we take for granted. They must consider that what seems so simple to us now – immunisation against infectious disease and the provision of clean, expert maternity services – will need a level of expertise and training. We would be hopeless at coping with a great pandemic such as the Black Death which kept the population almost level for three hundred years by its repeated assaults on the world. Sorry, Tom, I'm getting boring in my old age. Like your history of the 'searchers'."

"Don't worry, Julian, you have raised a number of hares; we simply have to chase them into the ground. I wish you well with big business. I have only had to deal with the likes of local councils and central government, and they're awkward enough, goodness knows. But this is infinitely bigger. At least it's something we can get our teeth into.

"Q has stirred up a small team from Reading to divide up the country into easily manageable sections. They will be, naturally, centred around cities or areas that used to have dense population. The organisers will have to choose days that are free of too much wind and provide loudspeaker vans to tell surviving people to come out into the open. That should help our viruses to have the maximum effect. Let's hope what is, after all, a desperate salvage operation, works."

Julian went to make tea, which was important for the morale of the team. Liu joined him. "How goes it, Julian? You did a fantastic job with Lucy's boys. I found some fishing rods at home and a tin of flies I remember making when I was their age. I felt slightly envious, I must confess. The thought of freshly caught trout from the lake by the power station makes my mouth water."

"And mine. Do you think anyone takes sugar? Or have you frightened them so much about diabetes, they daren't?"

"Most of my patients are much too sensible to be frightened by such rubbish."

"Thank goodness for that. Tell me, what does your professor friend from the university in Beijing think of what's destroying us?"

"You can ask him, if you like, he's staying with us. As soon as I phoned to tell him what was happening and how well you were dealing with the problems as they arose, he came straight over, and he's come to stay. Why don't you, Petra, Tom, and Carole come and have supper with us tonight? I'm afraid we are unlikely to be able to offer you trout just yet, but we might have something delicious in the deep freeze."

CHAPTER TWENTY

An attractive, forty-something year old dark-haired, short, well-covered lady met the four of them at the door of their substantial house. "Welcome, I'm Liu's wife, Ying Yue, call me Yue. Liu will be back in a minute. He phoned and said there had been some trouble at the surgery. Come in, come in. I believe you have already met our great friend, Professor Yi. He has actually been appointed as the senior official representative for China at our conference. I must warn you, he has a wicked sense of humour."

They were escorted to the sitting room with a wonderful open view of the hills. The colourful garden stretched alongside fifty yards of immaculate, mown grass. There was a small pond at the end of the garden and a low line of small, manicured trees to separate the property from the scrubland and heather in the rising ground beyond.

Yue announced the visitors. "Commander Julian Bailey, Professor Petra Bailey, Tom Mayhew and Carole, the school secretary. I'm sorry, Carole, I don't know your surname?"

"Don't worry, it'll soon be Mayhew!"

"Now, that's just wonderful, congratulations. I'm so pleased for both of you. Professor Yi from Beijing is an old friend of ours from years back. He taught me a huge amount of wisdom and did it with great patience."

The slightly bent, smiling white-haired old gentleman came slowly into the room.

He stood still for a full minute, switching his gaze from one visitor to another. When he was satisfied with what he saw, his smile blazed forth so that the whole of his face lit up like a beacon of good will. "I am very pleased to meet with you all again. I must confess that I have been appointed as the official representative to your international meeting – probably because I have come to know this part of your country through the Liu family. Carole, your news calls for a celebration; Tom is a very fine man. I have had wonderful conversations with him over the years, whenever I am invited to come and stay here. And Julian, it is a pleasure to meet you again. You have cured some people! And that, of course, is why we are all congregating in this little village at the other end of the world from my home country. How are you going to look after all your visitors? That is, if they can spare the time to turn up. I am all in favour of having a worldwide agreement to try to stop the unbelievable death rate. After all, it has never happened before. Even the Black Death was not like this. Although before the fourteenth century when it devastated Europe, there were reports in India and in my country of whole cities being abandoned to what was probably that same disease.

"Now, this idea of an international agreement …" The old man laughed at such a ridiculous happening. With tears running down his face he continued with no let up, "… words, words, words; it must be the background of all political discussions. And, my goodness, this could well be the most rambling of all political discussions. No nation will want to spend any of their miserable imagined wealth to help anyone else. There will be begging bowls by the hundreds hovering under the noses of the nations who have managed to survive this peculiar attack. But I tell you one thing. The first nation that agrees to mobilise its entire scientific materiel to produce enough virus to stop the

Archaea will take precedence over the rest. Once that is announced, most of the others will fall into line. Only the most belligerent of self-important nations will be determined not to cooperate. And they will perish. What say you, clever scientist, Julian?"

"You may well be right, Yi. I suspect we could name those nations right now. Another time, perhaps. Aha! Here is our host. I wonder what's been the problem?"

Liu came into the room holding a large glass of reviving liquid in his hands. He sat down heavily and turned to reveal a three-inch gash on his forehead covered with slightly soiled kitchen paper.

"Sorry I'm late, folks, we had quite a problem in the surgery. One of the, I suppose we still call them, mutants, instead of charging up to the top of the hills, must have taken a wrong turn and landed up in the front room of the surgery. Sonia, our tolerant secretary, went out to help. But she was attacked by the beast who was making an awful screaming noise. We all heard it and went to help the poor girl. My goodness, the strength of the beast. We were all damaged." He pointed to his forehead. "I suppose I should cover this properly. Have we any plasters in the house, Yue, rather than my grubby kitchen paper?"

Yue left the room and returned with a tube of antiseptic and an enormous roll of material that she expertly tied round the doctor's head. "There, that'll teach you not to get involved in fights. You should have grown out of all that years ago."

"We had to help poor Sonia. It took four of us to restrain the beast. Then the most peculiar thing happened. It simply disintegrated. The whole frame of the animal simply shrank to almost nothing. All that was left was a pile of brown dust and a mass of black hairs." Liu shuddered with the memory and had another gulp from his glass. "We imagined that because the beast had failed, whatever, or whoever, was controlling it simply wrote it off. Astonishing – there was absolutely nothing left."

Liu was shaking with fright at the memory. He looked at his friend for support. The old professor came over and knelt by the doctor. He put his arms round him until the shaking stopped.

Professor Yi pulled Liu to his feet and sniffed loudly. "I can smell the most delicious smells coming from the kitchen which must have been produced by my favourite chef. I suggest we move next door and enjoy the wonders of Yue's cooking, which I know for certain will cure all known ills and rid us of all bad memories." He looked at Yue who nodded her head.

"Time for lunch, ladies and gentlemen. Yi, can you lead the way? I have labelled where I would like people to sit and please help yourselves to white or red wine: the white is from China. We will be eating Chinese steamed bass with cabbage which is a favourite dish of my husband."

"And a favourite of mine," said Yi.

CHAPTER TWENTY-ONE

Tom patted his lips with his napkin. "That was as delicious as the first time you gave it to me. It must have been two years ago, Yue."

"I remember, that was when we were trying to impress you to take our two children into your school."

"I must say that wasn't a difficult decision, those two have always been the stars in their classroom. And your little girl, Sun – a lovely name, always beaming, just like the sun itself – is an extraordinary athlete. After all, she won the county athletic championship, streets ahead of all the others. I think she could have won the national event, but then this nasty little bug came along and ruined everything. You must agree, Carole?"

"I certainly do, and your boy, Min, could run the hind legs off anyone. And Dad is the best doctor in the area."

"You have both been very kind to us."

"Liu, how's the head?" asked Yi.

"Aches a bit but bearable now. I might take the afternoon off and have a sleep."

"Don't sleep too much." Yi lapsed into silence, but Petra sensed there was a warning note in his voice, and she said nothing.

The rest of the meal went sailing by with no hiccups and they went into the garden with coffee and the remains of their glasses of wine.

"If you will excuse me," said Liu, "I will go and have a nap."

"NO, you won't!" Petra shouted. She pointed to Liu's hands which were beginning to change colour. In the afternoon sunlight there was a hint of a grey discoloration. "Jules, we need … ah, you're off."

Julian was already heading for the car. They heard the car door slam and Julian came running back with a bottle of fluid and the atomiser.

"Sit down, Liu, and do as you're told. I want this stuff down to the bottom of your lungs."

"You don't think? Surely it can't be as quick as that."

"Oh, yes it can, and oh yes, you are to do as you are told. And finally, you're going to do precisely what I tell you to do. Inhale, dear boy, deep. Get this stuff where it's going to work."

A subdued Liu inhaled as deeply as he could. They laid him on the grass and, as if a magic wand had been waved, his normal colour began to return. Finally, Julian's fluid on his hands chased away the grey. Then they carried him up to his bedroom where he slept.

As the guests were leaving over an hour later, Petra turned to Yi. "What was it that moved you to say to Liu 'don't sleep too much'? How did you know something was going to happen out of the ordinary?"

Yi smiled. "I wondered when you were going to ask me that, Petra. There was a change in Liu that I find it impossible to explain to a European. It is a change in the demeanour of the person. In my country, we spend many hours studying a person's demeanour. It is an outward reflection of what you in Europe might tend to label as homeostasis. Sometimes it gives us a clue as to whether a person is ill or, as you say, pulling the wool."

The old professor laughed. "I used to teach other medical staff, both doctors and nurses and the rest of the hospital staff – even schoolteachers who could spare the time to come to my teaching sessions. A very useful indicator, and far quicker than all your clever tests. Don't get me wrong, Julian, your science is excellent and our science in China is excellent. But sometimes you need the icing on the cake."

"Well, Yi, you certainly added the icing today. I do hope we meet again before the great get together."

"We will, Julian, we will."

CHAPTER TWENTY-TWO

"Tom, what an amazing man is our professor. I wish we had more like him in this country. With that degree of insight, he would knock spots off most of our tame psychiatrists."

"Julian, there are quite a few like Yi in this country, but I'm afraid they're often branded as cranks and they become disillusioned and fade away. There is an obsession with instant answers which lead to instant labels. And once you have a label stuck on you, there is the standard treatment. The problem is that there is no standard person. Back to the present, what do we have to do next?"

"Tom, perhaps I'm learning from Yi, but I have a feeling that we should visit the surgery and see if anyone else is affected. After all, Liu was in a bad way having helped to restrain a mutant. Who else was he helping, Sonia, for a start? And he did say there were several of them involved in the battle? Come on now. The more I think about it, the more I feel we ought to check."

"I'm coming with you, two is better than one."

At the surgery they found Sonia slumped in a chair, crying softly and repeatedly blowing her nose. She looked up as Tom and Julian entered. "I'm so glad you came, I hoped you would. All I can do nowadays is answer the phone to one tearful parent after another who tells me that yet another child can't come to the surgery for their injections. I tell you, if too many children don't get their jabs, we are going to have an epidemic, especially measles. It's such a nasty germ, and I've been reading that measles destroys your whole immune system, so you might have to start chugging up your immunity from scratch."

Sonia blew her very red nose again. "It's making me feel ill; there's so much gloom around. Your Anthony came in this afternoon and said he had just come to see me. That was lovely, but his dog growled at me just as they were leaving."

Tom looked at Julian. "Are you sure about that, Sonia?"

"Oh, yes. Anthony did apologise and dragged the dog away for a walk. I think he said it was a bitch called Sheba, a lovely animal. Anthony is ever so proud of her. You are lucky, Julian."

"That's as may be, Sonia. How are you feeling? Any side effects from your battle when you helped Liu with the mutant that landed up in the surgery?"

"That was a battle and a half. He, or it, tried to bite my hand. Here, take a look. That's funny, the place has gone a dirty colour; I must wash it off." She started to rise from the chair but collapsed crying again.

Julian ran to the door shouting to Tom to stay with Sonia. "I need to get something from the car. Keep Sonia as quiet as you can."

Within two minutes Julian returned with a small bottle of fluid and the atomiser.

"Sonia, listen to me; I want you to inhale this tiny amount as far down in your lungs as you can."

"No! No! I can't have it! I'm not going to have your stuff. That's the stuff that's making us all ill. I've got to get home! Let me out!" Suddenly, Sonia had a burst of energy, rose out of the chair, brushed past the two men and ran into the corridor where she crashed into Liu and Quentin.

"Stop her!" shouted Tom. "We were trying to treat her when she erupted and flew off. We think she's a casualty of your fight earlier in the day."

Sonia was already at the front door and had torn off her dress by the time the four men were able to stop her.

"Shall I knock her out?" asked Liu.

"Try a small dose," suggested Julian.

The restraining was becoming more difficult, but Sonia became limp after the injection. It needed a lot of shouting to persuade the girl, in her befuddled state, to open her mouth wide. At last, Julian was able to pump the aerosol of curing fluid into her open mouth. She coughed several times and collapsed unconscious. They covered her with a blanket and waited while Liu listened to her heart.

"We must keep her warm, everything is so quick, damn it! I hope we're in time to stop the damage. Hang on, there's something happening – she had a racing pulse just a minute ago but now it is nice and regular. She's going to be alright. Can someone ring Sonia's husband and ask him to bring a clean pair of knickers and a dress. When she wakes up, she's going to feel really embarrassed."

Tom returned, worried. "There's no answer and they haven't got an answerphone. I know Jeff's at home as I spoke to him only an hour ago about my lawnmower. Not the most riveting of conversations, he simply wanted to borrow it tomorrow. But he said he wanted to watch some football match this morning. If he is doing that, he should be awake. And I know the telephone is just next to the television set and the match won't be that boring. I don't like the feel of this. I think, when Sonia is better, we should all go round to her house. We'll have to wrap her up and take her in her present state in one of our cars. She's not going to thank us one little bit."

No one came to answer the doorbell. But the door wasn't locked so they entered, and Julian called, "Anyone in? Jeff, are you all-right?" Silence. "Sitting room is on the left; Oh Lord! What a mess."

Jeff's clothing was torn and flung randomly round the room. The glass doors were slightly open, and Tom shut them. A strange sound came from the back garden and there they saw him. They saw him only too clearly when he knuckle-ran to the closed door and crashed into the glass. The glass resisted the attack and the ape-like creature looked puzzled.

"Oh my God!" murmured Sonia. "Has he gone too far? Julian, you can save my husband. Please save him."

"We'll do all we can, Sonia. But first we have to catch him."

Julian sat down hard. "How the hell are we going to do that? A net, of course! A large fishing net, thrown by an expert. Have we got any in this part of the county, or do we have to race down to the port to find one?"

"Of course, we have one right here!" shouted Tom. "There's a super Korean boy who comes from a family of fishermen; he is going to be ten years old next week. He showed us a month ago at the school how to catch a wild dog. It was a brilliant demonstration. Luckily, his grandfather had given him an old net as a present before he came to this country. I have his home phone number. He lives with his adopted family in this road. Hang on, I can dial him now."

"Hello, this is the school headmaster speaking. I have a very strange request which is very, very urgent. Can we borrow your adopted son, Sol, to do something dangerous? We need his

145

expertise at throwing the fishing net. If you could all come over to number twenty-four right away, he might be in time to save a life. You can? Splendid, yes, right now." He turned to the others in triumph. "You heard all that. He really is an amazing lad. His grandfather was a very famous fisherman. Surname, I think, is Kwon something."

The superbly confident Sol stood quite still, running the net through his fingers. He was very tense but the calm smile lighting his face and the visible pumping of the artery on the side of his head showed how excited he was.

"I can do that. Throw him something interesting, perhaps something to eat. He won't attack me because I'm too small to be a threat. But he won't like the sight of adults. Have you got something tasty in the fridge or a big children's toy?"

Sonia nodded towards a cupboard. Julian opened the cupboard door. "How about this?" Julian pulled out an enormous, bright orange cuddly bear, almost as big as Sol himself.

"That's better than a cold piece of meat," said Sol. "Good, give it to me and gently open the door to the garden. He can't escape, the walls are too high."

"Are you sure you don't want any of us to be behind you."

A very confident Sol laughed. "No, let me do this on my own. Watch me, but don't come outside until I tell you. Don't worry, I'm fine."

The door was opened, and Sol walked slowly out into the garden holding the teddy bear in one hand and the net in the other. The mutant Jeff approached and gently touched Sol's face. Sol handed Jeff the bear. Jeff seemed to be pleased with the gift and they heard him making a gentle rumbling sound.

With amazing speed, Sol stepped back two paces and, as if by magic, the fishing net leapt into the air and trapped Jeff. There was no reaction at all from the prisoner who seemed perfectly happy with his cuddly bear, both enveloped in the fishing net.

"You can come out now," shouted Sol. "Be quick, though. He'll go mad in about two minutes, but he can hear you."

Julian was first to the trapped Jeff. "Open wide!" Jeff opened his mouth, and the fluid was squirted into it and onto the rest of his hairy face and hands. Julian's instinct told him to look at Sol for instructions.

Sol, totally in control, smiled and gave the orders. "Everyone, be quiet, sit down on the grass and wait. Wait and see if this strange mixture of powerful viruses made by our scientist can do the magic trick and save a mutant at this late stage. We can only wait and see, Julian. Happy about that?"

"It might just work, but we couldn't have done it without your help, Sol. That was a fantastic throw. What age do you start to learn how to throw the net? You made it look so easy."

Sol smiled. "My grandfather started to teach me to throw when I was three years old. Dad was always out fishing, and Grandfather was the only person in the village who was a real expert at the throw. It comes easily after two or three years."

"Fantastic!" was the only word spoken by Tom.

CHAPTER TWENTY-THREE

Jeff appeared to be asleep, but there was a change; a very subtle change. Liu got up to be nearer, but Sol motioned the doctor to sit down. Liu blinked in surprise but did as he was told.

"Another ten minutes, please, something is working," said the little boy. He was humming an unusual tune with a curious mixture of half tones. It sounded repetitive to the untrained ear, but Liu recognised an ancient melody from the North of China.

They waited for what seemed to be far longer than ten minutes. Suddenly Sol stood up and gently took the net off the trapped body. He removed the teddy bear and gestured to Liu. "He'll be alright now."

A moan made the four turn to find Sonia in a deep faint. They picked her up and carried her into the house while Liu examined Sonia's slowly-returning husband.

"Normal pulse and these ghastly hairs are coming off in handfuls. I believe Jeff is recognising where he is. Tom, can you get a rug from the sitting room? Jeff is going to pretty embarrassed otherwise."

"Did Liverpool win?" Just a murmur, but the catalyst for a scream of delight from a clean, dressed, sweet-smelling Sonia as she rushed towards her husband. Sol put out a hand to stop Sonia.

"Gently, Sonia. Jeff is slowly coming round but there's an awful lot of repair work going on inside. Treat him very gently for the next week at least – especially his skin which will be very sore. Julian may give you an elaborate explanation, but the main thing is it appears to have worked. Close-run thing, though."

"Oh, I love you all." Sonia, crying tears of happiness, helped to cover her husband with the blanket from the sitting room sofa. "I don't know who won your football match, my darling, but we can find out using play-back. First of all, you need a bath and clean clothes."

Jeff frowned. "I had clean clothes this morning." He looked down at his pale body appearing as if from nowhere. "What have I done with them? What are all these people doing here? And this huge net?"

"Don't worry about that. Don't worry about anything. There's been a lot going on, we'll tell you about it later."

Jeff struggled to his feet and was helped into the house.

Sonia smiled uncertainly. "Thank you, all. I can cope now."

"We'll be off then," said Julian. "Some of us will be back this evening just to check everything's all right. Don't worry, Sonia, he's in the land of the living. It won't happen again – Sol says so."

"What won't happen again?" asked Jeff.

"Never you mind, my darling."

"Never you mind," said his wife for the second time, as the group were instructed how to roll up Sol's net. They left as soon as they could.

Back at the surgery, Liu opened a bottle with a 'pop'. "Our afternoon efforts deserve a glorious celebration, especially to celebrate the expertise of our Korean fisherman. Here's to you, Sol; you did a wonderful job. I hope you like a little fizzy wine."

"Thank you, sir. I've never tasted this before. My father and my grandfather used to make wine from rice, but I didn't like it. It tasted, sort of, like, some of their fish sauce – I didn't like that either. But this is nice … can I have some more, please?"

Liu laughed. "You sound like Oliver Twist. Of course, you can have some more – not too much, mind. We have to take you back home fairly sober."

Petra appeared. "Jules, I've been looking for you everywhere. Where have you been?"

"Resurrecting Sonia's husband with the fantastic help of Sol, who trapped Jeff with a fisherman's net, and we managed to spray virus into him just in time. He's recovering with extraordinary speed, hence the celebration. Have a glass on Liu." Julian paused. "You know, there was almost a mystical change in Sol. He became gently dominant and took complete charge of the rescue. We were, quite rightly, subordinate until the cure was complete. Quite amazing."

"You can tell me the whole story later, Jules. But just now, the girls are wondering when the first of the international lot are going to appear? We heard a small plane land on the hill about an hour ago, but there were no passengers. Perhaps it was a trial flight. Q, any clues from the big city?"

Quentin had been hoping to get a word in edgeways. He took a deep breath. "I can give you a little warning about arrivals. The first lot will be coming tomorrow morning. They will fly into Heathrow, take a flight to our local large airport north of here, and then take the final leg in a little plane to be able to land at our tiny local airfield. The first lot will be Europeans, then hopefully in the afternoon will be a batch from South America; they are very enthusiastic about meeting us. I guess some might come by helicopter. You never can tell, but they all must obey the local air traffic control.

"Flying at night is a mite too hazardous. The few electricians still around are having trouble with floodlighting our tiny airfield, as it's only a freshly mown strip of wild grass, but it's dry enough to take a bit of pounding. And, in a couple of days, the whole world will be here enjoying our simple food and drink. There's a chance, hopefully, that some of the visitors may bring some interesting bottles with them – there's always hope! How are the preparations in the tithe barn going, Petra?"

"That's a question of fun and games, all right. Chainsaws have been busy doing a mammoth job of alteration. The guys have been trying to get permission to make the alterations for years to stabilise the place, but the Heritage people always stopped us doing anything. The whole structure is in good condition, apart from its bottom. There are signs of severe rot in the some of the foundation blocks. The carpenters are working through the night to make the thing as safe as possible. Our treasured tithe barn will be all set up with a hundred and fifty seats and a decent sound system and a sort of gantry to take the film cameras. Some of the seats were rescued from their journey to the dump and are simple but we found a mountain of cushions in the warehouse. The lighting is a bit precarious; we've blown up the fuse box twice, but it should be working now. Will you be chairman of the day, Q?"

"If you're all happy with that." He looked around the little group and reluctantly had to conclude he was in the hot seat. "Thank you for your confidence in me." He thought for a while. "As audiences go, this lot will certainly have a degree of verbal diarrhoea. I suggest that we should allow every delegate to at least contribute something. But I'm inclined to let each person contribute only once. If you give them a second chance they'll go off at a tangent and there will be no stopping them. Delegates have a fascination with hearing their own voices, and they have to be stopped monopolising the time."

He stretched his old back and appeared to switch off. But his eyes lit up and he spoke again. "Now we have to decide on our approach to the international problem. The most important decision is the choice of someone chosen and agreed by all of us to convince as many as possible of those present of the extreme urgency to get overall agreement in the shortest possible time, so that we can all aim for the same objective. I know that might sound pompous, but we need to have a single voice that sets out the worldwide activity that is going to stop the elimination of *Homo sapiens*. Now, who is going to step into the hot seat and be incredibly persuasive? Liu, you are the most liked of the local doctors, and you have been involved with all our successes – would you feel happy about doing that?"

"I would like to ask the advice of my great friend who, remember, is the Chinese representative at this get together. Excuse me, while I phone him from another room."

"Well," said Julian when Liu was out of earshot, "I don't think Liu is very keen on the idea. I'm not so keen either. I don't mind talking about the science but by now they should all know most of it, just as well as I do – some of them, even better. There will be some serious experts coming to sit on those chairs and it would be like telling one's grandmother to suck eggs. Anybody got any ideas or suggestions? Even volunteers?"

Liu returned. "My friend Professor Yi thinks I would not be the right person. He has someone in mind but he's not telling me until you have your own suggestions."

Liu's statement produced an awkward silence.

Quentin frowned and was about to speak when Sol raised a hand. "Please, sir, can I say something?"

Quentin smiled and nodded his head. "Sol, if you can hold their attention as well as you held ours this afternoon, tell us what you are thinking."

CHAPTER TWENTY-FOUR

"Sir," Sol blushed wildly. "I, sort of, think … how about asking the first case to be cured? Anthony has a tongue in his head and sometimes it's quite difficult to shut him up. But he is one of my greatest friends and I would vote for him."

A stunned silence followed. Liu laughed out loud. "Anthony is the very person suggested by Professor Yi. Well, I never. Sol, beware of becoming too predictable."

Julian's face changed from astonishment to pleasure. "I can't possibly comment – well, I shouldn't anyway. Ant can certainly cope with barracking without getting flustered, he's a tough little devil. Petra, what do you think?"

"All I can say, is that I am so pleased that you have confidence in Anthony. I can understand the logic. He can speak from experience and we know he can be persuasive, and he won't be phased by a gaggle of mostly old men and women. Who's going to ask him, I wonder? Q, being the representative of our government, would you be prepared to ask Anthony?"

"Bad idea, Petra. I may be wrong, but I have the feeling that Anthony sees me as being too high and mighty. I have a much better idea; in fact, a combination of ideas which, I hope, won't blow your heads off." He turned and looked at Sol who blushed bright red. "Firstly, Sol, can you find Anthony for us? I think he is playing football."

Sol disappeared in the direction of the playground.

Quentin suddenly stood up. "No! I have a better idea, a much better idea. Liu, after you."

Liu laughed loudly. "I come from a country where the inhabitants are renowned for hiding their feelings," he said. "But, Q, it is so refreshing to find a very important person whose ideas are so transparent. Let me guess? You are going to suggest a combined panel of two young, but very bright boys, to persuade representatives from the whole world to act together to save humanity. Am I correct?"

"You are, indeed, Liu, almost quite correct. I take your personal comment as a great compliment. Transparent! Well, I never." Quentin laughed and was joined by the rest of them. "Petra, what do you think of that?"

"It's a lovely idea, but it has bypassed the original question. If both children are to be lined up in front of over a hundred experts, you can't ask one to ask the other – it's too much of a set-up. We all, this little group, must take the opportunity to ask them both at the same time.

"And I have another thought. How about little Ben who was apparently braver than all of us and led the poor mutants up to the hidden sanctuary in the hills to meet their fate? I know some of us feel he's sometimes not up to scratch, but, by any criterion he's bloody marvellous. Tom, any idea where the boys are now?"

Tom looked at his watch. "Most of them are milling around, fascinated with the work on the tithe barn. Remember they are survivors. I must say, those that are left seem to have a huge amount of energy; almost as if the original energy of the dead ones has been transferred to the survivors. You realise the cull amongst school children is rising ninety percent. I'll find them, wherever they are." He left with Anna.

Liu had tears in his eyes. "Sadly, the cull, as you call it, amongst the remainder of the population of this village is probably higher, especially amongst the old and frail. I might as well tell you that we have reached the stage when we don't need three doctors and a big surgery. There's so little to do except prescribe tranquillizers to the remaining adults. We all must come to terms with the realisation that there is one hell of a lot of catching up to do. And I don't mean that we should all breed like blazes. That's too simplistic. I suspect all the structures in this country have to adjust to much lower populations and standard of living, and do it fast."

Tom returned with the three boys in tow. They had no idea of the enormous burden they were going to be asked to carry.

Tom started. "Sorry, lads, we dragged you away from play time. By the way, which team was winning? Rounds or ovals?" He turned to the solemn little group of adults. "Those are the names of the two houses in the school. I have absolutely no idea where the names came from."

Ben responded softly, "Shape of the plates at mealtime."

"Thank you, Ben, I never knew that. Now, we have asked you three to come here because we have a very important question to ask all three of you. You can think about it before you answer, but we are asking you to do something very important. What is it, Anthony?"

"I think— we all think— thought, I mean." He drew a deep breath and looked at Sol for support. "You tell them, Sol."

Sol slowly looked at the earnest group of grown-ups. They were friendly, that he knew – he was as certain as he had ever been of the result – but what were they exactly going to be asked to do? The three of them had thought of an idea, but it seemed to be ridiculous. They had come to the conclusion in the playground that the little group of grown-ups had been plotting something – something big, very big. Was it to look after all the important people coming from all over the world, or was it something quite different and not such fun?

"We thought, between us, the three of us, that you were going to ask us to do something that was not dangerous. We've, sort of, had enough of that." The listeners had to laugh and, to some extent, relax. "We thought you were going to ask us to talk to the scientists when they were gathered in the big barn. Is that right?"

"You are absolutely right, Sol," said Anna. "I saw you three in a huddle in the corner of the playground. You looked so serious, I dared not interrupt such an important meeting. But you're right. Would you three, perhaps one at a time – you choose the first one – speak to the hopefully hundred and fifty-odd scientists? You will have to persuade them all to pour all their efforts into producing huge amounts of viruses to kill off the Archaea. Then to spray as many remnants of human beings as we can with the mixture of viruses from the air. We can help you compose the speeches, if you like, but the spoken words must come from you. You three are the most important people in this room. Ben was the first. He took charge of the fate of the first wave of damaged people and dealt with the problem in such a fabulous way.

"Anthony was the first to be cured in the initial wave of strange damage. Sol demonstrated that with ingenuity, individual advanced cases can be cured. You three are the proper ones to speak, as you will still be in the land of the living when us lot are all gone. That is important as you will be speaking on behalf of the next generation. How does that grab you, chaps?"

"Don't worry, we'll do it," said Anthony. "You OK with that Ben, Sol" Both nodded. "Just one thing?"

"And what is that?" asked Quentin.

"How about a demonstration, sort of, flypast. Gillian's father says he can borrow a little plane that has been used to spray crops. It used to belong to his brother, and it's been sitting in a hangar up at the airfield for the last two years. He says he can have it flying in a few hours. The plane has been checked every year so it should be all right to fly, and his pilot licence is up to date."

"What a super idea." Quentin was enthusiastic. "So, all we will need is someone to fly the thing. Julian, do you have enough viruses to fill the tank?"

"By tomorrow, the cider people will deliver several gallons at first light."

So, three relatively happy children were set-up to save the world.

CHAPTER TWENTY-FIVE

Quentin made a great attempt to be solemn. But when he saw the three faces in front of him smiling wider than cheerful, he had to smile too.

"Now, folks, we have to have a plan for how we're going to present our line of ambassadors in such a way as to help them persuade the international gathering do what we ask them to do – in their own interest, of course." He paused. "I know that I can be frightfully pompous."

Quentin looked at Julian. "I can guess what you're thinking; you don't have to say anything, Jules. But I must bring them all to attention. I will assume that they all speak English, for a start. I think a solemn introduction would be appropriate. Then, somehow, I have to persuade them that our trio is the best group to tell them all how far we have got in treating a very few people. But, and it is a very important but, we must hammer the fact that so far everything has worked – and worked fast – and they all have to work fast, too. Ideas please, Petra?"

"I think our trio have to emphasise the ghastly element of speed. The speed of development and the speed of cure. That's critical. But the main objective that we are going to push is the combined worldwide effort to protect the remaining people who are still alive in the major cities of the world. We are going to have to persuade the delegates at some stage that not only is it logistically impossible to protect the inhabitants of the countryside but, for some odd reason that we don't understand, it seems to be unnecessary, for the moment, anyway. As I said, for reasons that we don't yet understand, the farming community appear to be partially protected. Perhaps they are immunised in some way by wild Archaea that are all around us. Are you taking this in, lads?"

The three nodded. Anthony asked, "Are you going to write all this down?"

"I guess so but you won't be so effective if all you will be doing is reading from bits of paper. You are going to have to memorise some of it and then say it in your own words. Perhaps use some of your own jargon to liven it up."

Anthony and Sol laughed but Ben, his usual impassive self, sounded concerned. "I have to have something to read. Can Sheba be there?"

Petra heaved a sigh of relief; she was certain Ben's presence would be vital. "Of course, Sheba will be there, right next to you. She will need to be stroked and looked after, and you're the best person to do it."

"But she's Anthony's dog and I—"

Anthony, put his arm round Ben. "You can cuddle her for me." Ben smiled and looked a lot happier.

Quentin coughed and brought the tense moment to an end. "How long do you think you three will need to say your piece and prepare the ground for the boring bit about the logistics of preparing an extraordinary volume of viruses and then spreading it far and wide? That's quite important. We don't want our audience to get bored and fall asleep. After all, many of them will have travelled thousands of miles, often from the other side of the world. They will be jet-lagged and, remember, they may be grieving about relatives or friends who have died. They need to be given a huge amount of hope that we as a species have any chance of success. What say you, Julian?"

"I can give that to them in spades. Apart from the amusement of being soaked to the skin at the seaside, the technical details should be simple for all of them. Many of them will be much better qualified than we are to persuade big industry to cooperate to produce vast number of mixed viruses active against Archaea. I also suspect that many of them have their own pilot licences and will know far more than I do about spraying, by whatever means. It shouldn't be a problem to wind them up to speed."

"That's reassuring, Julian. Now, how about the barn. Does it have enough electricity? Roderick, can you help in that field?"

"Don't worry, Q, we've moved one of the big generators from the power station to the barn and there's plenty of fuel to keep it going for days, if necessary. Plenty of light with LEDs, heating if necessary, and air conditioning if it gets too hot. With that number of worried people, the place might well get overheated. Depends how much our three ambassadors can wind them up! Remember, there will be the faint noise of the television camera in the background. Most of them will be only too used to that. They might even expect it!"

They all laughed, and Roderick continued, "There's also plenty of power for the portable kitchen which will be right next to the barn. And I took the opportunity to ask the local publican to bring in a comprehensive bar next to the kitchen. Since most of his staff have died, we'll have to help serving both in the kitchen and bar. Never mind, the whole thing is free, thanks to Quentin."

"Well done, Roderick; I guess they'll be pretty hungry. For many, all they've got to look forward to is, at the end of the session – maybe in a few hours, but preferably after a night's sleep – flying thousands of miles home and working their butts off."

"Well, you three, do you think half past ten in the morning is too early for you to be on stage?"

"We'll be there, don't worry. I don't think we're going to get much sleep tonight," said Anthony.

"Splendid. Remember, make it emotional; it must come from the heart. You must pull their heartstrings until they almost snap. We'll give you notes, lots of them, but it doesn't matter a damn if you drop them and speak as you always speak to us. You are very sensible lads and we're sure you'll do a fantastic job. OK, lads?"

"Yes, Q. When do you think we should have the demonstration? The flypast?"

"After breakfast the next day the weather forecast is good, so loudhailers will have to be out a couple of hours before that to get everyone into the open. Good thinking, lads."

Quentin had always been a bad sleeper and he was the first to arrive at the tithe barn. He glanced at his watch; six o'clock, with the sun struggling to rise above the horizon. The television crew was setting up their system, trying to hammer what appeared to be miles of cable into wooden beams that were so hard, they were eventually forced to resort to sticky tape.

Quentin sat on a chair in the front row of the future audience, picked up a well-thumbed booklet and started to read: Income for the Rector partly came from the tithes paid by the local farmers; this was usually set at ten percent of their harvested crops. In 1535, Henry VIII's time, the value of one local tithe was £10 of grain and 18s/10½d of hay.

That was a lot to hand over then, especially to the rich priests; no wonder the king nationalised all the monasteries and said, "To hell with the pope!"

He read on: There were many tithe barns throughout Europe in the Middle Ages. They were built to store rents and, of course, tithes. They were mostly associated with monasteries and built in a similar structural style as hospitals or market halls. Ours was probably first built in the seventeenth century and must have originally been thatched. The county archives suggest that our tithe barn had to be rebuilt several times. One major rebuild, in the beginning of the nineteenth century, included a change of roof style from thatch to tiles. With the additional weight, they were forced to strengthen the roof structures. The original walls were of wood but later changed to rubble and stone walling.

Quentin looked at the obviously wooden walls. He was puzzled and continued to read: A complete restoration in 2013 replaced the bases of the twenty-five-foot oak beams, that mostly supported the roof, with upstanding brickwork. An unsafe small second floor was also removed, and the outside walls reverted to cladding with wood.

Oh good, that explains the present structure.

"That's better," he remarked out loud, and read on for a while: Compulsory tithes were eventually terminated by the Finance Act of 1977.

"So much for greed! What a fascinating little book. I wonder who has had the patience to keep it up to date?"

"You'll have to ask Carole; she's right here."

Quentin jumped. "Hello, Tom. I couldn't sleep so I've had a peek into the history of the tithe and tithe barns from this little book. The entries are quite superb, and I was wondering who could have been so diligent with the entries. Do you know who the scribe was, Carole?"

"I'm pretty sure it has mostly been Charmaine Bradley, the mother of Ben. She found the book, which must have been started in the seventeen hundreds, in the school library, and she's spent hours bringing it up to date."

"Well, she is certainly very thorough, and the historical references are excellent."

"She'll be ever so pleased if you told her direct. But for now, I have a thermos of tea for everyone, including the Baileys who have just arrived."

"Hello, you lot," said Julian. "I thought I would be the first, but now you are both here, you can help me. I need to clear three aisles between the chairs right up to our platform and preferably a clear run from one end of the building to the other."

"What's this all for, Jules?" asked Tom.

"Never you mind, I had hoped it would be a surprise."

They cleared the aisles and Julian slowly walked up and down each, carefully holding a black box recorder. At the end of each traverse, he tapped in further information. When he had finished, he smiled and muttered, "That'll do." He gave no clue to the others the reason for the peculiar manoeuvres.

"Right, folks; you can readjust to two aisles as they were before."

CHAPTER TWENTY-SIX

The three boys had been sleeping fitfully in a school classroom. Sheba was comfortable in her basket by the school entrance.

"You awake, Sol, Ben?" asked Anthony softly.

"It's only five o'clock," complained Sol, "and I've been awake for hours."

"Why did you wake me up, Ant?" asked Ben. "I like my sleep."

"Sorry, I thought I heard the front door open."

They waited for another five minutes.

"There's someone in the school kitchen," said Sol, "I can hear voices. I think it's Lucy and Roderick. Let's go and see."

They were met by the smell of toast and frying bacon.

"Come in, boys. We tried to be ever so quiet. Hope we didn't wake you up. There's porridge followed by a good fry-up. Rod is in his running gear and he has volunteered to take Sheba for her walk. She should find it fun to keep up with him this morning. So that gives you all plenty of time to enjoy a good breakfast. We are not due at the barn until nine o'clock."

"Can we go earlier and see how things are getting on, please Lucy?"

"Alright, but wait until Petra comes to pick you up."

Half past eight and three boys were sitting on the edge of the stage. A tired Sheba was lying in great comfort beneath them. She nuzzled Ben's hand as he stroked her.

After an hour, the boys retreated to a back room and the mass of delegates started to arrive, each looking tired after a night in strange surroundings and uncomfortable beds.

"Can't think why they look so bloody miserable," said Tom. "They all had a huge breakfast. How are we doing for time, Q?"

"Give them another ten minutes, Tom. If we leave it much longer, they'll be asleep again and start to lose interest."

Gradually the seats were occupied. The participants had no idea of the form that the so-called conference was going to take and there were wary glances between delegates from a few countries. As they warmed up and digestive fluids woke their brains, the chatter increased and their hosts started to relax. Perhaps this was going to work – it HAD to work. Otherwise, the whole world was lost, or at least the *Homo sapiens* part of it.

Ten o'clock on the dot and Quentin strode to the front of the temporary platform. He looked the part. Well over six feet in height, and an extremely fit eighty-five-year-old. Plenty of silver hair and a deep powerful voice, Quentin had presence, and he knew it. The audience hushed. "Ladies and gentlemen, thank you all for coming to this unique, simple setting to attempt to stem the vast number of deaths. I would like to present our three brilliant advocates to tell you what has happened here and how we have dealt with the consequences – I have to say, with some amazing success. Technicalities will come later."

Quentin sat down and waited.

In the back row, the three boys were just being boys. "You'd better go in first, Sol," whispered Anthony. "You're the oldest, by all of a week."

"No, you go, Ant, cos you were the first to be cured. But how about Ben, cos he's the smallest?"

Ben frowned. "But then Sheba must go in first, because she's the cleverest. No, it's you, Ant. You go in first."

"Oh, alright, then. I'll go in first; mind you follow close behind."

Anthony came in at the head of the little group of children. There was a sliver of applause and a few handclaps which quickly subsided as the audience realised this was not a joke. These three children were going to attempt to persuade representatives from across the world to adopt the same strategy to protect the remains of the species: well!

The three boys climbed the half a dozen stairs to the stage in front of the murmuring delegates. They turned to face the audience and stood silent for a minute. Anthony stepped forward with a ghost of a smile.

This is very strange. It's, sort of, like, um, a film or one of Dad's comics that he wants to keep up in the loft. Not sure I like being here; and I'm sure Ben and Sol don't like it much. Except Ben's never worried by anything, and Sol is such a friend, he would always be on my side, whatever happened. Better get it over with. You never know, they might clap at the end and give us a present. At least, I can talk as loudly as I like.

Anthony shrugged his shoulders and took a deep breath. "Ladies and gentlemen. Us three have no idea if there are any Lords and proper Ladies in here, but what we a going to say is to you, too. Now, this is not quite the result of a toss of a coin; but you will have to listen to us whether you like it or not." The audience appeared to relax and there was a gentle ripple of laughter. "Ben is eight years old and, at the beginning of the attack, Sol and I were nine years old. First thing that went wrong was that Sol and me and five others in the same class at school fell ill. It was pretty, sort of, slow at first, but we never seemed to be getting better. Most things we have at this age get better quickly but this didn't. The thing that worried us was that our wee smelt of rotten apples. So that was a bit odd as none of us like cider and this smelt like some of the rough stuff we make in this part of the world."

Now the audience did laugh – this cheered the three and they relaxed a little.

"We were looked at by our super doctor, Doctor Liu – behind us, in the red sweater – and he found out that we were all suffering from a funny sort of kidney disease. It wasn't that funny for us, as we all felt lousy. It was all very strange, and he organised that we had bits taken out of our kidneys at the local hospital which showed something very odd."

Anthony turned to Julian. "Well, my dad, the man in a blazer, is a scientist, and he found that a strange—" Anthony referred to his notes. "—Hang on; an odd piece of DNA had been inserted into our kidneys and that was messing up everything.

"He worked out, using miles of paper printout, that this peculiar piece of DNA most likely had come from the Archaea group of organisms." He looked back at his parents and was reassured that Julian was giving him a thumbs-up. "The question now was, where had they come from? Most of these little bug— Sorry, oh well! Most of these little buggers are all around us and are not supposed to cause any illness in humans. Well, not until now, anyway.

"Well, Tom, he's the headmaster at our school, and all the others behind us plotted the cases on a huge map. There didn't seem to be a pattern until our magical Ben, here beside me cuddling the dog, sort of, muddled along the map of all the cases around us. That's not fair. He spent a long time drawing long big black lines on the map. Then he stood back and said nothing. We all thought he had given up. But Ben never gives up and suddenly he pointed that the start of it all came from the nuclear power station. So then, with Roderick's help – he's the one in the black sweater – the source of the little bug devils was narrowed down to one point which was an air vent on the roof of the power station.

"So, we went on to the roof. I know you're not usually allowed onto the roof, but we had special permission from London. Mum, the botany professor, found this vent was stuffed full of the strange organisms, so Dad in his laboratory did their code." Anthony was running out of steam. He handed the notes to Sol. "Sol, please take over for a bit."

"My turn," said Sol gently, taking the notes and finding where Anthony had got down to. "Anthony's father, Commander Bailey, amongst many other things, is an expert on the genetics of a large range of living organisms including some of the very weird ones we are finding in the human gut. But he found the very unusual piece of code in our kidneys most likely came from, as Anthony puts it, these little buggers, the Archaea." He looked up and shouted, "We were all getting worse, and no one could do anything to help us!

"But Ant's dad worked out a way to knock off – sorry, kill or perhaps block – the invader. When he explained it to us, it sounded like a computer game. He said he could use something called CRISPR to do it. Well, that sounded more like a bag of potato crisps but then he showed us it was just a syringe full of a liquid stuff. We had a long and very boring explanation which I expect we understood at the time. The thing we did understand was that it might be dangerous.

"But you can't get more dangerous than death, and we were nearly there." He looked up and was pleased that his words had hit home. The audience was silent, waiting. "We all agreed to give it a try. There was nothing else and, as they used to say in the old days, we were guinea pigs. I hope I didn't smell as bad as the ones in my cage at home."

The audience laughed with a friendly rumble of acceptance. They began to relax – these lads were great!

"Well, it was all good and we all recovered completely and there were no bad endings and no bad effects. The other boys and girls were then treated, and they all got better as well." Sol looked up. "We were the lucky ones, and the only strange things were the weird dreams we all had. Anyway, right place and right time and right experts. But we understand there were others in other places who died, and it wasn't a nice death. It was horrid, they had a lot of pain and they just faded away." That brought any joviality amongst the audience to a grinding halt.

"Now, Ben doesn't much like talking in public; he's more of an action man which you will hear about in a minute. I will hand you back to Anthony." Ben didn't look upset and passed the papers to Anthony.

"You've got me again. As you know, another type of illness has hit people which makes them go all hairy and they go mad and die very quickly in a very strange way. Some of them become incredibly strong for a very short time. They walk on their hands or knuckles with a strange shuffling gait, sort of like chimpanzees. They often die of fighting and starvation. And the local farmers are saying there are strange effects on some animals and plants. This is a mainly farming community and some of the calves being born are enormous. The cows usually die but the calves are as tough as hell. They also say that plants are producing large numbers of odd mutations; I think I've got that word, sort of, right.

"So, now, I haven't read it yet, but I'm going to: *The Origin of Species* by Darwin. I was told that somewhere in that amazing book there is a statement where he writes that it's most unlikely that evolution will ever go into reverse. But listening to people talking, there are a lot of them who say this is happening here and now." He looked up and raised his voice to a shout. "As you know, it's happening over the whole world and the whole world is suffering! That's why you're here, to try and stop it. Sol, your turn again."

Sol collected the now rather messy sheaf of notes from Anthony. He tried to find the place but gave up and dropped the whole lot on the floor of the raised platform. "Shit! Oh well." He turned to the audience. "You'll have to have it direct from me." Nobody objected and most people seemed to like the idea. Sol had a powerful voice and could be as persuasive as Anthony.

"I would like to talk about Benjamin, we know him as Ben. Mostly he is not really interested in the lessons." Sol turned to Ben and asked, "Hope you don't mind me saying all this, Ben?"

Ben shrugged his shoulders. "Just say it," he suggested.

"Well, when the rest of his class suddenly turned into primitive apes, he was snatched out of the classroom by Van; the big man behind me. But then, Ben asked to be put back into the classroom, even though they had all gone mad and had broken up all the desks and the chairs. Ben persuaded the adults that he could lead all the class, all the wild apes, to a place in the hills. Van suggested that the apes should be attracted to one side of the class, with a box of fruit, and Ben could be quietly put into the classroom on the other side. It was all a bit tense and everyone was ready to charge in and rescue Ben for the second time.

"But I suppose everyone was proved wrong and, sort of, had to learn a lesson. Ben led them all to somewhere in the forest at the top of the hills. He came back and led children from other schools up into the hills as well. It was amazing, and Ben was incredibly brave."

"No!" Ben shouted. Everyone looked at Ben in astonishment. He took a while to calm down from a rare showing of emotion. They waited for him to stop shaking and say something. "Not brave," he said softly but then raised his voice to a shout. "You can't be brave if you don't have any fear! I wasn't frightened and I knew I could help them." He coughed, turned bright red and grabbed Sol's hand. "Please go on, Sol."

"You sure, Ben?" Sol asked kindly. Ben simply smiled.

"OK. This is much more important. What was not taken in was one thing that Ben said as he took them away – 'They won't last long'. Nobody was able to work out what that important thing meant. Well, as it turned out—" Sol looked up and spoke to the air above his audience, "—you all know, that turned out to be true. None of them have survived. Tom and Van went up to the top of the hills and found where they had been taken. There were very few left alive. There were bones of local wild animals like deer and foxes that had been killed by the apes and there was a suggestion that some of the bones were human. Then there were the two with arms round each other. Anthony, your turn." There were tears in Sol's eyes as he rescued the remains of the notes and handed them to Anthony.

172

"Sol was going to tell you about the two apes in a close embrace. They were both dead and Sheba sniffed them out as our Tom and Van were walking up into the hills. On their way back, they stopped at the place where Sheba had found the two bodies. The bodies had almost vanished. There was a lot of black hair and the earth that had been under them was a peculiar colour. The bodies had completely disintegrated and were now part of the earth.

"You might ask, what have we learnt so far? All we have learnt is that the dead had changed from modern humans to apes. Professor Yi has pointed out that the change was massive, bypassing the early hominids and straight back to more than five million years ago. That change was very quick indeed. Well, they were now animals, apes, which meant they couldn't even run, and they moved on their knuckles. Then the change from ape to death was also quick. So, whatever we were going to do had to be bloody fast.

"But then Dad, Commander Bailey, discovered that humans were being invaded by the whole organisms, the Archaea. To attack them we had to collect millions of viruses. And the best place seemed to be the froth from a breaking wave during a storm. Quite exciting, if you like getting wet and frozen stiff, and very nearly swept into the sea. But it worked, and, um ..." Having lost the thread of his notes, Anthony looked at Sonia, "Shall I?"

"Of course, Anthony, you're doing wonderfully. Give it to them. Give them the facts, man!"

Sonia's smile cheered him. He took a deep breath and abandoned the notes. "The lady behind me, she's a nurse at the local doctor's surgery, was beginning to show signs of hair on the backs of her hands and she was also not well. Very quickly, Dad made her inhale a whacking dose of viruses. She's alright,

173

but it was only just in time; everything happened so fast. Then we, well, they, thought we should check on her husband, Jeff. We went to their house and found that he was bad, very bad. Clothing all over the place and he was covered in hair, walking funny and rushing about the garden trying to get out. He was a full-blown ape and, for a short time, much too strong for us. But the walls were too high for him to get out, so what to do? Dad suggested that if only Jeff could be trapped by a huge net, he could be treated with the virus spray into his lungs and onto his skin. Headmaster Tom knew that Sol was a wizard at casting a fishing net because he comes from a family of expert fishermen from Korea.

"To go to the end of the story. Sol trapped Jeff and Julian cured him. But, again, it must have been just in time. And Sol seemed to know when we were safe to tidy up Jeff and make him normal again. Sol took charge of all of us. A close-run thing, all right, but it worked. No way can you do that to more than a tiny number of people. So, what can we all do? How can we stop the whole world dying?"

CHAPTER TWENTY-SEVEN

Anthony tried to piece together the scruffy remains of their notes but gave up and looked to Quentin for help. Quentin stood, and in the silence he spoke. "Ladies and gentlemen, I will say only a few words and certainly do not dare to take away from our three brilliant advocates. As you know full well, the world population has already been reduced by over ninety percent; probably up to ninety-five or even more in some locations, leaving a probable remaining worldwide population of only five hundred million. It is to be hoped that the few people left can keep most of our main systems going. Food and water supplies are adequate, certainly adequate in the countryside, and there is such a surplus of energy that it is terrifying.

"But this gathering of experts from around the world has to work out how to preserve the remnants of our species. I shall now hand you back to Anthony and Sol and Ben." He smiled at Ben and said, "Ben, I shall remember for ever you saying that one cannot be brave if there is no fear, or some such wording. I think that is profoundly philosophical. Thank you for that, Ben."

Ben's normally impassive face twitched, just a little. He looked at Anthony for support and was rewarded with a big hug which raised a cheer from the audience. Anthony, Sol and Ben took centre stage again. Sheba had made her way into the audience and was being stroked by those in the front seats.

"Thank you, Q – sorry, Lord Quentin!" said Anthony.

"Good Lord, Ant, Q will do very nicely. Back to you, Anthony."

"So, what we, you, everyone, have to do, is to try and flood as much of the world as possible with a mixture of viruses that attack or neutralise the Archaea." He referred to the rescued notes. "They are reckoned to be the first living things on this earth. Anyway, since they've turned nasty – or something has turned them nasty – we have to fight back."

Anthony frowned at the next page of the notes. "They say that if we only use one type of virus, it may not work, so we have to use a mixture – in fact, a huge mixture of viruses that can attack the different types of Archaea."

He looked up. "Hands up anyone of you who has been to the seaside in a storm and seen the sea break high over a lighthouse? One or two. Well, just the same happens anywhere in the world when the sea gets angry and, sort of, smashes itself up into the most amazing spray. That's where we told you they can be found, these viruses. Billions of them in each handful. But you do need to go with oilies, strong fisherman's gear, and don't get swept into the sea. It's a dangerous place. Sorry, I get excited about the sea – I always do! Sol, your turn."

Sol looked tired. They both were very tired, but they knew they had to persuade the audience to participate in a worldwide agreement. He picked up the script, absorbed the gist of it and stood ramrod sharp; keep going, keep going!

"Ladies and gentlemen, this is the crunch time. What is needed is an agreement with all the nations that have big laboratories to stop whatever they are doing and grow huge amounts of viruses that will be used to attack Archaea. We have heard from Anthony that a really good source of these viruses is the spray from an angry sea. Now, there's plenty of that around and there are plenty of people capable of collecting sea spray. I'm told that it will be very similar anywhere in the world." He picked up a brightly coloured paper from the floor. "This paper, for instance, shows that the gene structure of Archaea from two hot-spots on different sides of the world are almost the same: from Yellowstone National Park in America and from the hot springs of Kamchatka in far eastern Russia. That's about as far apart as you can get."

He looked up. "This is a fairly large village which has a nuclear power station on its doorstep but also has a big farming community. I, we, don't know how important the observation is, but it seems to us that the farmers appear to be more resistant to the invasion of the Archaea than the rest of the people. That's important. Think of it! To protect the whole world is not possible. So, how to cope? We suggest that crop spraying little planes can be used to spray places that used to have the highest populations; cities and towns and villages. It is not too difficult to modify small, prop-driven, powerful little planes to deliver a solution of mixed viruses to a huge number of people, in a reasonable time, to save enough people and keep what's left of our civilisation going. It may also be possible to use helicopters or even large drones that can carry up to a gallon of fluid. Those that know, say the very fine spray is the best, which may mean altering the spray nozzles. There, that's the proposition." Sol sat down, shattered.

The applause was tremendous and went on for a good five minutes. The oldest of the delegates, Professor Yi, stood up.

"Thank you so much, Anthony, Sol and Ben. You three gave us the most vivid, and the most realistic account of the beginning of this catastrophic outbreak. I call it an outbreak simply because it is associated with what appears to be an infectious agent. We have no idea how this agent has invaded and killed such a huge number of human beings. As to how, we have even less of an idea. It might as well have come from outer space. There are those who might take that statement as a possibility; others will treat it as a joke."

He turned to speak to the assembled experts. "Our three young lads have given us a wonderful and thoughtful account of the beginning of the attack on *Homo sapiens*. Then they gave us a dramatic account of the later stage and far more devastating attack which has now spread worldwide. We have been asked to come here to try to agree a strategy to stop the killing. Commander Julian Bailey has come up with a strategy which is not impossible if we all act together. It will need the nations who have the capability to produce, in their laboratories, substantial amounts of viruses, and mobilise large numbers of small planes, helicopters or even drones that can spread the viruses. These nations will have to work together and assist nations that are not able to mobilise in such a manner, to be able to spray areas of relatively high population density.

"Futile local wars and disagreements must not stand in the way of this worldwide project. If countries obstruct the project, there will be no point in trying to persuade them to do otherwise. It is more than probable that the entire population of such countries and areas will perish. We could simply have a show of hands, but that is too simplistic. We have prepared a document with every country present listed and the name of the representative expert. I am asking you all to come up and sign that document.

"I would also point out to you all that if only a few countries sign, they will be substantially ahead of the game of survival. If the majority sign, we can form a small group to hammer out the logistics to coordinate our efforts. Does anyone have a contribution to make to this discussion?"

One of the delegation from the United States stood up. In a sonorous voice he intoned his views. "I want my view to be heard. I believe that we are attempting to play God. Humanity has outlived its usefulness, is destroying the planet and does not deserve to survive. It is the will of God that we shall soon all die." He sat down to stunned silence.

Yi stood up to his full height, angry as hell. "Thank you, sir, for your views. You don't have to participate if you don't wish to …" Those near the objector started to erupt and a fight broke out, targeting the American delegation.

Tom motioned to the three boys. Anthony went over to him. He handed Anthony the school bell. "You might need this!" The boys went to the front of the stage. Their presence partially suppressed the rioting, but it was the sound of the school bell that finally shut them up. Anthony spoke to the naughty children in front of them.

"You are not behaving like grown-ups. It is an insult to children to compare you to badly behaved ones. Now, listen to Professor Yi and do as you are told. If you do not want to sign this document then, fair enough, don't sign. That's it, then. Now those in the front please come up first, followed by those in the second row and so on."

Before anyone could move there was a strangled, terrified cry from the middle of the crowd of delegates. The cry came from one of a group of Russians. Most of the nearest delegates fled to the sides of the barn, leaving a big man in his seventies standing, holding his hands above his head. The palms of his hands were grey and, as they watched, a mass of black hairs started to sprout from his hands and face.

"What on earth? It sounded like *bpharnaguite mnya*. What, in heaven's name, is that language?" Tom was shouting.

"Russian!" shouted Quentin. "It means help me. Julian, we need your viruses, and damned quick. Boys, help us to clear a way to poor old Mischa."

Mischa lurched forward, tearing off his jacket and shirt, followed by trousers and shoes. The disintegration was obvious to all the delegates, who quickly made way for the hoped-for saviours. Quentin, moving quicker than would have been thought possible for an old man, reached Mischa first but he was pushed away by the developing ape.

Anthony and Sol cleared the way to the stricken man while Julian primed the garden spray as he raced towards them. But they were too late. The animal stood up, over seven feet, and enormously strong. It crushed two of the chairs before advancing towards the platform. As Julian was forced to retreat, he looked back and saw Ben coming to help.

Julian had no hope of being able to squirt the virus solution from the tiny atomiser anywhere near the ape's mouth. "Ben!" he cried, "We need your calming hand!"

Ben came forward and his nearness calmed the ape who descended to its hands and knees. Putting his hand on the ape's head, Ben spoke softly. "Quentin, how do I say to him, open your mouth?"

"*Otkpon pot*. Say it softly and repeatedly."

The little boy whispered into the ear of the ape, trying not to sneeze as his nose was tickled by the mass of hairs. At last, the ape opened its mouth and Julian blasted viruses into its mouth and up its nostrils. Immediately, the ape appeared to relax and placed a paw on Ben's head. Ben left the paw in place and continued to whisper into the ape's ear.

Slowly, Mischa's dying eyes cleared, and his body began to shed the dreadful hairs. There was a tiny increase with minimal recognition and the Russian opened his mouth again. Immediately, Julian squirted more virus fluid into the open mouth. Another squirt of fluid was directed into Mischa's mouth, and the rest was emptied on his hands and face.

The boys pounced on the huge body and frantically pulled off handfuls of hair. They were helped by the nearest of the delegates.

"Tom, Q, rugs please!" shouted Julian. "There are some under our chairs. Or we will have a very embarrassed delegate from Russia who is the luckiest soul in the barn. Make him comfortable and get him as far away from the God-bothering nut as possible."

Two new chairs were rescued from the kitchen and the shaken delegates resumed their seats. Anthony rescued the school bell and rang it hard as the poor Russian delegate was removed to the temporary tent beside the tithe barn. Doctor Liu sat with him until he had recovered. A shattered Mischa looked round at the few people near him. He appeared to have a small memory of events and simply said, "*Spasiba*. Ben, *spasiba*."

Ben looked at Quentin for a translation. "He is saying, 'Thank you, thank you, Ben'."

Ben put a hand on the Russian who covered it with a little squeeze.

Quentin returned to the barn and stood up. The delegates sat quietly waiting for him to speak. "Ladies and gentlemen, you will be pleased to hear that Alexander, known as Mischa, our Russian friend, is fast reverting to his normal self."

The cheering took a while to allow Quentin to continue. "After that graphic demonstration of our ability to at least cure one or two people, let us continue the meeting. Now, Professor Yi's document. Can we start with the first row and work back from there."

And they did as they had been told. A second representative from the United States came to sign. Arthur McEward said, grinning, "You lads are quite fantastic. I am sorry about my colleague; Hooper is his name. We were dreading him saying something along those lines, but we couldn't stop him. He was part of our team because he's a very rich politician from the Mid-West. Sadly, he's as warped as hell. He even came in his own helicopter – you may have noticed he landed just outside the school playground. He shouldn't have done that, but he's not interested in regulations.

"He is so rich that he wasn't even bothered when his precious yacht sank. Half the crew suddenly started to become ape-like, just as you described to us. The captain lost control and steered his yacht straight onto a reef and sank the thing. Forty million dollars down the drain. He's as daft as, well, a brush! I hope the rest of us can make up for him."

"Thank you for saying that, sir," said Sol. "We need all the help we can get."

Yi examined the list and frowned as he noted a few absences. "The document will be on this table for another two hours," Yi announced severely. "It will then be removed and taken as the final evidence for cooperation or unwillingness nationally to take part in the project. A huge thank you to those gentlemen and ladies who have agreed to sign.

"On a lighter note, ladies and gentlemen, there is refreshment and simple food for you all available in the canteen which we have set up at the rear of this tithe barn. There is also a free bar next to the canteen. You will see us on the other side of the bar as most of the publican's staff have died.

"One word of warning. Tomorrow, around breakfast time, two cars with loudhailers will be touring our village. We have noted that the weather forecast is set fair with only a very light wind. The loudhailers are to tell all the inhabitants to come out of their houses and be waiting in the streets. Then a crop spraying plane will criss-cross the village with a spraying system actively covering the whole populated area with Julian's mixture of viruses.

"We thought you would like to have a simple demonstration before you all depart to your own countries. Thank you, ladies and gentlemen. I have one trick up my sleeve before we break for lunch. Julian, over to you."

Julian went to the end of the barn, removed the top from a wooden crate and took out a drone. He filled a small tank attached to the underneath of the drone and started the propellers.

"This isn't a joke, I have programmed this barn to be sprayed with the same fluid that cured our Russian delegate. Those who wish to be protected please stay for the flight of the drone. Those who, for various reasons, do not wish to be protected, please leave."

Only two delegates left, making derogatory comments as they did so. When they had left, Julian let the drone obey the programme he had prepared earlier in the day. As the little machine landed, spontaneous applause erupted with many of the delegates cheering noisily.

CHAPTER TWENTY-EIGHT

The local farmers had excelled themselves. Tables laden with the whole range of fresh farm produce – enough beef, pork, and lamb to feed an army – was swiftly demolished by the overwrought delegates, able at last to relax and enjoy themselves. And the drink flowed, even the cider which Anthony and Sol were beginning to like.

Arthur McEward, very red in the face, manoeuvred his way through the crowd towards Anthony and Sol. "Hello, folks, I've been thinking about your speeches. I reckon you were both better when you dropped the notes and spoke from the heart. And as for little Ben! Where is he, by the way?"

"I would guess he's back in the classroom," said Anthony. "Ben likes to have an ordered view of life. If it goes haywire, out of control, he likes to try and put it back into proper order. He never tells a lie – I don't think he would know how to, he's a good friend. What do you think, Sol?"

"Ben is terrific at getting us out of a mess. What's the phrase, something about oil and water?"

Arthur laughed. "How about 'pouring oil on troubled water'? That's what you did with the school bell. Very nice to meet you both again. I must go and sort out our religious nutter, try to stop him doing any more damage. We think he's a hopeless case. All his religious nonsense should be sent to the dump. That's where he would send us, given the chance. Come on, Sol, I'm hungry and there's a whole tray of bacon buns. If we don't eat them, they'll only go to waste.

"Hang on a minute, what on earth is all that noise?"

Sol laughed. "Come on, Arthur, I think it's called short-term memory. You have already forgotten we told you all that this afternoon the village would be woken up to the fact that tomorrow morning a little plane is to spray everyone in sight with masses of Julian's viruses. This big batch has been cultured in a cider factory. They have enormous stainless steel tanks that can produce millions of gallons of viruses. If you are here after breakfast, you can go outside and be sprayed as well. Just now, you can hear they are trying out the engine."

Lucy and Roderick appeared and started to mobilise the delegates.

"Ladies and gentlemen, we hope you have all had a good lunch and sampled the free bar. Give it another half an hour to have time to digest, then I suggest we can divide you up into groups and give you all a conducted tour of the interesting parts of the village. For the more adventurous of you, we could lead you up to the top of the hill, but we must warn you, there may be still a few remnant mutant apes."

"I can't vouch for the likes of Hooper," Arthur sounded cross, "but that sounds an excellent idea, fine with the rest of my little group. I gather we only have to climb a little way up the hill, and we will be at the level of Julian's laboratory and there should be a view of the sea."

"Excellent," said Roderick. "Later we can all congregate for a final meal and drink before bed. Remember to be up and out in time for the aerial virus spray."

After a great deal of persuasion, Quentin finally agreed to be the chairman of the group to establish the most practical

185

system to blitz the invading Archaeans. Other members of the group were to be in teams with specific requirements.

Quentin had a fine, deep carrying voice and swiftly took control. "I suggest the members of the first team to be Professor Yi, Yevgeni Porakov, and Arthur McEward, representing the three countries with the largest laboratories that can be motivated to produce immense numbers of viruses that could attack the Archaeans. On the technical side, I would like Commander Julian Bailey and Professor Petra Bailey; they have been involved since the beginning of this horror. You were told by the boys how Julian cured the first tranche of nastiness and went on to stop some of the later cases. A small team from each laboratory will to be formed to collect viruses from sea spray as quickly as possible. That will, I'm sure, be the fun bit!" Nobody laughed; the problem was too serious. Quentin shrugged his shoulders and continued.

"I realise that other countries, particularly in Europe, India, and Australia have first class laboratories, and they would have a right to send representatives to help the first team. Remember, distribution will be local and the choice of areas that have a high residual population will be chosen by the remnants of their respective parliamentary members. I repeat, if we all do the same, or at least similar procedure, it should result in protecting as many lives as possible. Finally, I would like to remind you that the current death rate is in the hundreds of millions, and this must stop!

"The next team will seek out national means of distribution of the concentrated virus for each country that has signed up to the document in the hands of Professor Yi. For instance, in this country and many others, the most obvious method is to use small planes that were, in the recent past, used to spray crops. We happen to be lucky in this village as a local has an

186

old crop spraying plane that he uses to satisfy his hobby which, curiously enough, is flying!

"An inventory of the availability of small planes will be needed for the whole country, together with workshops to produce the tanks necessary and spray equipment. For this team, I need a pilot, a farmer who has used a crop sprayer and a logistical expert. Any offers?"

The French representative, Alphonse Danet, raised a hand. "I have a pilot's licence and it happens I have done some spraying of crops on my own land. May I suggest we could do with someone from your own government who is familiar with the licencing system for private planes? That way, we can quickly see how many there are and if they can be modified. If we are short of planes, we can also use helicopters with the appropriate spray arms and even large drones. I know they have been used in Africa to try to control swarms of locusts. I prefer drones; the bigger ones can carry and dispense a gallon of fluid. The Chinese use drones to spray their fields of rice. The DJ1MG1S is the technical type they use mostly. I've seen them in action, and they are very impressive."

"Excellent, thank you, Alphonse. You are immediately in charge of this group – I said we had to be quick!" Alphonse grinned and shrugged his shoulders.

Quentin smiled. "Now, another member of this group will be Roderick. He has already proved he can manage a nuclear power station, and his was one of the power stations that produced the weird Archaeans. Van and his wife, Anna, will also be on this team to provide a civilian influence. We must also persuade a local farmer who, like you, Alphonse, is used to spraying crops.

"I have kept the most important job until last. I cannot possibly oversee every aspect of every team and I need a reliable colleague." Quentin was silent for a full minute. "Tom, will you help me in this job? I'm afraid you will have to hand over the running of the school to someone else, but I need your wisdom."

"Thank you. Quentin, I'll do my best."

Quentin turned to the listeners. "Tom Mayhew is the headmaster of the school where all the horror started in this country. He has steered us well so far, and we need his tact and diplomacy to help us to succeed. He will have unusual powers which some of you may object to. But there is nothing democratic in our present situation. The world population is probably down to around half a billion from a number which was reckoned as over seven and a half billion. We are dying fast and to lose many more will result in the failure of most of the systems that we have developed over the years to sustain huge numbers of *Homo sapiens*.

"If any of you don't like the structure which as outlined, naturally, is for this country, then it is up to each of you to devise your own system to suit the needs of your own. Your choice, my friends. But I must say, we are impressed and pleased that so many of you were able to come and participate. You can stay for a while to see if our structure might be appropriate for your country. Feel free to change anything to suit yourselves. If you need help when you return, I'm sure someone can be found to come and help you. But if the whole system is too difficult for you and there is the temptation to give up, there will be a strong probability of extinction.

"What say you, scientist, my friend Julian? On a philosophical note, what was it you said a while ago? That evolution is suddenly going into reverse. If that is true, what was the catalyst that started the process? Perhaps dear old *Homo sapiens* is past its sell-by date and its home is fed up with being destroyed and particularly fed up with being overheated. Poor old Gaia – we may well deserve to be annihilated. But we have the option of the get-out clause, just in time. Our children and grandchildren will be grateful for a cleaner, cooler and hopefully more rational world. Thank you, all of you. Let's hope many of us survive long enough to pull it off."

CHAPTER TWENTY-NINE

The tired group of delegates were out in the morning air waiting for the little plane to demonstrate spraying. The three boys were as excited as the delegates and loving the flow of admiration from all the nationalities that had attended the meeting the night before.

"There it comes!" shouted Anthony.

The bright red, noisy little single-engine plane came in low and the pilot opened the spray lever. A mist erupted from the backs of the wings and the slight, delicate smell was immediately apparent to the watchers. The residual local population cheered the little plane as it banked and performed another sweep of the village. Bill Makiver, the owner and pilot, had reckoned four passes would cover the whole village and a little of the surrounding area, to include both farms and outlying houses. With an empty tank of virus culture, the plane finally banked and landed on the strip of grass by Julian's laboratory.

"That was well done," remarked Alphonse. "Your Bill Makiver is a good pilot. He should be on your national team, Quentin."

"He's a good man. This afternoon he is going to spray the other two villages near us, then he might go down to the seaside villages and cover them as well."

With the demonstration over, the delegates started to leave the village. Most of them had got together to hire buses to take them straight to the local airport as transfer to the village strip of grass was becoming too congested.

A week later, a very tired Lord Quentin Ogilvie looked up from his desk, imported into the headmaster's office. "Tom, now that the impressive array of telephones on your high table has been silent for all of ten minutes, you can tell me how are the Russians liking the idea of tiny little planes overflying their major cities and squirting sea spray all over them?"

"Initially, they were not pleased at all, but I suspect the huge mortality, especially around the Kremlin, might have persuaded them. Any ideas about secrecy were ordered to take second place. Funny you should ask me at this stage. It may amuse you to hear that a degree of friendly competition has appeared out of the blue – you could even call it rivalry in the nicest sense. The big nations are trying to outdo each other. They are all juddering up to a sort of perfect dance. They're being ever so nice to each other and pinching each other's short cuts to perfection. I don't have to wield the big stick with any of the big ones, just a slight tweak of the tiller and it should be plain sailing.

"Some nations are a trifle tricky, especially those who failed to sign up to the original document. I think Professor Yi was a bit too generous, letting most of them sign up much later. But who am I to say? Some African states and overly religious countries in the Middle East, you know which ones I mean, are very willing to accept help, but do damn-all to help others. But we're getting there. Sadly, a few people have drowned. They were over-enthusiastic in their acquisition of sea spray and were washed away in the undertow. There not many life-saving organisations in the Far East. Overall, the system is working very well indeed, with spraying already started in some countries and scheduled to start next week in the rest. European countries and the whole of North America are the easy ones as there are plenty of little private planes available. The Far East is trickier. Australia and New Zealand are a doddle."

Quentin went to the coffee machine. "It's wonderful that this country, with all its minor difficulties, still has electricity and water and its drainage system still works. Coffee? Black or white, Tom, I can never remember?"

"Thank you, Quentin, I prefer black. Can I say that now? On a more serious note, what do you think we can expect after all the spraying has finished? Do you think we should work everyone up to give a second dose? Go on spraying until there are no more deaths?"

"We are obviously hoping that the death rate will plummet. If it doesn't, it'll mean one of several things. It could mean that the Archaeans have somehow become resistant to the mixture of viruses, although I can't believe that would be possible. Or a different infectious agent has taken over from the Archaeans. If that turns out to be the case, we'll have to start all over again. If the agent turns out to be a peculiar bacterium, we might be in the game of concocting a vaccine, but that takes a long time. It would take a hundred times longer than collecting buckets full of sea spray, and not half such fun. I would vote for a respray or two before we give up."

"Can we leave the washing-up? The water pressure is a bit low and we don't want that to run out. I remember during World War II we had to have a line painted on the bath and were threatened with hellfire and damnation if anyone had a bath above that level."

"Tom, who did you ask to run the school in your absence?"

"Lucy has kindly stepped into the breach. Apart from her nursing, she has a teaching degree. She's a very bright girl. Her husband has disappeared, presumed dead, but, as we know, Roderick was an old flame. I don't think we have to work too hard to rekindle that flame."

"That's nice, something cheerful coming out of all this at last."

Two telephones rang at once putting paid to more chatter.

"Tomato sandwiches again for lunch. Tom, who is the fantastic gardener who can grow these delicious ones all year?"

"Fred Jones, lives along the coast by a tiny sea inlet which keeps the temperature almost the same all the year round. He's over eighty but as spry as people half his age. Talking about spry – when you came in this morning, you were very low indeed. What went wrong with your weekend in the big city?"

"It was absolutely dreadful. For a start, there were very few people around, the roads were practically empty, probably because of the fuel shortage. And the few walkers were all slumped and dismal. I walked most of the way to my old flat. The lift was a dead loss and I had to climb up five flights of stairs. My invention, the voice-activated system to open the front door, failed and I had to find a key and the so-called secret place where I had hidden the key was full of mice."

Quentin laughed as he remembered something else. "I remember, vividly, when I was in charge of a tank regiment, one day, one of the crew was terrified when he found a live mouse in the tank. We spent hours chasing the poor little thing, and I eventually captured it in a spent shell case. They thought I was a hero as if I had defeated the invading army. I remember basking in that glory for the rest of the day. Happy days!

"But the electricity had failed and all the food in the fridge and freezer had gone off, so I had to rely on tins. I must confess, cold baked beans went down very well and brought back memories of a happy childhood before the Second World War. I walked to my old office, which was deserted, then to the Houses of Parliament. The House of Lords was a burnt-out shell and House of Commons not much better with embryo scaffolding just holding up the roof. And Big Ben had stopped chiming." Quentin stopped with tears in his eyes. "How anything is going to improve, I don't know. The death rate in the big cities must be well over ninety-five percent. The infrastructure is destroyed and will take years to restore. The country is going to be completely reliant on breeding a new generation of really bright children and we need teachers like you and Anna to get them going to repair the country.

"Even the journey back was difficult, to say the least. There were only two trains to this station scheduled to run during the whole of this week and there were no times given. I had to wait for half a day before I could get going. Getting back here was like heaven. Tom, it was all so depressing."

"Thank goodness you did manage to get back. I must report that this little village is a hive of industry. As you know, we did a preliminary spray last week and so far, touch wood, there haven't been any further deaths. The day before the spraying, we used a police car with a massive loudhailer to ask everybody to come onto the streets before the spraying.

"We have examined every house in the village and, sadly, we've lost well over ninety percent of people; that is adults and children. But the remaining inhabitants are working their butts off to keep civilisation going. The farmers are employing most of the inhabitants and paying them with food. It all boils down to a loose form of barter, and the survivors are remarkably cheerful.

"Now, all the delegates have returned to their respective countries, except those you, or I, asked to join the various teams. Arthur is a great guy, very sensible and practical. He's adamant that it is a pointless exercise to put much effort into persuading the non-participators to do anything. He says that as soon as they see that the death rate drops like a stone in the treated countries, they'll come running."

"Seems a perfectly reasonable idea. We don't have time to do anything different. Let's look at the results so far. And, I forgot to tell you, Anthony wants to be a passenger on the next spraying flight."

"That's the border city with Scotland, isn't it?"

"Correct. If his family agree we may have to reduce the amount of spray to make up for the additional weight."

"Are you strapped in, Anthony? We don't want you falling out of this tiny machine when we have to bank to make the alternate runs. I'm not going to fly too low as there are several power lines we must avoid because we don't know if they are in use. I don't fancy hitting over four hundred thousand volts."

"I'm fine, thanks, Alphonse. How much virus have we in the tank?"

"Around a hundred gallons and we can fill up with more from a local airstrip. By the way, you can call me Alph if you like. Pretend my name is Alfred."

"That's fine by me."

"Right, let's go. We can talk through the intercom, just press the button on the side of your mask."

The engine roared into life and the powerful little plane took off and made for the city. Alphonse's voice came over clearly.

"I'm going to fly back and forth in a grid based on that railway bridge."

He gestured towards the west. Anthony saw there actually was a very slowly moving train on the bridge.

"I hope they stop the train and get out onto the line. Not much use being shut up in the carriages."

The train did stop at that moment. Anthony laughed. "They must have heard me."

"Don't you believe it; I expect they've run out of diesel."

"That's too boring, Alph."

After half an hour of back and forth, Anthony was losing his sense of fun. He was also feeling slightly sick.

"Time to refill the spray tank. Are you all right, Anthony? You can swap with Sol at the refill stop, if you like."

Alphonse banked the plane and headed south for five miles. They descended to a small private airfield and taxied to a building where Alphonse killed the engine. Sol came running towards the plane and helped Anthony to the ground.

"Was it fun, Ant?"

"It's a bit boring just going back and forth and I was feeling a bit sick. Alphonse said you might like to have a go. We can change places while he fills up with more viruses and fuel."

"Oh, yes, I'd love to, I've never been in a little plane."

The two boys changed places and Anthony made sure Sol was strapped in.

"That's good, Anthony, give Sol a chance to feel sick. I suggest you go and lie down for half an hour. Don't worry about getting back to base. When this tank is empty, I can take you both back. I just must check one thing in the engine, it was misfiring occasionally and there might be a block in the fuel feed. I want you both out of the plane, just in case."

The two boys stood twenty yards from the plane while Alphonse fiddled with mysterious parts of the engine compartment.

He stood back, slammed shut the engine cover and called Sol back to his seat. "Anthony must have shown you how to belt up. Are you happy?" Sol nodded.

This time Alphonse talked very little and after twenty minutes he turned the plane back to the airfield. As it was landing, the engine cut out.

"Well, Sol, that was just in time! I have a nasty suspicion the fuel we've been given is on the dirty side. Let's see how Anthony is. Did you come across a kitchen in that building?"

"There's a kitchen all right. While we were waiting for you to come back, we made scrambled eggs and found a bag of frozen peas. Are you hungry, Alphonse?"

"No way! I want to use the kitchen sieve and paper towel to filter the fuel. I hope there is a strict ban on smoking."

"Now, boys, I need twenty gallons of filtered, clean as we can make it, fuel to complete the runs over the city. Set up a system so that we can pour the dirty fuel through the sieve, which has a liner of kitchen paper, and hopefully the clean fuel can be collected in a series of cans so that I can carry them to the plane. Now be very careful – no scratching of metal on anything that is likely to make a spark – we don't want the whole lot to blow up."

It took over an hour for the budding industrial engineers to complete their instructions. The plane was now ready, and they sat in the sunshine to clear their lungs of the petrol fumes.

"You look deep in thought, Sol, what is bugging you? Are you worried about my plane?"

"No, not the plane, Alph. Even if it goes phut in the air, surely you can glide it down safely? No, do you think all our efforts are going to work? There don't seem to be that many people out in the streets to inhale our lovely viruses. Ant said the few people on the train came out onto the track, but he said there were mighty few in the streets of the city. Even with a ninety-five percent mortality, we are going to need at least a thousand people to keep things running."

"I get your point, Sol." The Frenchman shrugged his shoulders as only the French can do. "We just have to hope and wait and see. It's good to see Quentin again, I've known him for many years. As usual, he is full of hope, and let's leave it at that. Come on, we have a job to do."

This time there were no mishaps, the rest of the city was sprayed, the plane returned to pick up Anthony, and they flew back to the little aerodrome at Pensfield Kingsley, pleased with themselves. They taxied to a stop and stood by the plane, both feeling slightly sick. The boys stuttered their thanks.

"Well done, boys. I couldn't have done it without you both, especially helping with the filtering. Well done, both of you."

CHAPTER THIRTY

Tom, Anthony and Sol were sorting out masses of paper onto the tables in the first classroom under the eagle eye of Anna.

She looked up. "Where's Sheba, Anthony? I haven't seen her for a couple of days. She often comes into the classroom with you and sits by my desk. I hope she's alright."

"The last time I saw her, she was with Ben. He was going to take her for a walk." He frowned, "And I don't think she and Ben came home last night. I expect it's alright, they often stay out all night. Can't think what they get up to." He laughed, but there was uncertainty in his laughter.

"I think we should go and look for her," said Sol. "She's our only detective that can tell when people start to go wrong. She's much better than we are. Perhaps when we've finished sorting these bits of paper, all these deaths, we should go on a hunt. Is that all right, Miss?"

Anna nodded her head. "The sooner, the better. In fact, we can do this later. I have torches here and warm clothes, we don't know what we're going to find. Where did Ben say he was going?"

"Something about a copse. 'Up to the copse,' I think he said."

"Oh dear, I think I know what that means. Come on, it's quite a climb and it's going to get cold if we leave it too late. Tom, can you come with us?"

"Of course I can. Anything is better than this paperwork. Coming? Ant and Sol. What is it, Ant? You look as if you have a question."

"So, it's just ... just that where they all go has been easy in this part of the country. They just go up to the very top of the hill and then disappear. What happens in the towns or other parts of the country, and the rest of the world?"

"Interesting question, where do they all go?" Anna thought for a while. "I suppose if they lived by the sea, they could simply try and swim until they drowned, but in the middle of big cities, as you say, Ant, there's nowhere to go. We did hear from Q that a few countries took fright and were shooting the mutants which made them disintegrate a lot slower, and that made the problem worse. We'll see if Ben has any better ideas, when we find where he goes. That's our problem just now and I do think we ought to get going. Just hang on a minute while I phone Van."

They waited for what seemed to be a ridiculously long time. Eventually the phone was picked up and Van announced he was on his way. Anna turned to the children with a worried expression on her face.

"He didn't sound his normal self. Something's wrong, I know it."

After a few minutes, a car was heard on the gravel outside the school, but the gentle noise ended with the sound of metal hitting the wall of the school. They rushed out to find Van slumped at the wheel of his car, which was firmly embedded in the wall. The children and Anna struggled to pull Van out of the remains of the damaged vehicle.

"Get the car rugs out of the back seat and lie Van on them."

"He's a funny colour," said Sol.

"Oh my God! Van's going grey – look at his hands," Anna pointed to Van's arms which were changing before their eyes. They watched as the mutation started to spread. Van's eyes dulled and a bubbling noise erupted from his massive chest. Van's muscles were tensing with the memory of the phenomenal weight-lifting victories from forty years ago. The watchers were spellbound as they saw Van's skin start to sprout the horrendous thick black hairs. Van stretched and tried to shed his clothes.

"What can we do?" Anna screamed at Anthony. "We have to rescue Van."

"Sol!" shouted Anthony, "phone my dad, say it's urgent. And then run and get your net, I think we are going to need it. Fast as you can."

But Van was changing too fast. He was changing in front of their eyes. He lurched between them, bent double and balancing on his knuckles, pushed aside two startled parents, and charged along the corridor to Anna's classroom. He stood up tall, now over seven feet, in the mayhem of destroyed classroom furniture.

Tom appeared and at once understood the situation. "The fact that Van headed straight to Anna's classroom must mean that there's still hope for him. We should be able to save him. Where's Sol? And we need Julian's viruses."

Anna answered. "Julian is on his way and Sol will be here in a minute with the fisherman's net. Somehow, I also think we need Ben – not sure why, but he seems to be able to calm the situation."

As if by magic, both Ben and a seriously growling Sheba appeared. Ben was out of breath. "I had to run down the hill," he complained.

"You can't possibly have heard us," said Anthony.

"I just knew and ran. I don't like running, but I had to." Ben's normally impassive face glowed through the sweat. "Sheba knew and we came back."

They heard Julian's car on the gravel as Van attacked the door to the playground. The door failed and the huge gorilla-like creature that had once been Van was loose outside.

Sol was waiting with his net.

"Please, oh, please, snare him, Sol," cried Anna.

Sol approached the animal, but he was quickly pushed away, and Sol had no opportunity to throw the net, so Ben came to his help. Ben slowly approached the mutant Van.

Tom put his arms round Anna. "Don't worry, Anna, we're going to win. I can see there's some recognition in Van's eyes and Ben is almost hypnotising him. He is amazing, and fearless. I just wonder if he is afraid of anything."

Ben touched Van's waist and reached up to his shoulders. Van collapsed down to ground level with Ben's little hands on his head. Ben was whispering into Van's hairy ear when Sol threw the net trapping both Ben and Van. Ben continued to whisper into Van's ear, louder this time.

"Open up, Van. Open your mouth and take in Julian's magic. Come on, Van, you can do it, there's enough of you left to breath in deep."

Ben's magic worked and, at last, as Julian squirted the virus culture, Van took an enormous breath. Almost at once, his eyes cleared, and the remaining tension vanished. He lay back onto the hard surface of the playground, resting his head on Ben's arm. Julian continued to squirt virus all over his hairy body and, wonderfully, the black hairs started to fall off.

Sol rescued his net and Tom brought out a cushion for Van's head, taking the weight off Ben's arm, while Anna covered Van's nakedness with the car rugs.

"That was bloody close," said Tom. "Well done, everybody, especially Sol and Ben."

"And Sheba," said Ben. "She was the one who told me to hurry back. And I hate running!"

The hint of a laugh came from the recovering Van.

Two days later with Ben and Sheba again missing overnight, Tom, Anthony, Sol, and Anna set off in light drizzle to climb up to the top of the hills. Tom had a backpack with bread and water and a supply of torches. He also had his favourite stave and sticks for the boys. Tom's mobile phone rang as they were about to leave the village. It was Van.

"Don't you dare to go without me. I'll be with you or catch you up. Won't be more than five minutes. I'll come prepared."

"Sir," Anthony asked, "what does Van mean by that? Being prepared?"

"I expect he means just that. Van is the sort of person who tries to be prepared for anything to go wrong. Don't ask me what precisely he has in mind, that's up to him. He may surprise you. In fact, I'm sure he'll surprise you. He certainly surprised me with the speed of his recovery. Concentrate, chaps. Has anyone the faintest idea where Ben and Sheba have got to?" The two boys shook their heads.

Half an hour later they stopped for a rest on a fallen tree trunk. Suddenly, Tom leapt up. "This is where we found the pair of apes wrapped in each other's arms. They were both dead and when we came back to this same spot there was nothing left except black hair and a slight change in the colour of the earth underneath where they have been lying. Where are they now?" Tom went a few yards into the trees and shouted, "This is the spot, but everything has disappeared. There's no sign at all, even the last of the hairs have disappeared. Weird. We ought to go on. You all right, boys?"

"We're fine," said Anthony and Sol. "How far is it, Van?"

"If we are heading—" Van stopped and looked around, puzzled. "—Or are we being drawn?" he continued, in a hard voice. "Drawn to the same place, we have another hour of hard climbing to go. When we get there, it's not going to be very nice."

"Don't worry, Van, Tom. Nothing has been very nice about the past few months. We can climb as far as you want. Don't you worry about us. OK, Sol?"

"OK by me, Ant."

It was a hard hour climbing to the plateau on the top of the hills. It was cooler and quieter. There were no planes powering overhead, the birds were stilled, and the only faint noises were the ones they were making themselves as they puffed along the track.

"It must be somewhere near here," said Tom. "Van what do you think?"

"I can hear—. Oh, wonderful! Sheba! Why are you in such a mess, you poor old thing, there's blood on your back. Anthony!"

Anthony cried as he cuddled his injured Sheba. "What's happened to you? And where's Ben? Van, Tom, we have to find Ben."

Tom and Van exchanged glances, and they were not happy ones.

"Where's that tree, Van?"

"About twenty yards, if you can see it through your tears."

"Oh dear, yes. Give me a hand up, Van."

"NO!" shouted Anthony. "We're much lighter than you two and we can climb higher and look over that great barricade of brambles."

From high up the tree, Anthony and Sol looked at the scene. "What are we going to tell them?" whispered Anthony.

"Just what we see."

"Let's get down first."

"What's the verdict, boys?" came the shout.

"Ben is still alive, but he's surrounded by a ring of twenty huge apes who are quite still. They are not making any noise, in fact there is no noise at all. It's as if they're stuffed and waiting for him to die. What are we going to do? We can't leave him there."

"Tom, there must be a way round this bloody barrier. That's it! That's where Sheba got so bloody. She knew we would come looking for her, so she waited for us – for two days. Well, old girl, we're here now and you can show us the way in."

The damaged dog stood up and slowly made its way, every now and then turning to see if the salvage team was following. After only a couple of hundred yards there was a slight thinning of the brambles and they started to force their way in.

"Hang on, folks, I should go first." Van produced a pair of secateurs and quickly cut a path through the brambles.

"I told you so, boys," said Tom, grinning. They grinned back.

Through the brambles and not more than fifty yards away was the scene described by the boys. The circle of silent apes was quite still, all facing Ben, who didn't seem to be particularly worried that he was tied with the same brambles to the remains of a tree trunk.

"What now?" whispered Anthony.

Two of the apes turned their heads slightly in the direction of the intruders but the others remained quite still.

"Do you think we should shout, or do something, Van?" suggested Sol.

"Walk very slowly towards them. We are going to have to play this by ear, literally. Here, hold onto these. If we are in trouble, pull the pin out of the little black box." He handed out two small black boxes, each with a cord attached to a pin which was stuck into one side of its box. "Don't do it until I tell you."

They were within ten yards of the group when the two apes, who had apparently seen them, got up to their full height of seven feet and slowly came towards them. The rest of the ring of apes did not move.

"Tom, you and I will point our sticks at these two giants, and we have to hope they will stop. Ant and Sol, hold the pins firm."

The giant apes stopped when the tips of the sticks held by Tom and Van touched their chests. The apes clutched the sticks and broke them to matchwood. They were within three feet of the two men when Van shouted, "Pull! Boys, pull the pins!"

Immediately the most horrendous sirens came from the hands of the two terrified boys. The apes crouched low, growling and whining, finally collapsing on the ground.

Van shouted, "Tom, Anna, boys, get Ben!"

"What about the others?"

"They're dead. Don't push them over, that's too demeaning. Just get Ben!"

Ben took some releasing from the sharp thorns. His few scratches were licked by Sheba. He smiled and stroked the dog as if it was all in a normal day's work.

"Can we go home now? I'm hungry," Ben said, as if he had just been on a fun trip to the seaside.

They passed the two collapsed apes on their way back to the hole in the briar fence. The apes were just as they had fallen, and Anthony went to touch one of them.

"He's cold. I think he's dead! He's dead, Van, how——?"

"If only, Anthony. If only any of us had the faintest clue to all this, we would all be the wiser. But we don't, so there, let them rest in peace."

On their way down, Ben recounted what had happened. "I went to see if I could do anything to help the animals. But there wasn't much I could do. Then two of them were fighting and I tried to stop them, and they tied me up and they all sat round, sort of, as if I was going to be asked to make a speech. But there was no asking. I think Sheba was worried and she ran away. Then you came and untied me after a terrible noise. The noise killed the last two. Pity, they were friendly, just slow. Thank you for the sandwich, Headmaster. But I'm still hungry."

"Let's get you back down the hill and you can have whatever you want, Ben."

CHAPTER THIRTY-ONE

Anthony was making a great fuss of Sheba and she was enjoying every minute of it. Washing, brushing, combing – how nice to be a dog! He looked up from his labours. "I don't understand. They tied up Ben and then left him there. If we hadn't come along, he would have starved to death. It was obvious they weren't going to feed him or give him anything to drink. What was the point of tying him up? Why did they do it, Headmaster?"

"Anthony, I do think in our present circumstances you can feel free to call me Tom. As far as the whys and wherefores, the easiest answer is that I haven't the faintest idea why they tied Ben up. Then most of them died in front of him with only those two still just alive. And they didn't last long when we blasted them with noise. That was a brilliant idea, Van. What's your interpretation?"

"Thanks for the compliment, it worked just as I hoped it would. Apes don't like sudden noise and obviously they are scared stiff by those panic machines. It is a horrendous noise. No wonder they were made to scare humans.

"Now, to try and answer your question, why did they tie up Ben? The only thought I have is that the apes liked him and wanted him to accompany them into their oblivion. Not a very nice thought for us, I must admit, but a sort of backhanded compliment to Ben." He paused and took another swig of beer from the can. "If you had looked carefully at the way Ben was tied up, he could easily have freed himself. Perhaps he was being tactful and would have stayed there until they had all died. We'll never know. Sorry not to be the fount of all wisdom. Not today, anyway."

"Interesting thought, Van," said Tom. "So that ring of apes probably won't be there tomorrow, just more hairs on the ground and little piles of dust. Dust to dust!" He laughed. "Similar to human burials but on a different time scale."

"How is Ben?" asked Sol, "And where is he? He should be here, having a slap-up meal. At least we know he's safe."

Ben appeared, looking puzzled.

"We wondered where you were, Ben. Have we satisfied your hunger?"

"I was in the classroom waiting for a lesson, but nobody came to give it. Thank you, Headmaster, I am not hungry anymore. I had no food at the top of the hills, but it rained a bit, so I had something to drink. I would like to lie down somewhere."

Anna put him to bed in what was now called the emergency ward. Sheba came and lay beside Ben and snuffled under his arm until he was asleep.

"Where were we with all these bits of paper?" Tom sounded desperate to get the paperwork in order. "China seems to be definitely up to the mark. They've mobilised what remains of the army and police to send loudspeaker vans to each city in turn to try to persuade all the inhabitants to come out into the streets so they will be able to receive some of the spray. Their count of the viruses in the stuff being sprayed is sky high. That should be a compliment for our friendly Professor Yi. Russia is only close behind China and America trailing a third. I gather the religious nuts are holding up the spraying as much as they can, but it's a rearguard action.

"Interesting, there are problems in the Middle East. If I can quote the history books to you; during the three hundred years of the Black Death, the Muslim religious ethic was that the Almighty had determined that it was not the done thing to run away from those that are dying. The Christians fled as soon as there was a whisper of an outbreak, but Muslims didn't, and so had a higher death rate. I am reading into some of these reports that a similar attitude has come about in some overly religious areas and they are refusing to be sprayed. Oh well, that's their decision. There may not be anybody left to regret that decision.

"The data we really need is going to be any change in the death rate. We have to hope it will fall rapidly, but that's only a distant hope, looking at all these bits of paper." Tom gathered up the work they had done and carefully put it into a drawer. "I do hope there was some point in gathering all this data and we haven't been wasting our time simply to fill a drawer. That's what used to happen with the previous statistics. I used to give the authorities my guesses for a couple of years, but I made a mistake. I finished the numbers with two noughts! That backfired when we all had to go over to computers – no money for training, of course."

"Sir, Tom, can I ask you something?" Sol was studying a tiny pile next to him.

"What is it, Sol?"

"It was someone almost at the beginning of the dying who said that it seemed that the farming community had a much smaller mortality. I can't remember who said it, but don't you think it should be followed up?"

"I do remember something along those lines. Let's think how we are going to study that idea. We can get a general breakdown of occupations from the County Council. Then we can analyse the occupations of those we know have died and somehow compare the two sets of data. There's a job for you two boys."

Van smiled. "That's one way to get lumbered with a job. But I do think it might be interesting. If it turns out to be true it might indicate that the farming community is far less likely to be in the firing line of the nasty Archaea. We have assumed until now that the little buggers were not scheduled, or perhaps primed to attack all humans. But it's all change now. Perhaps farmers become immunised with nice Archaea, and that might protect them against the nasty ones. Just a thought. It'll certainly keep you both busy for hours."

CHAPTER THIRTY-TWO

"Where have the boys gone this time, Van? Any ideas? They move like greased lightning."

"Sorry, Tom. The last time I saw them, they were in a tight huddle plotting something and muttering about the paths that were taken by the apes into the hills."

"Oh Lord! I hope they haven't tried to find another bolthole on the hilltops. I'm not too happy about the weather forecast. It's getting cold and it'll probably rain soon. I think we ought to take torches and warm clothing and see if we can find them. Don't panic, bring some of your screaming machines."

Anthony sat down on a fallen tree. "How far are we going, Sol? Don't you think we ought to wait until Ben has caught us up? At least he knows more than we do about the paths on the hills."

"Perhaps you're right. We'd better wait here. There should be another batch of apes coming this way in the next ten minutes. They seem to come in batches and then just, sort of, disappear."

After a few minutes that seemed like ages, they heard a noise. "Sol, I can hear Ben at last. So how did he know where we were going to explore?"

Ben appeared short of breath and sat down with the two boys. "I don't think we should sit on this tree. If you look closely at the ground, you will see lots of black hairs. This is where they rest until they get their breath before they go on to the lair."

"What do you mean, Ben, the lair? Where is it?"

"That's where they go to die and be at peace."

The three sat in silence for a few minutes. Eventually, Sol stood up and walked to the other side of the path. Anthony and Ben were about to follow when the first group of apes panted up to them. Sol found himself surrounded by twelve huge apes and looked very frightened.

"Don't worry, Sol." Ben shouted. "They won't hurt you. Keep quite still and don't do any sudden movements. We will slowly come over to you. Stay where you are, Sol."

Anthony and Ben held hands and very slowly weaved between the apes until they were with Sol. They looked back and it was as Ben had predicted, the apes took it in turns to sit on the fallen tree. One of the apes appeared to try and make eye contact with the boys.

"That is the only one that might be a worry," said Ben. "He, could be a she, hasn't quite gone the whole way. If she, and I think it is a she, starts to approach, don't say anything and stay quite still. She may want to touch you, either of you, but I'm certain she won't harm you. If she does, your only protection is to shout at the top of your voice. The only problem about that is that you will frighten all of them and then I'm going to have a big job calming them down. Above all, don't smile, look solemn as hell."

The ape slowly approached and put out a hand to touch Sol's face. The hairs tickled and Sol had to work hard not to sneeze, but he remained quite still. The ape dropped her hand and the boys saw tears cascading down her cheeks. She gave a low moan, turned slowly to join the others, and the group of twelve mutant animals went on walking up to the top of the hill. But thirty yards on, she turned to have a last glance at Sol.

Sol collapsed onto the ground, sobbing. "She looked so sad, as if she still had some *Homo sapiens* left in her. It was as if she was saying a final goodbye. I don't want to be here anymore. Let's go back, please!"

"You and Anthony go back. I expect you'll meet a search party on the way. I must see them to the lair. You can tell them not to worry, I'll be back before sunrise."

"You shouldn't be out here all on your own, Ben," said Anthony. "If you really want to follow them, I'm coming with you."

"Then I'm coming as well," said Sol.

"Tell you what – first we'll go and listen to the pipe man on the top of the hill. I heard him a few days ago and he sounded lovely. He's very nice to talk to. After we've listened to him, we can go on to the lair."

"I can hear the boys, Tom; they can't be far away."

"Thank goodness they didn't fall foul of the latest batch of apes. Some of them were huge and looked dangerous. Here they are!"

"And where do you think you three were off to so late in the day? What's the matter, Sol? You look as if you've been crying."

"I cried because one of the smaller ones, probably a female, looked straight at me and she touched my face. And she was crying. It all seemed to be so sad, as if there was still some part of *Homo sapiens* in her and—" Sol was shouting, "—she seemed to be asking for our help. I, sort of, think if we'd had some of

Julian's viruses, we could have done something for her, but it was hopeless." Sol's voice dropped. "And I cried."

Sol recovered. "Anyway, Ben was determined to follow this latest group to somewhere that he called the lair. We felt we couldn't let him go alone, cos we didn't really know what he was talking about."

"In that case, Van, I am all for exploring with Ben. Well, boys, we brought torches, warm clothing and a thermos of hot soup. That was Carole's idea and she insisted on coming with us. Well, Ben, you are the leader; lead on!"

Half an hour later and almost at the top shoulder of the hill, Ben motioned them to stop and listen. They sat and waited for five minutes until they all heard the sound. The sound of an unusual musical instrument. A glowing sound, almost mournful, which appeared to carry the music in the mountain air. It was coming from not far away. Another steep climb and there was the musician. He was a tall, gaunt man with flaming red hair, dressed in very old, once bright, clothing.

"Boys," said Carole, "he's wearing the Royal Stewart tartan. You can see the green very well in this light. That is one of the oldest tartans and it shows he and his family come from a clan renowned for its fighting regiments over the years. He's probably been playing for hours which is why he looks as if he's tiring. His pumping arm is not producing enough air to the bagpipes."

The musician turned towards the visitors and his face lit up with tremendous relief. "At last, there's someone alive!" exclaimed the man. "And friendly faces."

"Nick!" shouted Tom with delighted recognition. "Haven't seen you for a long time. How are things on your side of the

215

hill? And it's great that at last one of your ghastly instruments has come into its own. Why aren't you playing your favourite, the Northumberland small pipes?"

He turned to the others. "Sorry, folks. I should have introduced you to the chairman of the Parish Council of the village of Shotterhead on the other side of the hill. We meet so seldom, they might just as well be on the other side of the world. Nicholas Goodson, an accountant by trade, very helpful in checking my figures for the school accounts.

"Nick, good to see you. But what the hell are you doing up here? Is this the only place you're allowed to play?"

"Now, Tom, don't you be rude about my beautiful instruments. I need to play in the open. The Scottish bagpipes sound wonderful up here as the sound carries for an amazing distance. But my favourite, as you say, the Northumberland small pipes, are very special and difficult to play. They wouldn't be much use out in the open, especially up here, as the sound, although beautiful within a small space like a church or even a large room, would be useless in the open air. I came here in the hope that there were some other people alive. I thought yesterday that there were only ten left in our villages out of, I would guess, four hundred. Sadly, two of the survivors have gone mad and disappeared so there's only the eight left. We heard a lot of little planes going in and out the other day, but then nothing.

"What we can't understand is that the electricity is still on, and the water supply is still functioning. I know our valley is useless for telephone reception but the whole lot seem to be defunct. Mark you, the absence of television and the total failure of the internet is a blessing; I can't stand either of them. But it's the people we miss the most. We saw them all change into primitive apes, one household after another. Then they all simply walked up the hill, to oblivion.

"The change was so quick, it was terrible. Within ten minutes from being perfectly normal, you could tell that they were away with the fairies. Then they went grey and tore all their clothes off. By that time, they were covered, and I mean covered all over, with masses of black hair. We found we couldn't communicate with any of them. They just shuffled off with a peculiar gait." He stopped, trying to remember the awfulness of it all. "Where they all went, God only knows. Some of them went east towards the coast. We tried to follow a group of them, and they just walked into the sea and I suppose they drowned because we didn't see them again. Then my lovely wife—" But Nicholas couldn't continue.

"Ben here," Van put his hand on Ben's shoulder, "says he knows where the ones you said went up to the hills have gone and he was leading us to the spot. But he got side-tracked when he heard you playing and led us to this spot to find you. He said he'd seen you before and you spoke to him. He loves the sound of your pipes. He implied that the sound of the pipes added a wonderful normal human touch. The tune you were playing wasn't exactly jolly, but at least it was a normal human playing, and that was nice. Why don't you join us? I know it's getting late, but we've got enough torches and warm clothing."

"Not sure I like the sound of the suggested destination, but anything for the company of live people. If you like, I can play 'The Dark Isle', it's a well-known lament, when we get there."

Anthony interrupted, "What happened to the rest of the apes? It's too easy from our side of the hills. They simply march up to the hills and turn to powder, and that's it. What happens in the cities and by the sea? We don't know anything about all those dying animals. Animals that were once normal people."

There were tears in his eyes which he tried to brush away in embarrassment.

"We will have to leave that to the imagination, I'm afraid, old son. I guess that if they were by the sea, they simply went into the sea until they drowned. Nick said he saw some do just that. Otherwise, there must have been collecting areas." Tom stopped, not wanting to work up the imagination of the little boy. Too much thinking was not such a good idea.

CHAPTER THIRTY-THREE

It was a long walk to the far end of the little range of hills. Exhausted, they sat down in the dark and waited for the dawn. As the sun painted the sky, they saw they were within a quarter of a mile of an ancient disused quarry. Between them and the lip of the quarry were hundreds of silent apes who, although they were standing upright, looked as if they were asleep. Two of the apes turned towards the little group and went to drink from the dew pond. Otherwise, the visitors were ignored.

"They must be thirsty after a long walk," whispered Tom. "These ponds have been around for thousands of years. Some of them, and probably this one, will be spring fed and they never dry up. So, I wonder, could they have the cure for our nasty little beasties lurking in them? We are standing on the remnants of an ancient volcanic belt. So deep inside this little mountain, the temperature might still be high; perhaps too high even for the Archaea."

Anthony had been studying a pair of apes nearest to them. Suddenly he nudged Sol. "I think the one on the right of those two is the female who touched your face and cried. She is looking at you right now and not into the distance like all the others. She doesn't look so good today."

Suddenly, Ben shouted, "Sol! Sol! Go to her and bring her over here. Go on, hurry!"

Sol stood up and slowly approached the two apes. He was within a few yards of them when the female turned, and they were face on. They stood staring at each other. There was a definite spark of eye contact between them. She put out a hand and touched Sol's face. He grasped her hand and was plainly wondering what to do.

"Give us a clue, Ben. What do I do now?"

Ben came up to the pair. "Drag her over to the pond. If she won't go in, you go in and pull her in after you. I'm sure it's the right thing to do, it's something Tom said about the pond. Go on! Now, quick!"

With that, Sol twisted the female ape round, pulled her the few yards, and they both fell into the pond with an almighty splash.

"Make sure all of her is under the water," shouted Ben. "She must be soaked all over. I'll join you, Sol."

The two boys and the mutant thrashed about as if they were on a trip to the seaside. "Come on in, Ant," called the now hysterical Sol. "It's not cold, there's a really hot spring coming up from the bottom. I think she's enjoying it."

Drying was a problem, but the sun was rising and pouring warmth on them all. None of the great mass of apes had taken the slightest notice of the visitors, nor of the boys who led the now-bedraggled female ape back to the group of strangers.

"She's changing," said Carole. "I can see a difference, and she is looking straight at me. I don't believe it. Van, what do you think?"

"It makes me think that perhaps we don't have to go to the seaside to collect Julian's viruses. If this old spring, which must be heated from some deep volcanic process deep underground, does indeed have a mass of Archaea together with their viruses, then that answers one major problem. So perhaps we can forget our little seaside trips. But I don't have much hope in being able to persuade all this mass of apes to have a swim." Van pointed to the waiting hundreds of apes. "In my opinion, most of them have disintegrated too far. For the moment, let's look on the bright side with this little one. Sol, how is she?"

"She's, kind of jittery. Look! I can pull off great lumps of hair from her hands and she is looking at me with a strange mixture of hope and something else. It's, sort of, weird. I wish she would say something. Carole, can you help? If I pull off much more of this hair, she is going to need clothing!"

"Let me help you, Sol."

Gradually the naked body of a girl aged about ten years was revealed. Sol kissed her wet forehead and there was a hint of a smile. The girl shivered and they covered her with a blanket and pressed a mug of the, now, warm soup to her lips. She drank greedily and took a huge breath.

"I know who she is!" shouted Tom. "Her name is Gillian Makiver. She's the younger sister of one of the boys at the school. She's the daughter of Bill Makiver, our nearest farmer –; the one who has the plane. He said only last week that Gillian's greatest wish was to be the person in charge of the cheese making parlour."

He paused. "But I wish we could persuade her to speak –; this is worrying. The splashing about in the pond has been partially successful. We must take her back down the hill and get Julian to squirt his viruses into her lungs, that might do the trick. Sol, you've worked another miracle, and made another discovery. We should take some of this pond water back to Julian and see if it could be used as a source of his viruses. Let's rinse out the thermos and fill it up."

"Very kind of you to say so, sir, but it was, sort of, your idea. And Ben latched onto it – that the hot springs could help."

Sol stroked Gillian's cheek. "How are we going to get her back to the village? She can't walk with no clothes on. She'll get cold and have sore feet."

"Don't worry, Sol," said Van. "Gillian's not heavy and if she's wrapped up well, I can carry her on my back."

Sol smiled, breathed heavily, but said nothing.

Doctor Liu examined Gillian. "I can find nothing wrong with any of her systems. Reflexes are all in good condition and there are no injuries, but the absence of speech is peculiar. There's nothing amiss when I looked down her throat. But I can't see very far, and Julian's spray should be able to reach right down into her lungs. Give it a go, Julian. She can obviously understand what we're saying."

"Breathe in as deep as you can, Gillian," Julian ordered. "We can do this several times. That's good; and another one."

They waited until the girl had stopped coughing, bringing up quantities of foul-smelling material. But there was still no speech.

"Coffee time, folks." Carole entered with a welcome tray of steaming mugs. "Does anyone take sugar? If they do, I shall have to investigate the back of the kitchen cupboard."

"Yes, please," came a little voice. "I know it's supposed to be bad for me, but I do like it."

Sol gasped and sat down very hard. The cheers could be heard outside the school.

"Julian, what's troubling you? I can see it a mile off," Van asked.

"Just an idea, Van." Julian turned to the little girl. "Gillian, what were you doing just before you started to grow all that horrible hair?"

222

"Difficult to remember, sir. I know! Not much fun to think about it, but I was helping Dad clear out the cow-shit pond. It was a horrible job and I landed covered in the stuff. Dad hosed me down, but I still stank something awful.

"Then they left me outside when they went in to have some food. I cried a lot and then started to feel bad. My head hurt and I was hurting all over. Then I saw my hands and they were going all hairy, so I ran away and joined others coming up the hill. Then I saw Sol and, well, he has the loveliest eyes, and he was going to rescue me from a horrible something. You know the rest. Does that help?"

"It certainly helps. Well, it helped you and stopped you from disintegrating completely." Julian smiled, "Not, perhaps, to be recommended – spraying everyone with cow shit. But it goes some way to explain why the farming community is partially protected."

"So, if anyone is interested, I'm all for the cow shit!" said a very happy Sol.

CHAPTER THIRTY-FOUR

"Save it, Ant!" shouted Sol. But the ball skidded on the wet grass, straight into the net, and Anthony had missed it yet again. "I don't think you're much good in goal. What's your verdict, Gillian? You have a go, let's see if you're any better?"

"Don't you be so cheeky, Sol. You might have brought me back from the dead, but you don't own me!" She stomped away to guard the goal, saving three shots from her saviour. "How about that, Ant?"

"Now you're in trouble, Sol. That'll cost you at break time."

"Oh, shut up, Ant!"

"Change the subject – how about having a go at saving another ape from certain death? What was it Van said? Something along the lines that Gillian wasn't quite past the point of no return. The fact that she looked directly at you and she cried. This meant that she could be brought back. Or something along those lines. Where's the nearest supply of cow shit? We could rinse out Gillian's dad's muck spreader. Any volunteers?"

"Sounds a super idea, but no thanks. It was all very tense, I don't really want to have to go through that again." Sol stopped and looked with wonder at the girl. "But she is very nice, don't you think, Ant?"

"Hm! Gillian, what was it like, to be turned into an ape?"

Gillian took a while to answer. "It was very strange. The first thing I remember was that there was a dark, brownish mist. I don't know where it came from, but it hated me, and it wasn't going to forgive anything. That sounds stupid, I know, but that's how it felt. Then I felt all muzzy and my hands went numb. I looked at them, my hands, and they had gone a horrible bluey-grey colour and they were sprouting hairs.

"All my clothes itched horrible, so I had to take them all off. All my clothes, and there was nobody else around to help. So, I saw I was covered in all that black hairs. I felt I had to run away to the hills, but I was very slow, I couldn't run, and I had to keep my balance with the backs of my hands on the ground. I could go faster like that and I had to join the others going up the hill. It was tiring doing that and halfway up I saw Sol looking at me. It was then I felt I only had a short time and I cried."

Gillian was crying now, and Anthony wished he had never asked.

"Sorry Gillian, I shouldn't have talked about it."

Gillian smiled through her tears. "Don't worry, Ant, just wait till I teach you how to be a better goalie!"

And there it stayed for two hours. At break time when, as predicted, Sol lost his chocolate biscuit to Gillian, the two boys were joined by Ben. They put the question – did he think they should have a go to attempt to save another one. Ben, as usual, took some time to react.

Anthony stepped into the silence. "We never saw what happened to the hundreds of others up there. We should find out if they walked over the edge, or the ones at the back pushed them over."

Anthony and Sol both made a face and erupted, "Ugh!"

"If we did all go up again, I could show you what happened and, at the same time," Ben continued with no emotion, "we could look out for the odd one who might look at us and cry."

"Does that mean you like the idea, Ben?" said Sol.

Ben looked up at the sky. "There's another, about, ten hours of daylight. But we should take torches and the screaming machines if some of them are frightened and try and attack us. Of course, that might not be a bad thing, since, if they react to us, that means they are thinking along the same lines as we are – sort of! Could mean they're not too far gone. I don't know!"

"We should tell someone," said Anthony. "I don't think any of us are strong enough to carry even a child down the big hill. We need Van or perhaps Tom for that. Let's ask them now."

Van laughed. "You lot are getting delusions of grandeur. You'll be wanting to save a dozen or more in a minute." He checked himself when he realised they had taken his joke seriously. "No, I didn't mean that, but I do think we should concentrate on single individuals. Even that's hard enough."

The three boys spoke at once. "So, we can go, and you can come with us and carry back a saved one? That is, if we can find one."

"Come on then, lads, I'll ask Anna if she's free this evening and feels like a hike up the mountain."

Van returned. "Anna says she feels like a dose of fresh air, so she's on."

They reached the top of the mountain in record time and walked along the ridge until they came to the dew pond two hundred yards from the edge of the ancient quarry.

"I like that pond. There's something wonderful about it." Sol was glowing with the memory.

But when they looked further in the twilight, they could see the hundreds of silent apes not far away.

"What are they waiting for, Van? Do you think they're the same ones as yesterday, Anna?"

"I have no idea, Sol. A clue might be the twenty or so new ones who were following us up here. What do you think, Ben? You know all about this place."

Ben thought for a while. "The new ones will force their way almost to the front of this lot. Then they will start to push all these over the edge." He paused and looked at Anthony. "You don't believe me, Ant. I've seen them do it. Which is why I called it the lair. But I should have spelled it for you as l-a-y-e-r. We just have to wait and see."

It was as Ben had predicted, the newcomers, only twelve of them, forced their way through the hundreds of apes who did nothing to stop them. Most of the apes fell on the ground and appeared to be dead. Immediately, the newcomers started to push the non-responsive apes over the edge of the quarry.

"If it's any consolation," said Van softly, "it looks as if there are very few still living, and they are almost at the end of their sad mutant lives. What a dreadful sight!"

It took two hours in the failing light for the new batch to push most of the mutant apes over the edge. None of the originally standing ones pushed to their burial place appeared to object and the whole operation was conducted almost in silence. The only noise was a muffled thud as the bodies hit the bottom of the quarry. The new arrivals had some difficulty with the bodies on the ground but, eventually, the whole area was cleared. The twenty or so perpetrators of the pushing then sat on the edge of the quarry as if to wait their turn to be pushed.

Van had his arms round Anna who was crying softly, and cuddling Anthony and Sol. Ben sat on his own with his own calm thoughts wrapped in mystery.

"Reminds me of the stories of the Black Death," said Anna, "when the bodies had to be buried on top of each other to be squeezed into the last areas of consecrated ground." Suddenly she laughed. "Has anyone eaten lasagne recently? No? I thought not. The first use of the word was at the time of the Black Death. I believe it was an Italian countess who was describing the custom of burial with alternating layers of lime and dead bodies as a 'lasagne'! Now that'll give you all an appetite."

"Sorry, not funny," remarked Van.

Sol was a drooping picture of sadness. "I'm sorry as well, I didn't think it would be as bad as this. Let's go home."

Anthony started to lead the way when they were confronted by another group of shuffling apes.

"I suppose this lot will push those that are left on the edge into that awful burial hole." Anthony sounded upset. "None of them look as if they're worth saving. What do you think, Anna?"

"You're right, Anthony, not one of them looked up as they passed. They were almost dead themselves, poor things. Sol's right, let's go back to the remains of our civilisation. I can promise you the evening meal will not be a lasagne."

"Hang on a minute." Van shaded his eyes to look down the valley. "There's a single person following this sad lot. Oh Lord! It's the American God-botherer from the far west. His name is Hooper and he's bound to make trouble. I somehow feel it could be the last time he does."

"Hello there," shouted the newcomer. "I've come along to see you save a few more." He laughed an unpleasant, dry, disbelieving noise, as if to imply he didn't believe a word of the saving of lives.

Nobody said anything, but Hooper was not put off his mission. "I wish to see how the good Lord deals with this situation. Not interested, you lot?" Hooper turned away, ignoring the silent group and, humming to himself, simply followed the latest group of mutants towards the quarry.

The boys were not sure what to do and looked to Van for advice.

"We will follow Hooper, but at a distance." Van said softly. "Don't any of you interfere at any stage. Simply observe and keep silent. There's nothing you, or anyone else, can do to help."

They were a hundred yards behind Hooper when they saw him touch several of the mutants. Suddenly, four of the biggest mutants, well over six feet high, turned on Hooper. He tried to back away, but his path was blocked by the other mutants in the group. Gradually, they forced Hooper towards the edge of the quarry. By now Hooper was becoming frightened. He looked over his shoulder and saw there was only three feet left behind him and the edge of the quarry. Hooper waved his arms and shouted, "Help me, I don't want to die with these!"

They heard the scream and the drowning cry of "God forgive!" as Hooper plunged two hundred feet down into the mass of dying and dead mutants. Then they were all gone – over the edge to join the thousands of tiny piles of dust.

Van shrugged his shoulders. "And I hope your god forgives you, friend Hooper. You poor misguided fellow." He breathed a huge sigh. "Time to go back, folks. I'm not sure what the answer is but that was awful. Come on, we all need some of that nice brandy."

On their silent way down the last valley, Anthony stopped. "There's something I don't understand. That quarry must be full of bodies by now. I know the stone people stopped using it centuries ago so there must be an awful lot of accumulated rubbish. Then to push many thousands of bodies on the top of that, the thing should have been overflowing by now. But we heard the thumps as the bodies fell and they seem to fall a long way down. It doesn't make sense, Van."

"Don't you remember, Anthony, the few that have died almost in front of us, simply disintegrated into dust. So, essentially, there's nothing left except a pile of black hair, simply because the hair took a longer time to disintegrate. But even the black hair disintegrated quickly by normal standards. I can guarantee, when all this is over and Julian's spray has stopped people turning into apes, there won't be anything left in the quarry. Not even hair." He stopped and thought for a while. "Just think laterally. You're good at that, lads. How many people do you know who find it almost impossible to take off their wedding rings?"

"I know what you're going to say," said Ben. "In a year, if anyone took a metal detector into the quarry, they might be able, well, sort of able, to find wedding rings." He sneezed in embarrassment. "I don't like the idea. They might have names on them. The rings, I mean."

"That's a horrid idea," said Sol. "Forget that!"

"I second that," said Anna. "In a few years' time it'll just be history. Come on, we're almost back. Does anyone not like scrambled eggs on toast? We won't talk about the alternative."

CHAPTER THIRTY-FIVE

Two weeks of the frenetic noise of the loud hailers throughout the length and breadth of the British Isles, followed by the one-off spraying of massive amounts of virus by a motley collection of old single-engine planes with their wings peppered with holes, led on to a "wait and see" period. After seven days, confidence began to creep into the hopeful minds, as the nil messages were recorded by Carole and noted in the Pensfield School's headmaster's office.

Tom looked pleased. "No reports of deaths in our three villages for two whole weeks. That's the best news we could possibly ask for. We must hope that our single spray that Bill did at the end of the conference over our village worked, or are we being hoaxed by some higher authority into believing it's all over? Any thoughts, Petra?"

"I would be mighty wary to believe anything, Tom. Incidentally, Professor Yi has returned and is staying with the Liu family. We could ask him for first-hand information from China. We were told they were spraying with a much higher concentration of viruses so, surely, they would have stopped having new cases well before us. He might even have some original ideas as to why the whole thing started. I am sure he doesn't believe in your higher authority. Why don't you ask him over for lunch? If you can cope with us as well, we can sample your new wife's cooking."

"That's a good idea. I'll have you know, Petra, Carole's cooking is truly master chef standard – so there!"

"Of course it is, I wouldn't dare to question that for one moment."

Tom and Carole were at the door to welcome their visitors. "Come in, all of you. How super you all arrived at once. Yi, Baileys, Protheros, Lius, Lucy, Roderick, and the stars of the show, Anthony, Sol, and Ben." Carole looked down the road. "I wonder where the good Lord and Lady have got to?" She turned to the waiting guests with a sigh. "The weather's nice enough to have drinks in the garden. Make your way through the French windows on the left. Coats, handbags and other bits and pieces can be left in the hall. Ah, here they are." Two elderly people, breathing with some difficulty, leant their bicycles against the fence and, very carefully, walked up to the house, still breathing hard and rubbing their bottoms.

"Welcome both, Quentin, and—?"

"Carole, may I introduce my wife, Daphne. We have decided to come and live permanently in this delightful, quiet village. We do realise that quiet is probably not the most appropriate word – perhaps exciting would be more to the point. At the moment we are camping in one of the many empty houses. We are not sure how to tackle the house problem on a more permanent basis. Daphne thinks we will need a large one as there's an awful lot of stuff that, hopefully, will be coming down from London. I'm all for downsizing and getting rid of the rubbish that we have either never used or used so little we can't remember where it came from. Downsizing is a fashionable word for people of our age, especially with so many empty houses."

Tom came out to greet the two guests and laughed to see the bicycles. "Good Lord, Q, when did you last ride one of those?"

"If you really want to know, about seventy years ago when I used to cycle down to the river to row. It was the journey back that used to kill us, a climb of several hundred feet to get back before prep time."

"Delighted to see you both. Do come and join the party. Just one more to come."

"Who may that be?" asked Quentin.

"He'll be coming up the road in a minute, you should be able to hear him a mile off. Listen."

The sounds of 'Flowers of the Forest' came loud and clear towards them. A resplendent Nicholas in spotless clothing and a clean tartan came towards them. He was a happy man and the Scottish bagpipes were placed with great reverence on the chair in the hall.

"Welcome, Nick, glad to see your clean uniform. A cheerful song for a change!"

"Well, now," Nicholas responded, "if you feed me well, I shall play 'Amazing Grace', since I have just met a lady with the name of Grace and a spark has been kindled. She has also cleaned me up and, I confess, I do feel better for it."

"Come in, Nick, and be introduced. Now there are so few of us, we must do more to get the villages together."

Tom circulated with glasses of sparkling wine. "I raided the supermarket weeks ago, before all the horror started. There's also a freshly brewed barrel of beer which I hope has had time to settle. One good thing to come out of all our troubles is that the local pub is thriving, and a few little local shops have opened. There are even some who are boiling their own hams and selling cheese straight from the block. No more wrapping up little bits in miles of plastic, and to blazes with the regulations. Happily, the supermarket has closed as it was the cause of the failure of the original batch of local shops. They imported cheap rubbish and locals were persuaded to spend a fortune on fuel to save a few pence."

"I suspect the demise of the supermarkets is probably due to the lack of transport," said Julian. "Or lack of drivers. Even if there is any public transport, mighty few people want to go anywhere. They feel safer sitting tight until they're convinced they're protected against all known germs."

"Are we all protected?" asked Yi. "Do you honestly believe that *Homo sapiens* is, as you say, home and dry and we can suddenly breed up to the ridiculous number we were before? I don't have any equipment here, but I understand the carbon dioxide level has stopped rising and in some areas it might, perhaps with a little imagination, be falling. That is fashionably supposed to be a good thing. But bearing in mind we are at the end of the Holocene, a nice, relatively cosy warm period, we may be at the start of another ice age. There could be double trouble around the corner. The sea will perhaps stabilise at a rise of one or two metres, flooding most of our coastal areas, while at the same time the world temperature may drop like a stone. I cannot predict which is the more acceptable scenario."

Tom stood on a chair and made his announcement. "I have great pleasure in telling you all that Lord and Lady—"

Quentin raised his hand. "Stop right there, old friend. We want to put a stop to those now totally redundant words, Lord and Lady. My last place of work is a smouldering ruin and the whole structure of that central society will have to be reorganised. Happily, we are much too old to have any further part in it. Sorry to interrupt, Tom, carry on, please. You were about to say, I hope, something complimentary."

"I had a suspicion you were going to say that. I'll start again. Quentin and Daphne have decided to abandon the big city and come and live amongst us. They are camping in one of the empty houses by the school and hopefully waiting for stuff, in modern jargon, to come down to join them. Quentin says he wants to learn how to fish, and Daphne is looking forward to growing an enthusiastic range of herbs and other things in her own garden."

Quentin heaved a sigh of relief. *Here is a new life for us both, without the stress of the infighting amongst the self-styled experts and delusional self-satisfied politicians. What a relief – the supreme battle to fight the invasion of the primitive organisms has turned out to be a damn sight easier than we had all thought. Daphne keeps on telling me to relax.*

Quentin accepted a refill to his glass and noticed Anthony and Sol were sipping the same refreshment slowly and carefully. He went over to talk to them.

"Good to see you, boys, what have you done with Ben? Have you ever read the book *The Three Musketeers* by a Frenchman, Alexander Dumas?"

"I have," said Anthony. "Porthos, Athos and, um?" He looked at Sol who shook his head. But a little voice from behind said, "Aramis?"

"Ben! How lovely to see you! That's right, Aramis. And what was the name of the fourth musketeer who joined them?"

"D'Artagnan?" Anna chipped in. "Quentin, you must have done some teaching in the past, do you feel like having a go? Perhaps a couple of sessions a week. Now most of the local children have centred on Pensfield School, we have a decent number of pupils at all levels and there is a need for new teachers."

"You would have a much better chance with Daphne. She was a head teacher at a primary school when I met her. Yes, we could both have a go. Discipline might be my downfall, I'm fine with adults, but children?"

"Don't worry, Quentin," said Anthony. "We three will protect you and get you out of trouble."

"You're too kind, boys."

"Lunch time," called Carole. "It'll be a bit of a crush, but we're all friends and I'm sure we can all squeeze in together. First course is out here in the sun, a huge plate of nibbles, mostly prepared by my darling husband."

"Under instruction, you understand," said Tom.

Yi smiled. "In my youth, sadly, it wasn't the custom to teach men how to cook. And when I married, I was banned from the kitchen. But, I understand, it is now quite common for the man to cook and some are quite famous for their cooking." He smiled and looked up at the sky. "I can peel potatoes – I had to do that during the time of Mao. We were all forced to do jobs which were, at the time, thought by our rulers to be demeaning. I quite enjoyed myself, because you could talk at the same time and I could teach almost any subject then. Probably a bit rusty now, and well before the age of computers, thankfully! This is the most delicious dish, Carole, does it have a Chinese origin?"

"Afraid not, Yi, just a pretty standard sweet and sour from your average cookbook. I'm glad you like it. I tried to get some Chinese wine. The local wine merchant used to stock it but there wasn't any left."

"You can have some of mine," said Liu. "There's plenty in the cellar."

"Do many houses have cellars?" asked Quentin. "I've often been tempted to buy a house with a cellar, and then have the time, and the money, to fill it with wine. Anna, where do you and Van live?"

"Not more than a couple of hundred yards from the school. I have been thinking about the right kind of house for you both. I do know that all the inhabitants that used to live in the Manor are dead. All four of them were in their dotage and there's never been any evidence of relatives, so I don't see why you couldn't move into that. It is rather a rambling building and I'm sure it could be divided into at least three family homes. If you don't mind high ceilings, it's yours for the taking."

"Thanks for that, Anna. And I'm sure we can pull out the stops and help you with the teaching, at least at a relatively simple level."

"Speak for yourself, Quentin," said Daphne.

Their constitutions fortified and tongues loosened by food and excellent wine, they turned to more philosophical ideas.

CHAPTER THIRTY-SIX

Julian started the deeper discussion. "Come on, folks, get your thinking caps on. Just what or whom do we have to thank for all this killing? I can't believe there is some awesome creature out there, perhaps from another planet, who started it all. Professor Yi, we can rely on you to produce a canny answer to that kind of question. Give us your thoughts. Surely they will reflect – what was the interpretation of your name? Righteousness and fair play, I seem to remember. Was that the Confucian element of your surname?"

Yi smiled. "You will have to give me time to sort out an explanation which will persuade you of its logic. I need time to think, someone else must start the discussion. Anthony, you're full of original ideas, give us your views."

Pushed into the firing line, Anthony blinked as his mind struggled to be free of alcohol. "Dad gave me a glass of wine earlier on and he suggested that it would make me relax. The taste was lovely, sort of sweet, but not quite. But it left me with a kind of fuzzy feeling. It's not bad, but it's not quite good, either." He took a deep breath. "You have a go at it, Sol."

The Korean boy looked at the group of friends round him. "I feel very happy here. I had a glass of wine, but I feel fine. Which bit of all the disasters that have come our way in the last few months do you want answers for? I suppose the weirdest thing of all is why does it seem as if evolution suddenly started to explode into reverse, and so incredibly fast? I'm, sort of, sure that none of us will ever really know. How about thinking that we, *Homo sapiens,* have brought the whole disaster on ourselves? We're supposed to be so wise, but I don't think we are. We go to war – it seems just for the hell of it. We seem to enjoy killing animals and that goes on to killing people. Usually with the excuse of some difference of religion. Anyway, this mass of seven and a half thousand million humans is, I should say was, making a pig's ear … no, that's unfair to pigs! Making a complete balls-up of everything in this world – sorry about that!" He grinned and continued in a vague trail of thoughts.

"OK, we are making a complete mess of things, things that make up what we call nature, not some dreaded Dalek or some mystical god creature. Nature is what the earth is, and it was getting fed up with us. There! How's that for an argument?"

Yi's smile almost split his face in two. "Well done, Sol! That is brilliant. Philosophers for thousands of years have had to face up to and try to analyse what we would call natural happenings, however disastrous they may have been. Their analyses, back to, perhaps Spinoza, Confucius or the ancient sages from India, have tried repeatedly to put into words what you have explicitly said, in far fewer words than they did, why these seemingly dreadful happenings occur.

"There is a word that fulfils the meaning, I hope, of what you have said. That word is homeostasis. There is a complicated meaning to explain this word. A brilliant professor at the University of Southern California by the name of Antonio Damasio wrote a book about the origin of feelings and the development of civilisation. I will paraphrase. He suggests that homeostasis can be defined as the coordinated processes required to execute life's desire to persist and advance into the future, through thick and thin. He notes that no such process existed prior to the existence of life.

"Homeostasis has its origin at the simplest level of life. In other words, at the Archaean level. Cells don't have minds, but they behave as if they do. I would remind the academics amongst you that Spinoza wrote that 'each thing, as far as it can be its own power, strives to persevere in its being'.

"I don't believe anyone, given all the time in the world, will ever be able fully to explain the many weird aspects of what has happened in the last few months, but I am relatively convinced that the very recent enormous cull of human beings is the result of a fearsome backlash by the offspring of the original first organisms on this earth. There; we are on the trail of a long and probably boring repeat of what was said just now by Sol. I prefer your analysis, Sol, it's much easier to understand."

"But how do they do it? Yi, how do the Archaeans communicate?"

"We know they communicate by means of unusual chemical compounds, but that is all we know. Now, on the other hand, if we think they are merely puppets, we have no idea of the nature of the puppeteer – and, if there is one, how to disable it.

"One other thought. Anthony, in your speech you mentioned Charles Darwin. I met a neighbour of Liu's a couple of weeks ago. I can only remember her name as Helen. She had been mulling over the idea of reverse evolution – whether organisms, animals or plants could revert to simpler forms or perhaps even more complicated forms that existed many millions of years ago. Darwin was thinking that a change in circumstances like a marked change in climate or the failure of the availability of some necessary substance could so upset an animal or plant to send evolution into reverse. Isolation is the fashionable reason to suggest that evolution is not always a one-way process, but that's too easy. Darwin's finches might be an example – when they had been isolated on a series of islands, they changed amazingly quickly. Whether one could say this was reverse evolution or not is debatable. Then there's always the poor old dodo that lost its wings.

"But what we have just gone through is not in that league. This has been much too sudden and within the life of the animal. I find it impossible to think of any agent that could have produced such changes, so fast and in so many people. Not much help to answer your question, Julian, but I did try!"

"What a lot of thought! I must say, if outcome is the restoration of homeostasis for the Archaea, the operation has succeeded. The world population must be down to something like five hundred million, and the beginning of climate change will soon be solved when the carbon dioxide level is halved. All our power sources are set to rely on the sun to produce electricity – everything is all right for them. Big deal, so poor old *Homo sapiens* no longer rules the roost. Ah well!"

Carole stood up. "Coffee, anyone, all of you? Tom is always in charge of coffee. I can offer anyone a brandy – that's the remainder of the bottle we found in the school – I'm sure it tastes just as good in plastic cups."

"Even better," said Quentin. "I will help Daphne with her dose, she doesn't like brandy."

Anthony and Sol were not sure about the brandy and opted for tins of cola. The sun started its daily descent. There was a chill in the air and the guests crammed into the little house to have sweet cakes and reviving cups of tea. They left a very happy house.

Carole and Tom sat in the evening sun listening to the bird song. "We must be the lucky ones, my darling," said Tom. "All those people instantly transformed into primitive animals and fast disintegrating into the earth. Many of them we knew so well. Normal human beings, and now dust and forgotten in a disused quarry. Ugh!"

"My love, I have to hope they knew nothing about what was happening to them. After all, Jeff remembered nothing at all, and he didn't believe a word when we told him how he had changed into a primitive ape. It's, hopefully, all over, and we are the survivors. Let's leave the washing-up until tomorrow. Bedtime."

"That's the best idea this evening, my darling."

CHAPTER THIRTY-SEVEN

"One whole month and no more deaths, as far as we know." Tom sorted out the piles of reports on his desk. "That's a relief! Anthony, Sol and Ben are catching up with missed lessons at an amazing rate. I must say, the two Ogilvies are wonderfully patient with the slower ones as they bring them up to scratch. Petra, Julian – have either of you got any ideas about how many people are still alive in the three villages?"

"Probably less than one in ten of the original population have survived. Have you noticed ..." she hesitated. "I don't want to seem stupid, but did you get the impression that the Archaea seemed to attack whole households? They seemed to wipe out everyone, young, old, even small children. They all died at the same time. What do you think of that, Jules?"

"Typical of an infectious agent, I'm afraid. Very similar to the epidemiology of the Black Death. As far as survivors go, I think we should do our own census. A sort of modern-day doomsday book, if you like. Possibly we don't need to document the number of cattle or any other livestock, but land areas might come in useful to estimate the volume of essential crops we need to grow. I guess it's hopeless to rely on any help from central government. Before the archaean invasion, almost all communication with that lot appeared to be a sea of paper restricting almost anything we tried to do off our own bat. We won't be hearing anything from them for the next - how long? I would bet on six months to a year. At that stage we will have to look out for the paper-waving busybodies descending on us. I did wonder if whole households were getting wiped out in the rest of the country, in fact in the rest of the world. That would be logical with a highly infectious agent. Like the Black Death, yet again, but then they thought it was a miasma or some such influence. On a lighter note, here comes Quentin and Daphne. It must be break time."

"Good morning, folks," said the new teachers.

"Enjoying the teaching?" asked Petra.

"Very much so. It's tiring but when you see the brains absorbing information like sponges, it is very rewarding. Tiring, but great fun." The two sat down and accepted strong coffee.

"Jules is suggesting a new population census, just of our village and surrounding areas, especially the farms and little industries," said Petra. "I could even suggest that we, the whole community, might be self-sufficient. Advancing on that idea, we could use a kind of barter system, instead of cash or promissory notes which lose their value as soon as you look at them. What do you think, Quentin?"

"Law and order used to be one of my briefs. I am afraid not all our survivors will be wholly honest. There will always be one or two who are determined to rip off the rest and they will have to be put firmly in their place. If this community tries to be self-sufficient, it will have to appoint one, perhaps two people who can be relied on to keep the peace.

"We have been thinking about just that problem. How about, just for a morning, collecting the whole local population in one place – our well used tithe barn, for instance? Those that have survived in our three villages could do with a get together. And there must be more than just Nicholas and a few others still living in his village the other side of the hill. Where did he find his Grace, after all? They can be given the chance to appoint their own policeman or two. They would have to have the trust of the whole village, be fit and mostly able to do their job by gentle persuasion. Rather like the old-fashioned village bobby who knew everyone and everything that went on in the village. How about that, Tom?"

"I expect that could be arranged fairly quickly. At the same time, we could get tooled up to do the census. We could find out which houses are empty and can be stripped of anything useful, and perhaps knocked down to provide more land to grow food."

"Be careful about that, Tom," Quentin warned. "It sounds like an open invitation to thieves. We should, at least, try to determine ownership of empty houses before we write them off. If we broadcast what we hoped to do and gave our survivors a time limit to think about the problems as they see it, at least that would give prospective inheritors a chance to state their case. How about a month or two, or do you think that's too long? Remember we are jumping the law of the land, as it was only a while ago. We should tread carefully."

Roderick and Lucy came in, both out of breath. "Sorry we're late for coffee, Tom. I have been trying to teach Roderick to ride and look after a horse. He's fine on the mucking out bit, but in the saddle he's not so good. With the shortage of fuel, I think it would be a good idea for everyone to learn more about horses. We're going to need horses for ploughing and moving things. Elephants would be better, I used them in India, but the nearest zoo is miles away and most of those elephants have gone soft." Lucy laughed happily, at ease with the world. Her face shone with fresh air and reflected the adoring glances of her resurrected relationship with Roderick.

Tom looked pleased. "Don't worry, Lucy, nobody is ever late for coffee in this household. We were suggesting that we try and get the whole residue of our population, there won't be more than a hundred and fifty to two hundred, together. We can get them to meet in the tithe barn in, perhaps, two weeks or so from today. We can feed and water them, get lots of data, including about how many horses we have, and have a vote or show of hands to appoint a policeman or two. How does that sound?"

"Spot on," said Julian, who had been half listening to the conversation.

CHAPTER THIRTY-EIGHT

It was teatime, with the meal laid on tables set out on the school playground. Intense discussion was underway on what to do next.

Tom stood up to speak. "Two whole months and an almost clear desk – very few death notifications, as far as we know. Poor old Daleshott with nobody left alive. So sad, we all had a lot of friends in that village. Daleshott. It used to mean the corner of the land next to the forest, a shott means a corner. I suppose it would have been classed as a rotten borough in the Middle Ages, like Old Sarum. I guess the whole of that area will be open forest in a hundred years' time.

"We should integrate more with Wellmere and the few people left in Hawkley – that's Nicholas' village. Then slightly further afield there are the few houses that make up Brookbridge Farm, round Roderick's power station. That used to mean where the badgers used to cross the streams.

"What now, Quentin? You're the organisation man. Do you think we need to be organised, or are we better off simply drifting along in our own sweet way?"

"There's the tithe barn get together in a week's time which should sort out quite a lot of problems. I get the impression that several survivors have retreated into themselves and don't want to be organised. That's understandable, bearing in mind the suffocating attitude of previous governments. Regulations for years were coming thick and fast, producing either complete confusion or fury – mostly the latter. There are so few people. Our counters have found there are only around one hundred and fifty people left, so it would be logical to centre everybody on this village.

"There are lots of perfectly good houses with gardens which are empty and could be occupied by the remains of families from the other two villages. We also have the only school, our lovely barn and a few public buildings. How about that, Tom?"

"There are bound to be some who will want to stay put in the other villages. They might want to stay in a house that, perhaps, has fond family memories."

"I realise that. We must not be seen to force anyone to move. But it is inevitable that the public utilities will be on a knife edge and there will be failings in the water or electricity systems with nobody to mend anything. Houses out on a limb will not be much fun to live in. I'm afraid moving to Pensfield is the only real option. What do you think, Carole?"

"I think we should stick to the original plan and meet in a week's time with everybody present. Somehow, we must keep the conversations going. If we spring the idea of everyone moving to empty houses in Pensfield, I can imagine survivors from the other two villages will object and accuse us of taking over everything they have lived and worked for. No, the idea must come from them. Then we can smile and say, 'What a splendid idea'. We could, perhaps, start with the worry about the maintenance of public services. When that hits a brick wall, we have to hope they come up with their own ideas."

Anthony, Sol and Ben, who had been silent for most of the discussion raised their hands in unison. Anthony spoke first. "We've seen a number of people nosing around and asking peculiar questions. They seem to be acting like tourists, but we don't trust them. We don't think they are officials or anything like that, but they are very nosy, and we don't like them."

"How do they travel?" asked Tom.

"You've seen more of them, Sol, than I have."

"I guess half of them, say ten or so, come on electric bicycles. The others are usually driving tiny little vehicles which, I suppose, are electric cars. You ask them who they are and where they come from, but they don't give proper answers. We think they're spying on us. A couple of them spent hours with Gillian's father and asked him all about his farming and his aeroplane. He got fed up with them and chucked them out of his house."

Tom laughed. "They sound more like civil servants to me, with not enough to do except be nosy. Now that would be an ideal job for our new policemen – investigating suspicious strangers." He continued, "I agree with your sentiments, Carole. We need to collect twenty people per village, no more than that, otherwise any rational discussion will be strangled by too much chat."

The motley collection of chairs in the tithe barn creaked and groaned for the second time that year. One hundred survivors from four villages were pleased to have been asked to participate. Before the meeting was called to order incidental conversation started spontaneously. Quite a few made the point, forcefully, that Pensfield had not always been the largest of the villages; but they had to agree that it now had the highest number of survivors and facilities that the other villages did not have. Oddly, there was no mention, at least at the beginning of the meeting, that several of the Pensfield inhabitants had been instrumental in taming the worldwide disaster. And there was no mention of the fact that those now sitting in the uncomfortable chairs owed their survival to the efforts of those who had called the conference.

Tom, as chairman, stood up. "Ladies and gentlemen, thank you all for coming to this meeting. I, we, do hope you are happy with the choice of representatives from each of our five villages. We do seem to be a natural, you might even say, geographical, group and will be expected to have a say in our future organisation.

"I suggest, our first concern is the maintenance of law and order." He looked around the audience and there was nobody who disagreed with this proposal. "I would like to ask each village to choose two people, of either sex, and definitely of stable good character, to act as local police officers. We suggest they should act in such a way as to resemble the old-fashioned local bobby. Not necessarily in uniform but acting in a 'softly, softly' fashion to keep the peace. Years ago, the local bobby knew everybody in the village and everything that was going on, either good or bad. We suggest they should make a comeback. Does that meet with general approval?"

Most of the audience raised their hands.

"Are there any contrary views? If so, let's have them now."

A young man at the back of the audience raised his hand and spoke. "James Coldrey from Wellmere. Tom, can I ask what powers these policemen, sorry, or policewomen, will have? Can they arrest baddies? And if they can, what do they do with them? On a jocular note, which of our villages has its original stocks, and how many rotten tomatoes can we throw at them?"

Breaking into the general laughter, Tom had to shout, "James, thank you for that. Probably the most important question in front of us. Seriously, somehow, he or she should try and get some guidance from central government. We will have a go at that, but I can't predict when we will succeed. But as soon as we get a squeak out of them, I will communicate with you all."

"Thank you, Tom. May I suggest that each village has one person in charge of communication?"

"James, another good idea! You should be sitting in my seat. While we are on that subject, I suggest that the chair of successive meetings should circulate through the original inhabitants of our five villages. Good idea?"

They all nodded agreement.

"Now, to the schooling of our children. I am wary about being too dominant but the school in Pensfield was the latest one to be built. It is stuffed full of excellent facilities but has been left with a miserable number of pupils. In fact, we learn that the total number of children in all the combined village primary schools is just short of a hundred. And there are only two teachers left, apart from my school which has a surplus. I – we – suggest that all the pupils from our five villages and the surviving two teachers join up together and can be brought by bus into Pensfield daily. I have telephoned the bus station on the outskirts of our nearest city and they have offered two, almost new, single decker buses for as long as we need them.

"Sadly, none of their drivers have survived. But I have the appropriate licence and I know at least two other inhabitants of Pensfield who can drive a bus. I am hopeful that others can be trained up to be competent drivers. Quentin, sitting next to me, has driven tanks for a part of his life and is a qualified teacher. What do we all think of that idea? James? Any helpful comments, please?"

"I don't want to monopolise the discussion, but on the face of it, I hope it sounds a good idea. And, may I suggest we meet like this on a regular basis? I would have liked to suggest that we meet in each village, but Pensfield is the only one to have this old tithe barn. It really is a wonderful venue, perhaps for concerts or theatrical events?"

"Thank you, James. Of course, but for now I suggest that, firstly, you decide on a single person per village who is the person to deal with directly. When that perhaps difficult decision has been made, we can all make our way to the canteen and bar where there is enough food for an army."

Four representatives came forward and Carole noted their names and details before they broke to eat and drink.

James made his way through the crowd until he found Tom and Quentin. "Tom, I do hope my comments were helpful. You may have known that I am one of the two surviving teachers. We were wondering what to do next and you have come up with the ideal suggestion. Is it true that despite your being able to host the gurus from around the world, there hasn't been a dicky-bird from London?"

"On the face of it, James, you might think so. But it so happens that Quentin here is, or was, a Lord of the Realm and, given the right circumstances and timing—"

"And luck, and a certain amount of pulling the right strings—" Quentin stopped and left the two.

"Quentin has a wonderful ability to pour oil on troubled waters. He can also stir up an almighty storm, so beware, James!"

CHAPTER THIRTY-NINE

A month later Wellmere was running the meeting and James was in the chair.

"Thanks, everyone, for coming." He looked at the meagre audience. "Not so many as our first meeting. Never mind, we've got some good news for you that you can carry back to base. Two keepers of the peace – we will have to call them keepers of the peace – have been appointed. Average age of fifty-five, but they are fit and honest, as far as we know!" He paused until the laughter subsided.

"We can also tell you that throughout the whole of the country there haven't been any further mutations back to the apes so we can all begin to relax and start to form a new society. There's a hand up at the back."

"Harold Burbage from Hawkley. Nick asked me if I would be prepared to be one of your new bobbies. I rather like the thought of being an old-fashioned bobby. My question is this – has anyone from the so-called capital city had the courtesy to acknowledge that a tiny group of clever people from this area worked out how to stop the killing of all the remaining members of the species *Homo sapiens?* Has there been any communication at all from London, or perhaps Reading? I realise that the internet has collapsed and there is no such thing as email, but the old-fashioned telephone system is still working from time to time and the roads are clear. Does London still exist? In other words, parliament and the civil service?"

"Thank you, Harold. There may have been an attempt at communication, but I know nothing of it. Quentin, can you tell us anything about central government?"

Quentin stood up, looking weary. "I have to tell you that it is impossible to get through to London on the phone. But somewhere along the line, I heard that all the activities of central government have moved to Reading where they have taken over several large public buildings.

"I have to agree with Harold that it is mightily disappointing that there has been no acknowledgement of the efforts we have made in this tiny neck of the woods. You would have thought someone would have come here, simply out of curiosity, but perhaps they are afraid of our funny habits up in the north! But, sooner or later, we are going to have to obtain the all-clear to legalise our arrangements. There must be other tightly knit communities that have started to think as we have done. I must say, I am impressed so far and welcome you personally, Harold, as an upholder of the law." Quentin looked tired as he sat down.

Tom left the barn and returned with a worried expression on his face. "James, there's a car arrived outside. It looks a bit official. Maybe this is the answer to our complaints. Excuse me, I won't be a minute." Tom went out and returned with the newcomer; a short, dapper little suited man holding a new briefcase. He pranced to the front of the team running the meeting, without any apology or introduction.

"I have been authorised by the government to assess the situation in these villages and the state of the atomic power station." He bent down to retrieve a hardback notebook from his briefcase.

"Hang on a minute!" A voice from the back of the audience. "Who the hell are you, and how do you have the impudence to barge into this meeting without even giving us your name?"

"So sorry," said the little man. "My name is Lancelot Bordon. I am the under-secretary for the Ministry of Internal Affairs. As I said before, I have been sent to assess the situation in the countryside of the north of England. I shall need details of survivors, their National Insurance."

Lancelot was interrupted by a roar of defiance from the audience. They were shouting louder and louder with obscenities flowing fast and furious. Tom went to the back of the barn and returned with the school handbell.

"James, how about it?" He handed the bell to James who rang it as hard as he could before he was able to speak.

"Ladies and gentlemen! Whilst I have a great deal of sympathy with your reaction, I must insist that we deal with this situation in a civilised manner." He paused while the anger stopped boiling and descended to a mild simmer.

"Ladies and gentlemen, we have a visitor, and we are part of a relatively civilised society. So, we have a name and an organisation. Quentin, can you give us a clue as to the origin of this fellow."

"I'm not just a fellow," Lancelot squeaked. "I am an official government representative and I have come here at great expense."

Quentin stood up, an old but still impressive giant. He looked sadly at Lancelot Bordon. "Ladies and gentlemen, our newcomer has been sent on an impossible mission by a very newly created department of Her Majesty's government. It is run by a brash gentleman called Algernon, poor fellow. It was originally formed to keep several people employed in a useless field of information. You should have a little sympathy for our visitor, but the best attitude, I suggest, is to send him packing."

"You can't do that!" squeaked Lancelot. "Who the hell are you, anyway?"

"My name is General Quentin Ogilvie. I am a Lord of the Realm, Privy Councillor and Knight of the Garter. I am entitled to order you to go. Go back to Algernon and tell him from me to send someone who understands how to deal with highly intelligent persons who just happen to have saved a significant remnant of humanity. Now, GO!"

Lancelot collected his papers and left the barn without looking back.

"Well done, Quentin." Tom's voice was drowned out by the cheering audience. A tired and disappointed Quentin sat down. Tom touched his arm and Quentin managed to raise a bleak smile.

"Sorry about that, Tom. I hate pulling rank, especially with a complete nonentity. On a lighter note, Daphne and I would love to explore the Manor this evening. We are looking forward to having a permanent living space."

"Of course, we'd love to show you around. Come to our place and have a drink first."

"That sounds very civilised, Tom. Six o'clock?"

CHAPTER FORTY

Lucy stood on the school steps, looking worried. She relaxed when Roderick drove up.

"What's the problem, Lucy?"

"The problem is that both of our bus drivers are at that meeting in the barn. I don't like to interrupt, but the children are hungry, and they want to get home."

"Don't worry, Lucy, I can solve your problem for you. I've got a Public Service Vehicle licence and, you might not believe this, but our friend Gavin used to be a bus driver in a former life – before he discovered we paid a decent wage and had a much more interesting job just waiting for him. Only at the last minute did he tell us his lifelong hobby had been the study of weather systems. I'll give him a ring since his workload halved when we shut down. My phone should be under the seat."

Roderick shuffled through a mass of rubbish and found the phone. "Here we are, it should work if I plug it into the car battery."

"Gavin, how would you like to drive a bus again? The school buses are sitting here with no drivers, Tom and Quentin are both at the meeting in the barn. They're taking much longer than expected, so I have volunteered us both. I hope you don't mind. I can come and collect you right now. Great! See you in a minute."

Roderick turned to face his old love. "Problem solved, Lucy."

She smiled, wrapped her arms round him, and kissed him hard and long. "Oh, Rod, I enjoyed that. Now, the children …"

"No more, not now, love. I'll be back from the school run in an hour. I must collect Gavin.

"Don't worry, children," he called to the hungry girls and boys. "Back in five minutes, then we'll have two drivers." They cheered.

An hour and a half later there were two empty buses in front of the school and Roderick had returned from Gavin's house. A sweet-smelling Lucy was on the school steps, with fresh lipstick, a bright smile, and a palpitating chest.

"Can I offer you—"

"No, you can't. Get in the car, we're going for a drive, to somewhere high up where we can breathe lots of fresh air." He stopped and studied her. "You are looking lovely this evening; much more than I can put into words."

"Thank you, Rod, you look pretty good yourself."

"I did tidy up at Gavin's. I need a kiss, right now. It'll make a mess of your lipstick."

"I hope so!"

"What a wonderful view! I can just see the sea and a few fishing boats. You're right, love, the air is breathable." Lucy was wondering how to begin what she was dying to say but the bland chatter was not helping. "I need a kiss now. To hell with the bloody lipstick."

"Lucy, two hours ago you started to say, 'the children' – you didn't say yours or those waiting to be taken home. Please continue from there."

"Oh, Rod, I was trying to say my children love your company. you're so good with them." She swallowed. *Now for it, for all our sakes. Let's hope and pray.*

"Go on, love," he said.

"That's the word I want. Oh, Rod, I – we – love you … please come and live with us. I know it's not my place, but I really want … oh, dear, I don't know how to say—"

"Of course I will! I should have proposed first, but I don't think it matters nowadays. Wonderful! Yes, yes, and yes. Give us a minute, I've something in the boot of the car."

Roderick returned with a bottle and two stainless steel beakers. "It should still be pretty cold." He opened the bottle with a satisfying pop and poured the frothing liquid into the beakers. "Cheers, my love, to the four of us. This is the happiest day of my life."

"Me also. We both have stories to tell, but—"

"But, some other time, Lucy, not now. Let's live for the moment. And another thing."

"More excitement?"

"Back to my old job. The central powers have asked me to start the power station up again. I have been asked to supply all the local villages and the whole of the next town and the supply will be free. Think of that, free electricity! They have at last realised that this tiny village, and the clever people in it, have done a bloody good job in the last year; and all of us, we deserve a break."

"Cheers! This is very nice. I wonder what persuaded you to put a cool bottle of champagne in the boot of your car?"

"Simple, my love, a little something your children let slip. They let slip that you hinted that you wanted to ask me something very important. Just that! I've been worrying myself, but I don't have children to talk to. So, you were ahead of the game. Just as well, my love – I might not have been brave enough, having failed dismally so many years ago."

Lucy cried and cried, tears of joy and tears of sorrow for the missed years. They held each other tight for a long, long time, until the sky started to change colour and dim into the twilight. At last, they separated, smiling shyly and Roderick switched on the engine. He drove slowly back to Lucy's house as she clung to his arm, so happy she could burst.

At the sound of the tyres on gravel, two boys crashed through the front door, bubbling with too many words. "How did it go, Mum? How did it go, Roderick? You both look good; must be time for a drink. We did hope … so, it's all ready, and the nibbles. Come in, come in, come in! This is so great!"

CHAPTER FORTY-ONE

Quentin looked thoughtful. "Tom, tell me who lived here last, and how long ago? What happened to the Lord of the Manor and his or her family?"

Tom laughed. "As far as we know, the last occupant left here about two years ago, so it may be a trifle damp. The actual building was built in the early eighteen hundreds, and was thought to be modern at the time. Within the last five years a huge sum of somebody's money has been spent redoing and upgrading practically everything. They obviously spent far too much and the guy who was living here on his own went bankrupt and left in a hurry. Various odd relatives came and went and last year we, the Parish Council, we were told that they had all died of some strange hereditary disease. There was nobody left to claim ownership and because various bills were unpaid the whole thing came to a grinding halt. So, the place is under the care of the Parish Council. In effect, it is up for grabs, and with so many empty houses in the village the Manor is essentially worth nothing. If you like it, it's yours for the asking. What do think, Daphne? Carole has been around it and everything is in working order."

The two men looked at Daphne and Carole. Carole nodded and Daphne smiled. "Seems like a fait accompli. What do you think, Carole?"

"Don't worry about the size, Daphne. Half of the building can be shut off and at least one other family could live here."

"I suppose that's a good thing. Alright, I'll give it a try. The position is excellent, right in the middle of the village, and the garden's not too big. Come on, Quentin, let's explore our new home."

The Manor was immaculate, and all the essential services appeared to be in good order. They wandered into the oak-lined dining room.

"Where did these wonderful carved wooden panels come from, Tom?"

"That's quite a story. After the battle of Waterloo, the higher ranks of the ordinary soldiers were allowed free range to plunder all sorts of items from the houses of the defeated French. They often stripped off carved hardwood panels like these and I suspect that's their origin. They were usually taken by the lesser mortals in the hierarchy of the army command. Apart from the wonderful carving, they should make the room nice and warm. Sometimes you'll find they land up being painted, but I think that's a pity. How do you like it so far?"

"Did you have witches in this village, about the time of Waterloo or later?"

"Why on earth do you ask that?"

"See these round marks, just above the fireplace? They're symbols that were meant to stop witches and other beasties coming down the chimney and causing a nuisance in the family."

"That, I didn't know. Perhaps that's why we have never had witches in this village. Everything else to your liking? It's going to be splendid to have you living so close."

"I think Daphne and I will live here very happily. How do we manage to get ownership with all the complications you've told us about?"

"It's yours for the asking. I've been given powers that are quite extraordinary from those who now seem to have settled on Reading as the centre of power in the land. They phoned me yesterday and I can cheerfully say it solves a huge number of problems. Something to do with the Privy Council."

"Oh, them! About time they paid back for all the work I put into the modernisation of that lot. Things are looking up at last. How many other problems are you able to solve in a twinkling of an eye?"

"What to do about tourists."

"What's that got to do with this community?"

"That wonderful thing, the verbal grapevine, has told me that there was a bus full of visitors seen a few days ago in the village. When someone asked them what they had come to see, the driver shrugged his shoulders and remarked that as far as he could understand, we seemed to be famous, and should be turned into a tourist resort. We should have banners at the entrance to the village with placards shouting, 'saviours of the world'. Those were his comments, take it or leave it!"

"What a horrendous idea." Tom paused. "On the other hand, we could put on a mini exhibition in the tithe barn that included the film and anything else we can think of. Then at the door we could ask for donations to help us bring all the abandoned land back to nature. How about that, Q?"

"Go on, Daphne, I have the feeling you are working us up to one of your, with respect, unusual ideas. Perhaps you can help Tom and stop him worrying."

"Well, there's a huge problem with the farming community."

"What's the problem there?"

"The problem is that since the farmers don't have to punish the land so harshly to squeeze out the last ounce of food and meat to feed what was an unsustainable population, most of the land is now worth nothing and the natural process is that it will revert to scrub very quickly. That means the hillside will be covered in brambles in no time at all. Also, the farmers' machinery is now so huge that it's not suitable on much smaller farms. On the other hand, I can't imagine anyone might want to go back to walking behind a plough being pulled by a couple of oxen in the pouring rain."

"Q seems to think, Daphne, you have an answer to the problem of redundant land."

"Tom, I have been interested in that sort of problem for some time. The answer does need a fair amount of money. How about using the contributions from the tourists? I certainly can solve Tom's problem. Have either of you heard of rewilding? It is better to be called wilding. Encouraging nature to revert to a savannah type of countryside which was probably the case a thousand years ago. I've got several books on the subject. There must be several thousand acres on the west side of the village, right up into the hills which would be ideal. Wilding takes a few years to accomplish but it does mean that everyone in our little group of villages must make the effort to be involved. The first thing that we must do is refresh the land which has been plundered of most of its minerals ever since the beginning of the last war. I don't mean simply letting it lie fallow – the top rubbish grass must be sacrificed and the land rid of its load of herbicides and pesticides before the proper insect and bird population will return. I could go on but, as I said, the whole population round us has a right to be informed and, preferably, asked to take part in the exercise.

"Tom, you seem to have the ability to undo the purse strings, and it will cost quite a lot of money. But we are suddenly in the ideal situation to improve the well-being of all of us. With the work involved, all the able-bodied people can take part and we could all be a lot healthier."

"Wow! I seem to have opened the floodgates. Daphne, why don't you take charge of the idea and I'm sure we will all support you. Looks like another conference. You might need the three lads to help!"

CHAPTER FORTY-TWO

Every seat in the tithe barn was occupied to hear the new Lady of the Manor. Only a few of the audience had a clue as to what she was going to say. The bar had been open and well used for half an hour, and the audience was looking forward to hearing her words of wisdom.

"Thank you for coming to listen to me. The subject has been a hobby of mine for a number of years, and it is, at last, fashionable." Daphne took a deep breath and in a strong voice, ignoring her notes, started to speak.

"Wilding, as a concept, has been around for some time. The latest offering in this country is a book by Isabella Tree published in 2018. Her story revolves around a family farm in West Sussex which appeared to be profitable – but over time it began to lose money, no matter what they did to improve the return on their capital. Suddenly, they realised that they couldn't see any way to solve the problem. It was a working farm with neat hedges and fields, constantly in use, but, fundamentally, it was on very poor ground and fast becoming a biological desert. The family discovered very quickly that the 'back to nature' mantra was not just a process of abandoning the land. A lot of effort had to be expended to do this correctly and they had an enormous amount of help from experts in Denmark where they have been wilding for some time. The essence of the process is to encourage large herbivores and carnivores to control the ecosystem from the top down and restore it to a healthier, more biodiverse state.

"We and, I guess, large parts of the countryside throughout the country, are suddenly presented with the problem of huge areas of land which will have to be abandoned. This land is therefore valueless and, unless a certain amount of care is used, it will all become a useless wilderness which has no beauty, no function, and no biodiversity. We want to see and hear the return of the birds and bees that were a feature of this island a thousand years ago before the land was forced to produce more and more food.

"Now most of the population have died, the same amount of food is not needed and, therefore, the land can be allowed to recover from years of intensive farming, which must have been started – for perfectly good reasons at the time – during the Second World War.

"The idea is not simply to revert to a previous state, because there never has been a so-called previous state. You may well ask, before what rough date? We can't go back to the seriously giant herbivores such as the mammoths, wild rhinos and other primeval animals because they no longer exist. On the other hand, the reintroduction of large predators may provoke objections from people worried about their own safety or the safety of their animals. This is understandable and is why the whole population of the area must be involved.

"One thing we do not have to worry about is interference with economic activity. A year ago, the local farms worked flat out to supply our towns and surrounding villages with as much locally grown food as possible. This had to be achieved with the help of considerable quantities of herbicides and insecticides. The result is an almost sterile land which has a huge load of unwanted nitrogen and phosphate and a variety of poisons.

"Once the enormous area of abandoned land has been given new life, we can all adopt a more sensible lifestyle. I have already talked to the few remaining local farmers and they are happy with my ideas. Their residual farming activity can be channelled into local activities such as ice cream, butter, yoghurt, and cheese. That will be a lot easier now the overbearing supermarkets have vanished. Come on now, get reading all about it. I have several books on the subject and you can take them away. There is no charge, but please share them with your friends."

The audience crowded round Daphne, bursting with questions. Mostly, they were enthusiastic – none more so than the farming community. All the books on the table were borrowed with earnest promises to circulate them and eventually return the precious books to Daphne.

"Well done, old girl!" said Quentin. "You certainly got the message through loud and clear. Now, Tom, we have thought up some subtle plan to milk the generosity of the tourists to pay for it."

"How about a tithe on every tourist who comes to the outskirts of the villages? A conducted tour of Pensfield and perhaps other villages could be organised if there is a bus full of them. Remember, thanks to the boys, there is a film of the international conference that could be on one of those continuous systems in our tithe barn. And for a fee, perhaps Bill could be persuaded to take one or two of them up in his little aeroplane. Any other ideas, Julian?"

"I could show a few of them around the non-secret parts of my laboratory and then blind them with science to explain how we did it, and beat the little buggers, as Sol would say. Who is going to be the fund raiser? You need an enthusiastic person."

"How about the boys? Anthony and Sol are enthusiastic enough and Ben and Sheba can be the stars of the show. How about persuading the big bookshop to set up a stall and have lots of books about wilding? Then we could take a small percentage of the profit? Tom, you probably have a contract to buy schoolbooks … suggestions, please."

CHAPTER FORTY-THREE

"How old will you be, Quentin, in a couple of weeks' time?"

"Kind of you to ask, Tom. Daphne is better at mathematics and says I shall be ninety years old. Should have been put down years ago! Past my sell-by date, and all that."

"Don't you dare to speak like that! You of all people are bound to reach a ton."

Quentin simply laughed. "I have heard rumours that she is plotting some sort of a party. One of my oldest friends from the big city wrote to me to ask when it was going to be. So much for secrets!"

Tom looked at his diary. "I don't think any of us are any good at keeping secrets. Some friends of ours were plotting to give their father a surprise birthday party. But the whole thing fell flat because they forgot to send birthday cards – obvious, really, as they were going to be present.

"Well, I might just as well tell you, it is going to be on June the tenth. I know that because she asked me to make sure the tithe barn had enough heating, and did the roof leak? There were a few other things which apparently depend on the weather. There you are, no more secrets. How is London being resurrected, by the way?"

"I'm told the underground is not functioning yet and the flood defences are not up to scratch. Let's hope the two don't mix. Once the underground is flooded it would take ages to empty and get working again. The problem now, of course, is that there aren't enough people to get the systems running. Poor old *Homo derelictus,* as we christened them, have a lot to answer for. I get the impression my friends are hoping that all the government offices will be transferred permanently to Reading."

"At least it's not at sea level. How high do you think it is? Twenty feet above sea level?"

"Twenty feet, perhaps. It could be good idea. I mean to transfer the nuts and bolts of government upstream. Daphne could occupy herself wilding all those royal parks and flattening thousands of houses. I like the thought of a few beavers trying to block the Thames."

It was a cool morning with the summer sunshine fighting the dew but failing to penetrate the deepest shadows. The village tent, erected the night before, stood firm and indifferent to the damp. The early workers, swaddled in their nice warm clothes, were walking to the old barn where they struggled with the new doors that had been recently cut into the original twenty-foot doors. It was unlikely the original barn doors would ever open again. There was no need as the horse-drawn wagons overflowing with hay were long gone. But the retired custodian of the barn had insisted the wooden hinges were still to be greased, just in case. The case, perhaps, related to the huge combine harvester laid to rest in a back corner. The two farmers were ever hopeful that a big slice of their arable lands could be salvaged from the wilding.

Next to arrive was a tractor and trailer with heaped tables and chairs. The few remaining strong men who had walked to the barn started to unload to a recording of a cheerful tune from Nicholas' bagpipes. One of the school buses made its way to the barn, filled with cutlery, plates, cups and saucers, and, most importantly, cases of wine glasses. The men transferred their efforts to the tent where their wives were huddled round the simple heating system, getting ready to be bossy. Tables were needed from the barn; the men should have thought of that! And so on, as ever will be.

Coffee time arrived, along with more helpers. The chat level rose slowly as the barn warmed up. A welcome present from the French of a case of brandy was broached to reinforce the coffee. The case of schnapps from Austria was reserved to liven up the afternoon.

Next was an excruciating practice session of the school choir, led by Sol whose musical sense was only slightly better than Anthony's. Nicholas had been volunteered to accompany the songs with his electric piano and the conductor was the long-suffering Anna. Ben and Sheba were observers – Ben said he wasn't into singing, thank you.

The second school bus arrived with lunch which quietened down both the adults and children. Someone, it could have been Van, suggested they try the white and red wines. The wives were not so sure, but it was going to be a special occasion and certainly the red wine should be placed next to the heaters to warm up, just a little bit. And since the bottles had to be moved, it seemed sensible to at least loosen the screw tops and perhaps even try ...

Six o'clock, in the dark cool of the evening, was to be the grand opening. Outside lights were switched on to welcome the "belle" of the ball and his guests. A London bus had arrived the night before and hidden in a cattle shed outside the village.

The evening was still and relatively warm. Anna had chosen a dozen of the children to be the welcome event as Quentin and Daphne arrived in style. An old friend was driving them in a 1928 Lagonda to which he had attached streamers, as if for a wedding. They were greeted with strains of 'Happy birthday' which brought tears to Quentin's eyes.

He looked up, and above the barn doors was a brightly lit sign indicating his age.

"Oh dear, I'm not sure I'm going to enjoy this."

Daphne looked at her fast-ageing husband and shook her head. "Three people above all that you must have sitting at our table. Have a guess who they are."

"They're my favourites, the three musketeers. Well, that's nice."

Quentin and Daphne entered the barn to the sound of 'Happy birthday' being sung by the whole school choir. Before they sat down there were great cuddles with the three boys and a pat for Sheba. For the first time in his life, Quentin was unable to speak, and Daphne took up the reins.

"Thank you, all, for such a glorious welcome, and especially the school choir. Quentin is not as young as he was and will give you a speech when he has been wined and dined, especially the former."

Then it was the turn of his old mates from his tank regiment, followed by friends from the political times in London. Each one was greeted with full recognition and memories of past times. But the strain was beginning to show and after he was forced to rise and cut a beautiful cake, he stumbled and nearly fell on his way back to the table.

Tom instantly took the weight of the old man. "Steady does it, Q; alright now?"

"Thanks to you, Tom. A bit dizzy, but I'm all right. What is the next jollity on the horizon?"

"Nicholas on his bagpipes. He is going to play 'Amazing Grace' to celebrate his new lady."

"Oh, bless him."

The speech started well. Quentin took a deep breath. "Friends – for that is what I insist on calling you all – you have welcomed Daphne and I to your village. You have given us the most wonderful place to live and contributed to the most exciting time in our lives. . .

. . . thank you all, from the bottom of both our hearts for such a wonderful birthday party and thank you, boys, for your company at our table. Your conversation is bright and, in your own jargon, 'with it'. It is time for us to retire and leave all you lovely people to continue into the night."

Quentin sat with the sound of clapping. Tom and Carole then escorted the old couple to the waiting car.

"I know, my love, that I usually have a brandy before bed, but tonight I feel I have had slightly more than is wise and the thought of relaxing beneath the sheets is too tempting for words."

"Quentin, you garrulous old wonder. Bedtime it is."

"Just one thing, Daphne. Before we left, Anthony said he thought they might go for a swim. I forgot to tell you at the time. Do you think he meant it?"

"Don't worry, my dear. I can give Petra a ring on her mobile and make sure they are all right."

CHAPTER FORTY-FOUR

A flustered Petra, holding her mobile in one hand and a glass of brandy in the other, found a tired Julian. "Have you seen Ant? I've just had a strange call from Daphne saying that Q had forgotten to tell her that Ant said they were thinking of going for a swim."

"That's ridiculous, it's still dark, although there's a full moon. And where were they planning to go for this swim? There's only the sea or that tiny little pond by the edge of the quarry."

"Well, they aren't in the barn and nobody has seen them for at least half an hour."

"Ask Ben, he'll know where they are."

"There's no sign of Ben either, or Sheba. And Gillian Makiver has also vanished. Find Roderick and Lucy. Last time I saw them, they were in a cuddle in the moonlight. They might have seen where the children went."

The two went out and found the amorous couple.

"Roderick, have you seen any of the children? We've had a call from Q to tell us Anthony was suggesting they, the children, were thinking of going for a swim before the sun came up."

"I did see a group of them about an hour ago. Ben and Sheba were leading them by the usual route up to the top of the hill. They were very cheerful and making quite a noise, so we presumed it was all above board. Anything the matter, Petra? Aren't they getting a bit old to be called children? They have had a tremendous bellyful of growing up recently, they are acting more like teenagers. You should be careful not to mother them too much."

"Oh well, I take your point, Rod. Anyway, there's plenty of light by the full moon and it'll be dawn in an hour's time, then we can check on them."

Roderick shrugged his shoulders and muttered to Lucy, "It's all part of growing up."

"We need towels, rugs and containers of hot drinks. Come on, Jules, no more of that schnapps. It'll do you good, a healthy climb up to the top of the hills in bracing dawn air. How many are coming?"

"Tom and Carole, Roderick and Lucy, Liu and his wife, Van and Anna, and us. That makes ten in all."

They changed into more rugged clothing and set off. An hour and a half later, they were on the summit path walking silently towards the quarry. The air was still, and the path often obscured by wisps of morning mist that waved in front of the walkers.

Carole stopped. "This is eerie. Why is there no noise? I was expecting some remnant of the dawn chorus, cheering us along. But not a bit of it." She waved her hands in front of her. "Do you think these moving wisps are the ghosts of all those thousands of mutants who died up here? What do you think, Van?"

"My only thoughts are worrying about the children. It's not far to the pond."

"There it is," cried Petra. "And I can see something by the edge of the pond."

They silently crept nearer and saw Anthony, Sol, and Gillian huddled together between the warmth of two ponies. Seated bolt upright behind the three children was Ben, with Sheba's head on his lap. He looked up as the visitors approached and pressed a finger to his lips. They waited for Ben to speak.

"Don't worry," he whispered. "They had a lovely swim and were very noisy. That's when the ponies came to keep them warm. Then when they lay down, I could reach over and pull the warm mist from the pool to keep their warmth in. It's a very friendly pool and it let me do it. They've been asleep for more than an hour so they should wake up soon."

"What a happy picture, Jules, I should have brought a camera."

"Try your phone, Petra. And while we are about it, don't forget to thank Ben for looking after everyone. I think it's hot drinks all round."

The first to wake were the two ponies who stretched, stood up, and wandered off, as if what they had contributed was all in a day's work. The four children accepted the hot drinks and quietly dressed. The pool retrieved its blanket of warm mist.

CHAPTER FORTY-FIVE

From his comfortable bed, Quentin looked up at the intricate plasterwork. It was a relief to be without pain and the sleepy result of the opioids was just what the doctor ordered. He remembered the last time he had been in pain was when his tanks were seriously outgunned and there was no other option but to go full tilt at the enemy.

Although the battle was won, it turned out to be an expensive victory and almost all his men suffered multiple wounds. This pain was different – a dull, gnawing pain, as if he were being eaten from the inside.

"We can't blame the dreaded Archaea for my problem, Doc. But I can understand why some people become addicted to the 'unhurting medicine'. It certainly works. Poppies have a lot to answer for!"

A gentle sound disturbed the silence. "Come in!" Quentin shouted. "Visitors are welcome at any time. We are told there isn't much of that left – time, I mean. Carole and Tom, how nice to see you. Help yourselves to a glass of something from the table. There should be enough to suit any palate." He pointed to a magnificent array of bottles, an ice bucket and drinking vessels enough to wet the whistle of an army.

"How are you, old son?" Carole asked tearfully.

"Much the same as many ninety-two-year-olds. Daphne is not far behind me – we usually do things together. Give the old thing another year or so. In the meanwhile, to give you something useful to do, I will have a large gin and tonic with very little ice."

"Are you allowed—" Tom started.

"Allowed, by whom, may I ask? At this stage, I do as I bloody well please."

Quentin accepted the glass and took a sip. "Just right. Thank you, Carole."

Doctor Liu smiled, touched Quentin's hand, smiled at Daphne, and left the room.

They watched the wonder of the shooting stars through the open window. Carole handed Quentin another gin and tonic at midnight and, very soon after, with a smile on his lips and an empty glass in his hand, General the Lord Quentin Ogilvie died surrounded by his friends.

Daphne decided Quentin's funeral celebration – no black ties, please – should take place in the tithe barn, the place in which Quentin had seemed to enjoy himself the most and the place where he had steered them all to win the battle to save the residual numbers of *Homo sapiens*. Quentin's will had already been welcomed by the inhabitants of the surrounding area. After enough was put aside to keep Daphne in comfort for the rest of her, sadly, short life, the remainder was to be used to promote the wilding of the entire area of the hills. This wonderful addition to the coffers of Tom's trust fund, several million pounds in all, was to be spent to take account of the many projects that would, in time, add up to the proper wilding as proposed by Daphne.

The celebration service was attended by many of Quentin's old colleagues and friends. It resulted in a substantial addition to the trust fund.

The four children, trussed up smart, were looking forward to the feast, and not enjoying their fame and their rumbling tummies.

Anthony turned to Ben. "When we were waking up after that swim, you said the pond had a name. What was it?"

"The pond was given the name as the sun came up: peace. You can tell everyone now."

Acknowledgements

With thanks to my son Tom, a teacher, who helped me to understand the spectrum of autism.

Also I would like to thank Julie O'Donnell for her help and advice.

And to my publisher for their assistance in bringing this book into the world.

About the Author

John Pether was born in London in 1934, and later moved to Buxton. His mother left when he was four and when his father went off to the war, John was raised by his grandparents in Bournemouth.

Haileybury, Oxford and Middlesex Hospital Medical School were next and then house jobs before moving into the field of pathology, where he subsequently chose to specialize in microbiology. Research in London was followed by 30-odd years running the microbiology service for Somerset.

An author of more than 60 papers, he spent a career discovering unusual germs and caught over 300 wild rodents for study at Porton Down.

Retiring in 1995, he took up silversmithing and started to write science fiction/fantasy.

Printed in Great Britain
by Amazon

64259825R00170